An Inconvenient Acquaintance

CONVENIENT RISK SERIES, BOOK 5

SARA R. TURNQUIST

MOUNTAIN
SUMMIT PRESS

If you would like to stay up-to-date on this and other series from Sara and receive a free ebook, sign up for her newsletter:

https://saraturnquist.com/list

For my son, Andrew.
You always make me smile.

CHAPTER 1

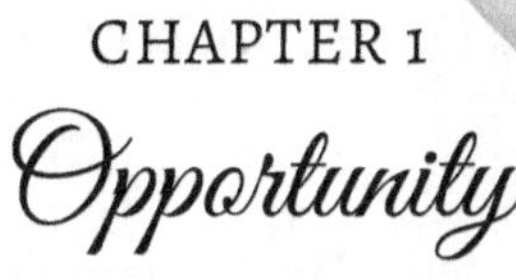

A train platform was a terrible place to catch one's breath. Much less one as busy as this. Ada Clara Miller had been knocked and bumped too many times to count. What a way to treat a lady!

She shifted and attempted to move out of the main path of travelers. But that didn't seem to help. No matter which way she looked, people bustled about, hurried, and harried.

Where was her train? Her platform? What time would it leave? How much time did she have to linger? For certain, she was making no progress as it was.

Grabbing for her timepiece pinned near her collar, she checked the hour. Had it truly been twenty minutes since she set foot off the last train? And all that time, she had been floundering about? Some grand adventure-seeker she had turned out to be...couldn't even manage her way through the train station.

What would her brother think of her, now? She frowned. He'd likely send her, trunks and all, back to Richmond with a promise never to leave again.

No. She could do this. She would.

Another bump from the side found her fighting for her balance.

"Excuse me," she all but screeched. Who would be so thoughtless?

She released her timepiece to grab her carrying case. But encountered resistance.

Glancing up, she met the glare of a scraggly, rough-looking young man, who had taken hold of her case and was pulling at it. His grip was firm, and his mouth was set in a scowl. Had he run into her on purpose? As a ruse to distract her?

What a fiend!

Gritting her teeth, she jerked on the handle of her case and kicked at the man. Her foot flung wild but connected with something solid.

The man hollered as she fell backward, holding naught but the torn handle of her case. She looked up as she pushed off the ground to a sitting position only to see his back as he ran off, maneuvering through the crowd, clutching her case in his arms.

"Stop that man! He stole my bag," she yelled.

A few heads turned and looked after him, but no one moved to pursue him. Nice town.

She pulled out a handkerchief and blotted at her eyes. How could she ever have thought she'd make it out here?

Swallowing against the lump in her throat, she tried to pull herself together. She must be a sight—sitting here on the platform, fighting tears. But she needed the moment. Not that anyone cared.

She took in a couple deep breaths. It was time. No more of this.

Two pairs of boots stopped in front of her.

What could that mean? What could these men want?

She looked up to see the rapscallion who had taken her bag. He was held in place by another man grasping his collar.

This other man, perhaps a couple of years older, but definitely more clean-cut with a confident air about him, watched her. "Ma'am, I'm afraid this ruffian has something to say to you."

She sniffled. Really? Right now?

The man gave the would-be robber a good jerk.

"I'm sorry, miss," the bag snatcher said, though she could tell his heart definitely wasn't in it.

But her gaze had been set on her rescuer. He had kind, blue eyes that shone concern. The inward tilt of his eyebrows hinted at a determination that warmed her. His face was strong with a firm jawline and a nose that had length to it, but not unpleasantly so. Now the hair, that was difficult to see beyond his brown hat, but she would guess it to be dark. His frame was solid, and he was certainly taller than she.

He turned to the scoundrel who had accosted her and ground out, "Drop it."

The thief hesitated, frowning.

A slight movement from somewhere between the two brought about a hoot from the stubborn man.

Her bag plopped onto the ground.

"Now, don't cause any more trouble," the man said. Then he released the rather uncomfortable-looking younger man, who then stumbled and rushed off.

Ada's gaze darted between her bag and the retreating figure. And she sensed more than saw the other man move closer. Turning toward him, she was met with his extended hand.

"My apologies, miss. I hate that you've received such a poor reception in Tucson."

She stared at his hand for the length of a breath.

"Please, let me try to remedy that." His voice soothed her, and his presence was more calming than it should be considering what had just happened. She couldn't help but wonder where he had been this whole trip.

She slid her gloved hand into his calloused palm.

He helped her to her feet with ease. She was upright quicker than she'd expected. So much so, that she found herself closer to him than she'd prefer.

He braced her arms. "Whoa, there. You all right?"

Her face warmed, as did the whole of her, it seemed. From damsel-in-distress to fainting flower. My, my...wasn't she a storybook cliché?

"Yes." She took a step back, removing her hands and arms from his. Though she was reluctant to do so. Tugging on her traveling jacket, she faced him again. "That is, I'm just fine. A little shaken is all."

She groaned inwardly. Why must she share that? As if the situation weren't awkward enough.

The man's eyes flickered over her features. Could he be as kind as she imagined? Or was that a product of her situation?

Then she stopped herself. What was she thinking? She didn't know this man any more than that rat who'd attempted to steal her bag. Fine independent woman she'd make, indeed. She ran a hand down her skirt, smoothing over wrinkles that would have to be pressed out. "I...thank you for your assistance retrieving my things. But I—ah—have a train to catch."

And, as a fact, she did. How soon? Had she missed it?

The man's brows furrowed. Had her growing worry been displayed on her face?

"Can I help you find your train car? Get aboard?"

As if the one mishap made her completely useless! She straightened, squaring her shoulders that were much smaller than his, which appeared strong and very capable. "No, I thank you, sir. I am quite capable. I just need to gather my..." She crouched and picked up her suitcase. "Bag."

It was rather cumbersome to pick up and hold without the handle attached. But after some moments, tipping it this way and that, she managed to maintain her grip on it.

"All right then, miss. I guess I'll be on my way." He tipped his hat and turned.

She dipped her head and fought the urge to stomp her foot. How childish! He was only trying to help. Indeed, he had helped her. And this was how she repaid him—with her schoolgirl stubbornness and an attempt to prove something.

"I..." she called after him.

He shifted and looked over his shoulder.

"Thank you." She peered at the ground as her face heated. "For your assistance."

He nodded and when she glanced up, shot her a smile before continuing on his way.

She was thankful he had turned away, as her knees had weakened at his smile.

What an adventurer indeed!

Slim maneuvered the horse and cart through the wilds of Arizona. His short time in Tucson had been quite enough for him. He much preferred the quieter, slower pace of life in the much smaller town of Wharton City. Even more so, the set aside Miller ranch.

Although, that pretty blonde had been quite enough to turn a fella's head. With her large brown eyes and dainty features, she'd found her way into his thoughts often during his ride.

He smiled to himself. She had seemed rather uncomfortable receiving his help. But the way her features colored...no, she definitely enjoyed it, too.

And that intrigued him. More than it perhaps should. Why would her reaction stir him so? Or was that even it? Was it something else about her? The fact that she'd needed help and he had been able to rush to her aid could endear her, perhaps. But the way she had fought against that thief...

Slim had spotted her from a short distance away, pulling at her case and kicking at the man. To her credit, she had landed a solid hit on the man's knee.

She was no typical lady, he mused. She had fire in her. And that enticed him. But that didn't mean she was within reach.

Her clothing spoke of her refinement. Yes, she came from money. And that was not something Slim wanted to be mixed up with.

Either way, it wasn't as if he knew who she was, where she was going, or even her name. It wasn't likely their paths were ever to cross again. Best to put her out of mind.

If he could.

Another train platform, another city. With this stop, however, Ada had reached her destination—Tombstone. It was for the best. She had long tired of traveling. What kind of adventure was that? Brandon hadn't mentioned how arduous the trip would be—multiple train cars and being shuffled about, herded like cattle. Not quite what she'd had in mind.

Yet here she was. So far from home. A dream come true. Why didn't it seem so dreamy then?

She was worn, ragged, and weary. Ready to remain on solid ground and find a comfortable bed—one that didn't move that she could lie down in for two nights together.

Closing her eyes, she couldn't help but see her mother's face and the worry lines etched there. She wished all of this hadn't been so difficult for Mother. But Ada had to take this chance—this one chance to do something for herself, to be something. Thankfully, Brandon had given Ada his support. Maybe Mother would come around in time.

Only...

Things were different now. Father had passed. There wasn't anyone to watch after Mother. Their cousin had agreed to come for a time and stay with Mother. But would he care for Mother as she would have? See to her every need and comfort?

But Ada had to do this. For herself. Was that so wrong?

Many thought so. Men had every prerogative to strike out on their own. But a woman? 'Empty headed nonsense' was a phrase she had heard more than once.

Ada shook her head. Maybe things would be different someday.

There was little she might do to change those opinions today. So, she turned her attention to her own plight.

Looking to the hastily written names she had jotted from her brother's last letter, she then scanned the platform. How would she know who these people were? Brandon had given little to go on—such the male way of thinking. Maybe they would know how to find her?

Because, try as she might, she could not spy a couple—this Dan and Lily Hayworth—that appeared at all to be seeking her out amongst the crowd. Just her luck. She turned back to the train and searched out the men who were unloading trunks and bags. The dark-haired of the two had grabbed one of her trunks and shoved it to the other.

"Careful," she called out while rushing toward them. Why did they insist on tossing her valuables about?

"These yours?" the one man said with lifted brows.

She folded her arms. "They most certainly are. And I'll thank you to be more mindful how you handle them. They contain things necessary for my classroom."

"Classroom?" He tossed a strained look at the man assisting him.

"Yes. My classroom. Many are the things needed to aid in the broadening of the minds of—"

"No wonder," the other, taller man said as he smiled. "With them highfalutin' words and all."

"I beg your pardon, sir?" Her face heated as the man with the brown hair snickered.

"Nothin' to worry yer pretty head about, miss." The taller man winked at his friend.

Her discomfort grew, reaching a level that bade her extricate herself from the situation. "Either way, please do take care, gentlemen."

"We'll do our job," the first man assured her. Then he turned away and grabbed for the next item. It was the trunk containing her books on history, literature, and all manner of subjects. If possible, her face warmed all the more. It would be quite heavy. Dare she linger? Dare she not?

The man grunted as he lifted it. "You aimin' to teach about bricklayin'?"

"No, sir, I..." Her words faded into her embarrassment.

As the man twisted, preparing to fling the trunk, he lost his balance and dropped it. It banged open, and the contents spilled onto the platform.

Ada stuffed her fist against her mouth to contain a shriek. She then hurried over, skirts flapping, to collect the precious cargo. Grabbing for the books, she attempted to stuff them back into the damaged trunk.

"Allow me, ma'am," a voice said from behind her.

A man knelt beside her, making quick work of sweeping the volumes back within the confines of the case.

Ada settled back, fighting tears. "Thank you, sir, I..." She eyed the damaged trunk. Was it hopeless?

"Did you drop this, miss?" a higher pitched, but still calming voice soothed.

Ada turned in that direction.

A woman with pinned up reddish brown hair stood with Ada's bag in her arms.

"Yes, ma'am." Ada stood. "I...must have forgotten it when I..." She could no longer fight the emotion welling within. All of her efforts had come to naught—she was tired, at the end of her rope, and not even able to accomplish the simplest tasks.

"I don't think this trunk is salvageable." The man's voice cut into her moment of self-pity.

She could only nod.

"Dan," the woman with the red hair admonished.

"Huh?" he fired back. Then, "Oh."

Ada appreciated the woman's attempt to spare her. But it did not, could not stop the thickness that welled in her chest, continuing to rise. She grabbed for her handkerchief—her father's. Though masculine and out of place in a lady's possession, it gave her some sense of his presence.

"I thank you, sir, ma'am. Your kindness is much appreciated." And try as she might, she was not able to muster even the smallest smile for their efforts.

"It's no trouble." The woman's kind voice continued to offer comfort. A delicate hand pressed Ada's shoulder. "Why don't you let us help you get where you're going?"

Ada sniffled. "I only wish I could. But I'm waiting for..." She dragged herself out of her stupor. "Did you say, Dan?" Her gaze jerked between the man and woman.

"Yes," the woman said, looked to the man. "This is my husband, Dan Hayworth. I'm Lily."

Ada felt all the tension release from her being, and her spirit lifted. At last! Something had shifted her way. "Thank the Lord!"

The woman's features scrunched. "Ada Miller?"

"Yes." Ada wanted to collapse right then and there or throw herself into Lily's arms and just sob.

"You poor thing." Lily laid a hand on her arm as she steered her away from the busted trunk. She exchanged a look with her husband and jerked her head toward Ada's stacked things. "Dan will take care of this. You look like you could use some fresh air, away from this monstrous thing." She eyed the locomotive.

Ada nodded and allowed Mrs. Hayworth to direct her. The woman's sweet voice and gentleness were such succor for her worn nerves. "Thank you."

She might should celebrate that she had made it, well and whole, to Tombstone. And that she had, in fact, found her brother's friends, who would see to her care and safety.

Even so, she felt more lost and hopeless than ever in her life.

The Miller Ranch came into view. Slim let out a deep breath. He could already taste Cook's beef stew. Well, he could hope. Maybe that was on the menu tonight, maybe it would be something else. Whatever she made, it would be good. They had the best eatin' this side of the Rio Grande. He had been determined that no matter what Brandon needed him to fetch in Tucson, one thing was for sure—he'd be back by chow time.

He might have had to push the horse a little harder than he'd liked, but they made good time. And he'd be filling his bowl with some of Cook's vittles within the hour. That was something to celebrate.

The outlines of boys sprinting about the barn greeted him. Samuel? Done with his chores already? And would that be Nisto? Slim smiled. Those boys had become thick as thieves over the last few years. And they had grown. Their heads nearly came up to Slim's shoulders.

As he came closer to the largest structure on the property, the boys turned toward Slim's approaching cart and waved.

He raised his hat in their direction. Maybe he could pawn off the job of putting the wagon away. It'd be good for them. "Hey, boys!"

They hooted and hollered, running up alongside the cart the last several feet until Slim slowed the horse to a stop beside the barn.

"Thanks for the fine welcome back." Slim grinned.

Nisto reached for the mare's mane.

The horse tilted its head toward the native boy, letting him rub her muscled neck and nose. Nisto sure did have a way with the animals. He'd make a fine rancher one day. Though Slim hoped the boy could chart a better course for himself. Be more, perhaps. Though...in this world, with its prejudices, he might run into limitations that were outside of his control.

"Where've you been?" Nisto asked, looking up at Slim, his deep brown eyes seemingly almost black.

"To Tucson." Slim hopped down. "Mr. Miller had a new saddle for me to fetch."

"A saddle?" Samuel crinkled his nose. "What'd ya have to go to Tuscon for? Can't Mr. Handal get a saddle in?"

Slim walked to the back of the cart. "This is a special saddle. Came in on the train. Mr. Miller needed it special delivered."

The boys came to the tailgate where Slim stood. They peered around his broad form, trying to get a glimpse of the prized piece.

"Shoot, boys. Ain't nothing to see here. It's all covered up."

Both faces fell.

Slim turned and leaned down just a bit to meet their eyes. "You know what, though? I bet Mr. Miller wouldn't mind if I give you a peek once we get it inside."

Two sets of widened eyes lit up.

"That is, if you two don't mind putting the horse and cart away while I get it settled."

The boys looked at each other then back at Slim, and nodded.

"Yes, sir," Samuel shot out, before turning to Nisto. "Get the bridle."

"Whoa, there." Slim put a hand to the youngster's shoulder. "Let me unload that saddle, first."

"Sorry, Slim." A sheepish half grin split across Samuel's face.

Slim tugged at the boy's hat and turned back to the cargo.

In a matter of minutes, Slim had the saddle in its new spot among the others. The boys, as well, made short work of getting the horse in its stall and the cart in its place. They now pressed in on either side of Slim, clamoring for a look.

"All right, all right," he said with a laugh. "But keep your fingers off." Then he lifted the canvas covering and watched them admire the fine silver-studded leather piece that even he had been caught gawking at in Tucson.

"Is that the kind of saddle that sheriff in your story would have?"

Slim scanned the area around them quickly. His stories had always been something he just did for himself. He never thought he'd ever share them with anyone. Had it been four months ago—no six—when the boys became aware of Slim's stories. Since then, he found he could entertain the boys quite well with them. Though if Brandon or any of the other ranch hands found out...

He'd just rather it stay between them.

"I think Sheriff Tex Maynard would be right proud to have a saddle such as that." Why did it still embarrass Slim for the boys to admire his tales? It just didn't seem they should.

"Did you come up with another story?" Nisto's eyes were deep and serious. Not a hint of humor. Nothing but genuine interest. "I just have to know what Sheriff Maynard's next adventure is!"

Slim licked his lips. He always had a dozen or so in the back of his mind. But he'd only just started to be comfortable telling them with any regularity. "I might."

"Please, tell us! Please!" Samuel's desperation seeped into his voice. Was he really so wanting for these tall tales?

Slim looked between the two boys. How could he say, no? "All right," he said, re-covering the saddle. "But only a short one."

Then he leaned forward and shared the story he'd concocted on the drive to the ranch—one inspired by the saddle. He took out a few details to shorten the tale.

When he finished, the boys continued to stare. Did they not realize he was done? Was it not a suitable ending? Had he messed it up somehow?

"That was quite the story," a voice said from behind. The voice of his boss.

Slim swallowed. Hard. And his face warmed.

Brandon was not supposed to hear that. No one was...not really.

Slim turned, slowly. Very slowly. And grimaced when his eyes confirmed what his ears had told—Brandon Miller stood just inside the barn, leaning against a post. Where had he come from? And when?

"You...heard that?"

Brandon pushed off the post. "A bit of it. But not quite enough. That was something else."

Slim closed his eyes. Was it possible for him to disappear?

His boss clapped him on the shoulder. "It was...really. And you kept these two hanging on every word."

Slim glanced at Samuel and Nisto, who now looked between the two men, as if gauging what to do, or if they could leave. Could he?

"I think Cook might could use a hand with the table," Brandon directed the boys. They dropped their heads but headed off.

As Slim watched them go, Brandon moved to stand beside him. "You had them completely captivated. That is a rare gift, indeed."

"Boss," Slim said, keeping his eyes trained on the retreating youngsters, unable to make himself meet Brandon's gaze. "Could we just forget that I—"

"Nonsense," Brandon cut in. "You have nothing to be so shy about. Why, if I had your gift, I'd share it with anyone who would listen."

Slim shrugged and stared at the ground. "It's not like that. I just, well..."

"How is it, then?"

Slim shuffled his feet, trying to find a stance that wouldn't make him feel so vulnerable. But then again, that feeling had nothing to do with how he was standing. "Those things I make up...they're silly little stories. More for me. The boys caught me writing one down a few months ago. And ever since, they've been asking me to share more."

When he looked up, he saw that Brandon was nodding.

"But honest, boss, I think they're just trying to make me feel good."

"Let me tell you something, Slim. Here's the truth. If you've got more stories like the one you just told, they are not just being nice. That was a well-spun tale. And I wish you'd consider trying to sell one to a newspaper or other publication."

Slim jerked his head from side-to-side so quickly it hurt his neck. "I could never do that."

Brandon watched him. Was he considering Slim's words? Preparing to naysay him and pressure him anyway?

"Just...don't tell anyone." Slim looked down. "I couldn't survive it."

His boss's eyes never wavered. "If you won't submit them, hear me out on this. My sister is the new schoolteacher in Tombstone. Why don't you let her read your stories to the children there?"

That was the craziest thing Slim had ever heard. He could never...

Slim opened his mouth to protest.

Brandon held up a hand. "Just...listen to me. You would never have to see her or those children. Send her a couple of stories. Then, if they like them as much as I think they will, you'll agree to send one to a newspaper."

He eyed his boss.

"Deal?" Brandon pressed.

"I don't think so, I—"

"I won't take no for an answer." Brandon folded his arms across his chest. He appeared rather resolute.

Slim watched him. His boss was a good man. And even in this, it was his strange way of believing in Slim. Even as much as he wished the man would leave him alone. Perhaps he could send the sister one story. Would Brandon leave him alone then? It was appealing, this idea that he wouldn't have to face the woman as she read it.

"All right. I'll send her one story."

Brandon quirked a brow. "I don't like the sound of that."

"One...or none."

Brandon stuck out his hand.

Slim grasped it. "Deal."

His boss shook his hand with a firm jerk. "I intend to hold you to it."

Slim nodded. What had he just gotten himself into?

CHAPTER 2

Unexpected

Ada tried to settle her mind as aptly as Lily Hayworth had worked to settle her in the humble home's great room.

"This should help with those lingering nerves." Lily smiled as she passed a steaming mug to Ada.

Coffee. Why did everyone think that was the answer?

Ada offered her hostess a polite smile. How was the woman to know that Ada found the beverage detestable? Even so, the warmth in her hands and the smell of the brew did help soothe her.

"Thank you, Mrs. Hayworth, I—"

"Lily."

Ada nodded. "I am forever grateful for you and your husband. I was quite at my wit's end."

In spite of herself, Ada's face warmed once more. What was wrong with her? She brought the cup's rim to touch her lips in an effort to fill the void. The aroma became all the more pungent. Fighting the urge to balk at the now strong smell, she stilled herself and lowered the mug.

"Your brother mentioned you were to be traveling all the way from Richmond. I can imagine you'd been tossed about and shuffled around quite enough. Anyone would have been put out."

Ada let her lips lift slightly. Despite Lily's reassurance, Ada wasn't convinced any of that gave her reason to fall apart as she had. She was supposed to be brave, to take hold of this opportunity, this adventure. Why, then, did she crumble so easily?

"I...encountered some trouble in Tucson when changing trains." She blurted it out before thinking otherwise. How would that excuse her behavior? Perhaps, that had contributed to her state of mind... having been mishandled and nearly robbed. If not for the man who had rushed to her aid...

"Trouble?" Lily peered at Ada over the top of her own cup as she sipped at the dark brew.

"Yes. A man, well...a ruffian, to be truthful, tried to lift my bag. Right out of my hands." The memory of it became more vivid—the sounds of the crowd, the way she had felt confused, discombobulated even, on that platform. And then there was the thief, trying to wrest her bag from her. Had she truly fought back?

"Oh my!" Lily held a hand to her chest. "You were robbed?"

"Almost. Well...yes, actually, I was. But a man came to my rescue. He brought my bag back to me and made the scoundrel apologize." The man—her hero—appeared in her mind's eye. In truth, his visage had not been far from her mind since the incident—his square jaw and blue eyes, the chiseled lines of his features, and his arms, which held the criminal fast and easily lifted her to her feet. It was enough to make a lady go weak.

Lily gasped. "You poor dear! I don't know how you managed to get on your train and continue by yourself."

Ada's gaze met hers. As a fact, she had gotten on the train. On her own feet, by her own grit. And then she'd gotten to Tombstone.

Now, she sat in the home of her brother's friends. Then why was she ill at ease? There was nothing to be ashamed of. Or to be concerned about. All had turned out well. And all was well.

If only she could shake this sense that something was wrong.

The morning had faded into noon as Slim and Eli rode in for their midday meal. Slim had grown accustomed to the man. Eli had fit in well at the ranch. More so than the two newest additions. Or was it more that Slim begrudged Dan's absence too much to give the men a fair shake? He hadn't liked it when Cutie moved on after marrying to pursue his and Mariena's dreams of starting a school for the Tohono O'odham children.

And Slim had seen the writing on the wall when Dan and Lily tied the knot last summer. Still, he had thought Dan would stay—ranching was in his blood. Slim wasn't wrong. Dan and Lily struck out to start a budding ranch in Tombstone.

So, Slim was left behind with these new recruits. Would they ever be the friends and brothers to him that Cutie and Dan had been? It was doubtful. But there was some hope when it came to Eli. The man was good company. And easy to get along with. He did his fair share and kept his nose clean.

Slowing his mount as they neared the barn, Slim nodded to Eli. Moments later, they had dismounted, secured the horses in the side paddock, and turned toward the homestead.

"Heard about that saddle you fetched yesterday," Eli said, glancing in Slim's direction as they walked. Did he think it was necessary to fill these silences? It wasn't.

Slim shrugged. "Yeah."

"Is it as nice as all that?"

"I s'pose so." This whole line of questioning made him a little uncomfortable. It wasn't Slim's saddle, after all.

Eli nodded. "I'm hoping to get a peek at it later."

"I wouldn't go making any certain effort about it. I think the boss has something special in mind for it. And I think he aims to keep it a secret."

"Do you know what his plan is?" Eli's gaze stayed on Slim.

Shaking his head, Slim pushed out a breath. "Can't say."

"Can't?" Eli's brows rose. "Or won't?"

He was caught there. So he shrugged again and lengthened his stride. They were only a few feet from the front porch. Would the young man wise up and hush about it?

As they climbed the stairs, the door to the house flung open, and

Brandon stepped out. Their footfalls causing creaks on the old boards must have drawn his attention. Brandon's gaze darted between them.

"Come on in, fellas. Cook's got a hearty meal ready for some hard-working hands."

Slim slid his hat from his head and nodded. But as he and Eli passed in front of Brandon on their way into the house, Brandon caught Slim by the arm.

Eli paused when Slim was halted.

"Go on in, Eli. I got business with this scallywag." Brandon's smile widened.

Eli threw Slim a glance, amusement on his features. Then he nodded and moved off into the house.

Slim swallowed. And prayed there would not be a repeat of the conversation from the previous evening.

Brandon dropped his hand but backed farther from the door. Did they have need of such privacy? What did his boss need to share? He turned to Slim, his eyes serious.

"You need anything to write that letter?"

Slim dropped his head. Not this. "Boss, I—"

"I fully intend to hold you to your deal. I just wanted to ask if you need paper or anything else to get that story written down. And posted. Whatever you need...you let me know."

Slim pushed out a breath and raked a hand across the scruff on his face. "I..." He wanted to put off his boss, had hoped Brandon might forget the whole thing in a few days...but that didn't seem likely now. "Give me three days. I'll have it done. Then you can post it yourself."

Brandon's eyes lit up. Did he think he would get a chance to read it for himself?

"In a sealed envelope, that is," Slim added.

Brandon's mouth downturned.

Slim stepped to the door once more and shrugged. "I never said you could read it." With a wide grin, he let the door shut behind himself.

"Yes." Ada turned. Were her features still colored? She prayed not. "I apologize for delaying our departure."

"Nonsense." Dan offered a smile. "You think you're the only woman here that takes a few extra minutes to get ready?"

Lily shot him a look and swatted at his arm.

He captured her hand and rubbed his thumb across the back. "Not that you need any of it. You always look beautiful to me."

Ada averted her gaze to descend the stairs, affording them what privacy she could.

"You think you have all the right words, don't you?" she heard Lily say.

"Don't I?" his voice was softer, more difficult to hear.

Ada became more uncomfortable. Perhaps she should retreat back into the house. But as she turned at the base of the stairs, Lily pushed back from Dan and ran her hands down her apron. On Ada's account? She did so hate to disrupt their tender moment. Still, she did not think it prudent for such to continue in her presence. She risked great embarrassment, at the very least.

Dan grabbed for Lily's hand and pulled her back toward his chest.

Ada halted and held her breath.

He kissed Lily's hand. "Until later." His words held such promise.

Lily smiled at him, her eyes glistening. "Until later."

Then he loosed her hand and turned to Ada. The rancher was in place then, not the soft eyes she had just witnessed upon Lily. But the roughened rancher with a good heart and kind ways. It put her at ease.

"Shall we?" He held out a hand.

She let him help her up to the wagon's bench. Then, as she settled her skirt, the cart tipped slightly as he hauled himself up beside her from the opposite side.

Lily stepped to the wagon and looked up at Ada. "Good luck with Mayor Clum. He's a good man. He'll treat you right."

Ada smiled. "Thanks."

Lily lifted a hand to wave and moved back as the cart lurched into motion.

The ride into town was pleasant. Dan offered comments here and there, but their conversation remained sparse. That was only to be expected and she imagined, appropriate. She had been eager to hear more tales of her brother, though. And Dan had spent several years under his management and had, as she could imagine, come to know Brandon well. But she couldn't bring herself to ask anything overtly personal.

Sooner than she expected, the cart rolled onto Tombstone's main stretch. Dan maneuvered the wagon to the far side of town and toward a smaller building. The schoolhouse? It seemed suitable. Well situated. And the door was open. Was the mayor already inside? Had she arrived late?

She tugged at the timepiece near her collar and glanced down. No, it was yet ten of eight. They were, in fact, early. Perhaps, the mayor preferred to be early, as well.

Dan reined the horse in just short of the entrance. He turned to her. "Looks like you're not the first one here."

Ada could only nod. Her pulse had sped once more, and her breathing had quickened.

Dan didn't move for several minutes. Would he not help her down?

Ada didn't speak or make a move to get down, either. No, she was too focused on getting control of her breathing.

"Listen," Dan said after some moments had passed. "It's none of my business. And I don't really know you..."

She shifted and looked at him. What was he about?

"But I do know your brother. And he's from good stock. I gotta think that means you are, too."

She stared. Where was he going with this? Was this some kind of attempt at encouragement?

He swallowed. "What I'm trying to say is...if you're even half the man—er—woman your brother is, you're a better person than most everyone I've met."

Her brows furrowed. What a strange compliment.

"You don't need to fret about Mayor Clum. You'll do well. And everyone here will love you." He pushed out a breath.

After he stopped rambling, she decided she rather appreciated his words. They did help put her at ease. She had merit. While she might not have earned this man's regard—even as much as he meandered around the subject—she was worthwhile. Wasn't she? She could do this. And she would. To the best of her ability.

"Thanks." She offered him a smile.

He managed a small smile back. "I think it goes without saying that your brother is the best man I know."

She nodded. "Me, too."

Dan settled the reins, turned, and dropped out of the cart. Then he was on her other side, lifting a hand to help her down.

Once she was on solid ground, she faced the open door. There was no indication of whether the mayor would come out to greet her or if she should go in. Either way, one thing was true—she was more ready to face him.

"Let me walk you in," Dan said, holding an arm up in the direction of the door, indicating that she should lead the way.

"I don't think that's necessary, I—"

"I insist." His voice was firm.

She jerked her head around to face him.

He was all seriousness.

Perhaps he was concerned about her reputation. It probably would be better for her to not meet with the mayor alone. Or was he worried after her safety? Regardless, she doubted arguing would get her anywhere.

So, she nodded and then stepped to the schoolhouse. At the open door, she peered within. Beyond the rows of desks, a chalkboard and teacher's desk sat at the far side of the room. And, among all the things spread about, a woman swept the floors. Swept the floors? Was the mayor not yet here then?

She turned back to Dan. "I think we did beat Mayor Clum."

At her comment, the woman within looked up and called, "Miss Miller?"

Ada faced her once more.

The woman was perhaps fifty or so, her dark hair well salted with gray and white. Her figure had curved and plumped in places, but in a pleasant way. She set the broom to the side and stepped to the door, wiping her hands with her apron.

"Miss Miller?" she repeated.

"Y-yes?" The hesitation surprised even Ada.

"Are you Miss Ada Miller?" the woman's brown eyes sparkled.

"Yes, ma'am. I am." She looked around, trying to take everything in. "I'm sorry to intrude. I have a meeting with Mayor Clum at eight o'clock."

"I'm here in his stead." The woman smiled. "He will not be able to meet today."

"He won't?" Was that a statement of how unimportant she was to him?

"I'm afraid not, dear. Nothing personal. There are...circumstances beyond his control that take him away for the moment. He asked that I get you acclimated with the schoolhouse and help get you settled in your new accommodations."

"I thank you. But that won't be necessary. My friends, the Hayworths, have volunteered to get me to the boarding house by week's end."

"Mayor Clum didn't tell you?"

Ada's throat tightened. She did not like surprises. "Tell me what?"

"You won't be lodging at the boarding house."

Now, her throat constricted. She tried to swallow and found herself unable to. "No?"

"There's no reason you can't—" Dan inserted himself.

Ada cut him off and shook her head. "I don't want to trouble—"

The older woman held up a hand. "If I might. The town has, of course, made other arrangements."

Ada's brows rose. "Oh?"

"Yes." The woman's smile spread across her face. "With me. You'll be staying with me."

This was the moment of truth.

Slim sat in the barn. No one around. Just him and the animals. It was his favorite place to think. And he needed to think. He had promised and promised Brandon to write down a story for his sister, and it was high time he delivered. But which one? What would be the least likely to embarrass him? What was his best?

Would the one about Sheriff Maynard and the band of renegade Comanche be his favorite? Or the one with the gang of horse thieves? Slim liked this larger-than-life hero he'd created. He was pretty perfect, the sheriff —not afraid of anything, always knew exactly what to say and do, and there wasn't anything unbecoming about him. The stuff legends were made of.

But he needed to settle on which story, or he'd never get it done. Perhaps, the one with the bank robber. That was a good one. And it was short. He could keep it simple...make it even shorter. That would be best.

He touched the pencil to his paper but stopped. Should he introduce himself? Or the tale? Or just write the story?

It wasn't as if he wanted to make friends with Brandon's sister. He wasn't likely to ever meet her. What, then, was the point in introductions? Brandon had asked for the story and only the story. It was up to Brandon to explain what was going on.

But he planned to give his boss the pages in an envelope. What if Brandon just postmarked and mailed it? Then he'd be sure to tell Brandon to include an explanation. Just the story it was then...

Although... Slim stopped himself again. He didn't want to talk about it any further with Brandon. Couldn't he just hand over the envelope and be done with it? Yes, then it would be best to write a sentence or two about what this was all about. Just in case all she got were these pages.

Hello. I'm Slim Dagley, one of your brother's hands on the ranch, and he thought your class would like this story. I hope you find it useful.

There. That should be enough. He read over the lines. They looked pitiful. Should he start over?

No. Best to leave it as it was and just keep going. If he started second-guessing now, this would take all night. So, he moved onto the story. He wrote out the tale he had once told Samuel and Nisto.

It was about Sheriff Maynard, of course, and his stopping a bank robbery in progress. To top it off, he also rescued a woman kidnapped in the process...wrong place, wrong time...as sometimes happens with folks. But Sheriff Maynard, valiant and brave, saved the fair lady and the day. And once more brought peace and prosperity to the small made-up town of Dayton City.

When he finished, he let out a long breath and read over his work. It wasn't the best he'd ever written. But then again, he was not in the habit of writing his stories down like this, from beginning to end. And certainly never with the intent that someone else would read it.

This would have to do. It was what it was. And, with any luck, it would get Brandon off his back and be the end of this whole nonsense.

CHAPTER 3

Exchanges

The house was quiet. But that was all right, as far as Ada was concerned. It seemed she hadn't had a moment to herself, save to sleep, since she'd left Richmond. She did enjoy and appreciate the Hayworths' hospitality. And she found Mrs. Wilmont to be an absolute delight. Still, she did so tire of being the focus of everyone's attention and concern. How much longer would it be before things calmed and a routine fell into place? Until she was no longer a novelty?

She sighed and continued to wipe down the table. Mrs. Wilmont had left nearly two hours ago on an errand to the General Store. It wouldn't be long before she returned.

Ada hoped to make good use of her time. No sense dawdling. She could enjoy the quiet and be useful. Thus far, she had fluffed pillows, swept, and wiped down counters. Her back ached enough for twice that amount of work. It became all the more apparent that she wasn't accustomed to so much time on her feet or doing even these simple chores.

That would change. It would not do for her to shy away from the more taxing things about life out here. She refused to be viewed as one who couldn't carry her own load. Not to mention, working with her hands kept her mind focused...and away from the things that she'd rather not think on. Such as how her students might receive her. What they may think of her. Or the parents...

How did she think she would win over these hard-working folks if she maintained her pristine ways and fine manners? She must be willing to get dirty. And be as any other frontierswoman.

And she would.

The door creaked.

Ada hung the cloth and moved to greet Mrs. Wilmont.

The woman came in with a small crate balanced on her hip.

"Oh my, let me take that." Ada rushed forward. She reached for the burden.

"That's not necessary," the widow protested. "It's not so heavy."

"Please, allow me." Ada met Mrs. Wilmont's gaze. How could she have been so obtuse? She should have listened better and met the woman outside.

Gripping the sides of the small box, she tugged.

Mrs. Wilmont relinquished it.

Ada stumbled backwards, then nearly fell forward under the crate's weight. How had Mrs. Wilmont handled it with such ease?

"You all right, dear?" The woman stepped toward her. "Let me get that."

"No need," Ada said, shaking her head as she jerked on the weight. She managed to get it higher, but not quite to waist level.

Mrs. Wilmont stood nearby, hands out, ready to help.

Ada struggled, certain her arms would pop out of their sockets. At last, she made it to the center of the dining space. With great effort and a heave, she got it onto the table. But not without knocking into a chair that clattered to the floor.

Turning to Mrs. Wilmont, Ada offered a sheepish look. "My apologies."

"It's no matter." The woman couldn't hide her chuckling. "You do mean well."

Ada looked away and bent to set the chair to rights. Then she turned toward the far side of the cabin. "I'll just...be in my room. Trying not to cause any trouble."

"Wait just a minute there," Mrs. Wilmont called.

Ada spun. What further embarrassment could she create for herself?

"You have a letter." Mrs. Wilmont reached into the small bin, grabbed an envelope, and walked it to where Ada stood.

"I...thank you." Ada accepted the precious piece of mail. She turned it over as her heart did a little flip in her eagerness to determine the identity of the sender. There, even before looking at the return address, she saw it—her brother's handwriting. What tidings would he have? For certain, he would share news and encouragement. He always did know just what to say.

She glanced back at Mrs. Wilmont, who for her part, had begun unpacking the crate.

"I'll...um...read this in my room."

"All right, dear. Go ahead. It's always good to hear from loved ones." The woman smiled at her.

Ada nodded before turning back toward her room. Once inside the small quarters, she sat on the bed and ripped at the seal. A note and another envelope were inside. She examined this letter within her letter. It bore no markings or any other indication what may be in the envelope. Perhaps Brandon would explain what it was.

Picking up the pages bearing his penmanship, she poured over his words. Indeed, they did speak of how he, Amanda, and the children fared. As well as the ranch and the town.

Over all this time, Ada felt as if she knew the place as well as anyone could. Even the hands on the ranch, Cook, and, of course, the Uncle Owen she had only met a handful of times. Yet, she had come to love and admire him all the more through Brandon's letters. Knowing Dan before meeting him a few days ago was rather awkward. And she had well felt it.

Now she had to learn about new ranch hands. As was everyone else on the ranch—especially Brandon and Slim, who had to work alongside these men each day. She prayed the bonds that they had known with Dan and Cutie would form soon and be solid. For all their sakes.

Brandon wrote of how glad he was to hear of her safe arrival in Tombstone. She had omitted the part about the would-be robber. No need to worry her big brother. He also asked after her classroom and living situation. How was he to know things had changed in that regard? She must inform him that all was well.

Then he wrote about the envelope. Apparently, it was from Slim.

Slim? Why would Slim write her?

Her heart thumped a hard beat. What was Brandon's intention there?

Brandon explained that he discovered Slim created stories. Then he detailed how he cajoled Slim into sharing one with her new class—a hopeful welcome of sorts.

How nice! That would be a wonderful way to start off in her class.

She picked up the sealed envelope and studied it, taking a deep breath. And, for whatever reason, some of her earlier concerns about meeting the students and that first day melted. There was this story. It provided a point of connection. For that, she was grateful.

The only question: to read it now, or wait?

Slim checked on his mare after leaving the homestead. Another fine meal from Cook. What would they do without her? With any luck, they wouldn't have to find out. That's what he'd keep in mind. Firmly in mind.

He patted the horse's neck and rubbed her nose. "How about it, girl?"

The animal stared at him. Still, she seemed to understand him more than anyone else at this ranch. Well, anymore.

"She knows you have that carrot in your back pocket. You bring one every night."

Slim kept stroking down the front of the horse's head. He didn't so much as give his boss a smile. It just wasn't in him tonight. And he didn't even know why.

"C'mon, Slim. Why hold out on her?" There was laughter in Brandon's voice.

But Slim didn't make a move to do as bid. Then he sensed more than saw his boss move closer. Until the man stood in front of the next stall.

Slim glanced in that direction.

Brandon stood facing Slim, arms crossed, leaning back on his heels.

"Can I help you with something?" Slim said on an exhale.

Brandon shook his head. He brought his hand up to rub down the side of the horse's neck.

The mare continued to sniff along Slim's hand and arm. Yes, she knew about the carrot. He reached behind himself and pulled it out. "There ya go, girl."

The animal crunched and swallowed it in a matter of seconds.

As she did so, the two men stood in silence. Until it became more awkward than Slim could stand.

"I guess, I'll be turning in." He tipped his hat to Brandon and moved off in the direction of the bunkhouse.

But as he passed by, Brandon grabbed for something out of his own back pocket. "Got something for you."

Slim looked down. It was a letter. With decidedly feminine hand-writing. "What's this?"

"What's it look like?"

Glancing off into the night to keep himself from saying something smart, Slim bit at his lip. Then he offered a calmer answer. "Looks like a letter."

"It is." There was something a bit hard in Brandon's gaze. "From my sister."

"Your sister?" No way could his boss be more surprised than he was. "Whatever for?"

Brandon shrugged. "I don't know. Maybe she wants to thank you for the story. Maybe she wants to ask for another."

Slim stared at the envelope for a moment then looked at his boss.

The man's gaze did not soften. "I didn't read it."

Slim swallowed. "I don't mind if you do, boss. It's—"

Brandon cut in. "It's addressed to you."

What could he say? Would Brandon find reason to be cross about this? Wouldn't he be? "Listen, boss, I never asked her to—"

"I believe you. I just came to deliver it."

That wasn't all his boss came to do. Slim hesitated but reached out and took the letter, certain that color crept into his face. Was he embarrassed? Or worried? Perhaps both?

Without a thought to further engage his boss, he picked up step once more.

"Slim," Brandon called.

"Yeah?" Slim stopped but didn't turn.

"I've noticed you've been...different...lately."

Slim looked to the ground. He didn't want to talk about this. How could he share with Brandon how lonely he had been? How much he missed Cutie and Dan? It would sound like he complained.

The silence stretched.

"Change seems to be the only constant in life." Brandon's tone had cooled somewhat.

There was shuffling behind Slim. Had Brandon shifted to face Slim's back?

"But don't let it change who you are."

Something inside Slim ached. A little too much. But why? He opened his mouth to offer Brandon a polite goodnight but found himself unable to. Instead, he simply nodded and moved off. Nothing stopped him then, and he held his own until he was at the bunkhouse.

The other ranch hands were within. Not only did the lights give them away, their voices were audible through the thin wall, though somewhat muffled. He couldn't go in. Not yet. No way could he face them. So, he settled on the lone bench outside and watched the stars.

There was something peaceful about it—the way the stars blanketed the night and each had their own place. Night after night, they marched up into the sky, no need to find a reason, no need for change. They just were.

As he moved to cross his arms, the letter crinkled.

What was he going to do with this? It clearly made Brandon uncomfortable. But why? Because he worried after his sister writing a fella? Or because that fella was Slim? Did Brandon think Slim was unworthy? And why shouldn't he? She came from money. Lots of money. And deserved every opportunity in life. Much more than Slim could offer.

No matter her intention, he should just burn the letter and forget the whole thing. But then...

Would that be fair to her? To make such an assumption and act on it? Her letter may well be completely innocent. After all, the one he sent her was. No underlying motive. No intentions. Maybe he could give her the benefit of the doubt.

He looked at the envelope. Her handwriting sure was nice. And the way she wrote out his name—made it look fancy. Like he was important. Taking in a deep breath, he made his decision and tore open the thin paper. Two pages were all that lay within. At least it wasn't some long-winded declaration.

Slim,

I must thank you for your story. I was able to share it on the first day of class. The students loved it. Sheriff Maynard is a hero already. They especially liked the way he figured out where the bank robbers were holding the fair maiden. What a clever Sheriff! They are eager for the next tale. I do so hope to inform them that another is coming.

It does seem a bit strange to write to you. I feel as if I know you already from my brother's many letters. In fact, I feel as if I know everyone at the ranch. Even that old dog Daisy.

I hope things are well with you and the new ranch hands. And that Cutie is well in his new life. I am happy to report that Dan and Lily are healthy and in a good situation, even if they do miss everyone in Wharton City.

Please, let me know how I might best encourage more stories. I cannot tell you what just this one meant to my students.
Sincerely,
Miss Ada Clara Miller

Slim stared at the salutation for a moment and the sweeping lines of her pen strokes. He didn't want to read between the lines, but there was something familiar about her, about the way she addressed him. Almost as if he knew her, too. Perhaps it was nothing more than his familiarity with Brandon. That must be it—the siblings were alike.

But she hit on some of the very things that tugged at his heart even now—Dan and Cutie's absence and his struggle to adjust to the new ranch hands. Though she didn't say it, he wondered if she could know how difficult it was for him. And more than that...she liked his story? Her students wanted another one? Would he oblige?

The ranch hands became louder in that moment. He held his breath and listened more closely.

"I'm glad to have this job," one of the men said. Though which he couldn't be sure.

"Me, too. This is a fine set up. Good boss, great food...awful generous."

"We lucked out. What with all these immigrants running around... willing to take half the wage..."

Slim's heart froze. What did they think of him? Or did they not know? How could they not? He ran a hand over his hair. Yes, it had darkened into a deeper shade of auburn over the years, but he well remembered when it was a brighter red, when his Irish heritage was easier to identify.

He remembered all too well the names, the jabs, the outright abuse he took in school. All because his parents had sought a better life here... for the hopes and prosperity promised in these lands. Little did they know their son, Francis Dagley, a man most would call Slim, would spend his life wondering if it was worth the cost.

Ada stood as directed by the Reverend. Mrs. Wilmont rose beside her. They joined with the congregation and sang a closing hymn. The words did not speak to Ada as much as the melody. Or the fact that numerous voices were lifting together to praise God. What a picture of heaven! She always loved this part of the service.

She closed her eyes and let that wash over her. It gave her chills, even on such a warm day in this crowded church. The tingles on her skin were unmistakable.

As the last lines faded, she bowed her head until the Reverend finished his closing prayer. Then they were released.

"My, wasn't that a fine sermon," Mrs. Wilmont said, turning toward her.

Ada faced her new friend and caretaker. "Yes, ma'am. I especially liked the part about Abraham's faith being credited to him as righteousness. Just think, there isn't anything we can't accomplish through Christ if we have faith."

Mrs. Wilmont nodded. "I like your enthusiasm, dear. It will carry you far." The woman's smile was genuine and sweet. "Come now, let's see if we can't meet some of the townsfolk before heading to the café."

Ada nodded and followed the widow out of the pew and into the aisle. Mrs. Wilmont looped an arm through Ada's and steered her toward the back door. They stopped here and there to chat with various folk. Mrs. Wilmont was indeed mindful to introduce her without putting undue pressure on her to carry the conversation. For that, she was grateful.

But as they neared the exit, a man stepped in front of them, blocking their path. "Aunt Lottie, don't think you will get by me."

"Oh, you startled me!" Mrs Wilmont put a hand to her chest. "What do you mean, coming out of nowhere, scaring old ladies?"

"You are far from old, my good woman." The younger man, who was probably only five years older than herself, Ada wagered, flattered Mrs. Wilmont. Indeed, the woman did not act or appear as old as Ada had come to discover her to be.

Mrs. Wilmont turned to Ada. "Ada, I would like to introduce you to my nephew, Mr. Stanford Wilmont."

"Stanford A. Wilmont, III," he corrected, quite nearly speaking over her. But his eyes were on Ada's face.

"Stanford, this is Miss Ada Miller, the new schoolteacher."

His brow rose. "Schoolteacher? No. You appear much more... refined than I would have expected for a schoolteacher."

What did that mean? "My father is the last in a long line of prominent lawyers in Richmond."

"I see." His smile was warm and inviting. It put her at ease immediately.

Mrs. Wilmont's voice broke into her thoughts. "I saved you a seat. Did you only now make it to service?" Her gaze on him was hard, admonishing.

"I...slipped in a few moments late, but I arrived long before the sermon started. I enjoyed Reverend Jones's pontification on Abraham walking out his faith."

Ada quirked a brow. Had he just voiced the very thing she had earlier?

Stanford's eyes fell on her once more. "It is interesting to see how one lives out their calling."

"Through faith," Ada finished for him.

"Yes, of course." His brown eyes moved over her features and turned her stomach to porridge. Had he been so distracted he'd let his sentence trail?

"We were about to continue into town toward the café," Ada said, looking to Mrs. Wilmont.

"Oh," Stanford said, the disappointment evident in his voice.

"Stanford, what is it?" Mrs. Wilmont appeared the slightest bit exasperated with her nephew.

"I was hoping to catch you and beg my way into your kitchen for some of your dumplings." If possible, his eyes deepened in that moment as his features drooped. What kind of charm was this he played out on Mrs. Wilmont?

She gave him a sideways look. Would she not relent?

At last, Mrs. Wilmont threw her hands up. "All right. But only because it's Miss Miller's first Sunday lunch with me."

"Of course. If you will allow me, I will treat you both to lunch at the café next Sunday."

"I will see you do." Mrs. Wilmont winked at him.

"Allow me to see you lovely ladies to your wagon."

The group of three managed to exit the church, and Stanford assisted the women into their cart. Then they made the trip to Mrs. Wilmont's home in short order.

Stanford's cart pulled in soon after they were inside.

"You must allow me to assist you," Ada said, as she pulled off her hat.

Mrs. Wilmont jerked around. "That...um...won't be necessary."

"But I don't mind." What was Mrs. Wilmont concerned about?

The woman bent down to grab flour out of the bin of goods she retrieved the previous day from the store. "Goodness me!"

"What is it?" Stanford questioned as he stepped through the front door. "Everything all right?"

Mrs. Wilmont bolted upright. "Yes. I just...lost track of these letters that came for Ada."

Ada stepped forward to receive the envelopes Mrs. Wilmont stretched toward her.

This handwriting, addressing the first letter, was not her brother's. But it came from Wharton City. Slim, perhaps? It looked a little like his penmanship. Curious. Was everything all right? The second appeared to be from her mother.

"Are you unwell, Miss Miller?" Mr. Wilmont touched her arm.

She looked up. "I...yes. It's just...these may be important."

"Oh. I'm terribly sorry. I feel awful." Mrs. Wilmont stepped toward her.

"No, it's all right. I simply mean that I might need to excuse myself to read them. I don't wish to be rude." She glanced between the two.

"Of course not," Mrs. Wilmont said. "Go, read your letters. I'll get lunch started."

"Thank you." Ada nodded. "Excuse me, Mr. Wilmont."

He nodded back to her.

Ada slipped into her room and ripped at the seam of the second letter. Her mother inquired after Ada's ability to settle into life in Tombstone and asked after her new accommodations. Nothing too pressing.

Turning her attention to the first letter, she opened the envelope. The papers within were written in the same script and hand that the address had been. She pulled them out.

Glancing over them, she let out a breath. It was from Slim—a response to her letter and another story. Wouldn't her students be thrilled! But he had also written a short letter. Perhaps a simple response to her words? Or an introduction to his story? She looked at the note.

Miss Miller,

Thank you for your kind words. I did not think my stories would ever be read, but I am glad you like them. I have included another. I hope you enjoy it. And your students.

Things here at the ranch are not the same without Dan. Or Cutie. But the new hands are getting along just fine.

She stopped. There was something he wasn't saying. Something important. Maybe it wasn't for her to discern. So, she shrugged and kept reading.

Daisy is a character all her own. Maybe she should be in one of the stories. Or become a repeating character?

Next time you see Dan and Lily, give them my best.

Your friend,

Slim

He had signed it your friend. Was that what they were? Friends? They weren't enemies. Were they acquaintances? That was a type of friend.

Maybe she was just thinking about it too hard. Much more than she should.

Still, she found that a smile had made its way onto her face. And she couldn't rein it in. But was that because of the letter? The new story? Or the rather good-looking nephew to Mrs. Wilmont that was not five feet away, just beyond the wall to her bedroom?

Slim worked to clean the last stall on his round through the barn. He rather liked the quiet work. Time to think. To imagine. To dream up more stories. And that's exactly what he did. By the time he'd finished, he'd have a solid one done.

Most other tasks on the ranch didn't allow for that—too many distractions. Add to that the flapping gums of the other ranch hands. Why were these new hands so talkative? Couldn't they just relax and let things be?

"Slim," a voice from behind said gently.

He startled, jerking around to face any manner of attack.

Amanda Miller stood just outside the stall, eyes wide, hand raised to block any onslaught.

"Sorry, Mrs. Miller, I...well, you surprised me."

"Truly? That's not like you." Her brow furrowed.

He pulled off a glove and ran his bandana over his forehead. Could he ease his pounding heart? "Did you need something?"

She looked as if she'd been caught sneaking candy before supper. "I...just came from town. I picked up the mail. There is a letter for you."

"A letter?" His heartbeat quickened. Had Ada written him so soon? There was barely time for his letter to have made it to Tombstone and another to travel back. He let out a breath. Perhaps, she was only polite and timely with her correspondence.

Amanda held out the envelope.

Indeed, the address was in Ada's hand. He hesitated only a moment before rubbing his palm against his pant leg and reaching for it.

Amanda held to it for a moment.

He looked at her.

"I did not mention this to Brandon."

Slim's brows gathered as his eyes dropped to the letter. Why would Amanda not speak of it? Would Brandon be upset? He remembered his boss's unease with the last letter Ada had posted to him. Maybe this wasn't a good idea.

He set his gaze back on Amanda, swallowed, and gave a slight nod.

"I haven't, but I will."

Again, Slim nodded. It wasn't his desire to come between a man and his wife.

Amanda released her grip on the letter. "I just want to give you a chance to decide what you'll say to him. Because he will want to know what's going on." Her words were firm.

Slim couldn't look at her any longer, so he shifted his gaze to the letter, examining the fine pen strokes.

"Do you know what's going on?" Amanda's voice was softer. Her words were measured.

He peered at her. And shrugged. Had Brandon told his wife about Slim's stories? It was likely. "I'm sharing some stories with her school children."

Wasn't that all? And hadn't Brandon started this thing in the first place? Why then would he now be suspicious?

Amanda nodded. "All right."

The silence that fell between them became awkward. Why shouldn't it be? She all but expressed that Slim had best not have intentions where Ada was concerned. Even Amanda must see how unevenly yoked they would be.

She let out a breath. "See you at supper." A small smile passed on her features before she turned and left the barn.

Slim removed his hat and hit the side of the stall. These were the people he admired the most in the world. If they didn't think he was worthy...maybe he wasn't.

He shoved the letter into his pocket. It would be best if he got rid of it later. Perhaps, he could talk with Brandon and have him tell his sister that Slim was just too busy to share any more stories. Yes, that would be best.

Though he was resolved, he couldn't deny that the thought cut at him. Because he already enjoyed her warmth? Or because of the insult to his person?

He made short work of finishing the stall. Then he stopped by the bunkhouse to wash up. Hank and Junior walked up while he stood at the pump, finishing.

"Wonder what Cook's got for us tonight," Hank muttered.

"I'm just looking forward to a cool glass of tea," Junior said, but his voice seemed grated. He did sound parched.

As usual, Slim wasn't in a hurry but didn't wish to linger. He stood upright, nodded to the two men, and moved off toward the homestead.

Hank tipped his hat back to Slim and stepped to the pump.

"Hey, what's this?" Slim heard Hank's voice clear and loud.

He spun.

Hank held up a rather familiar-looking envelope.

No! Slim moved for his pocket. It wasn't there. How had it fallen out? Did it even matter?

"It's addressed to Slim." Junior had come up behind Hank and peered over his shoulder. "And that handwriting is awful purty."

Hank snickered.

"Open it." Junior bumped Hank with his shoulder. "See what it says."

Slim took two strides to close the distance, but Hank backed up as Junior moved into Slim's path. "Now, boys, that's enough. Give my letter back."

"Why? You got something to hide?" Hank sputtered, fighting laughter as he looked down at the letter once more. "Miss Ada Clara Miller!"

"You don't mean the boss's sister, do you?" Junior's eyes were wide, but not as wide as his grin.

Slim tried to push past him. "I'll thank you to return my property and leave this be."

"Hear him, Junior?" Hank said, shuffling back a few more paces as Junior continued to frustrate Slim, blocking him. "Seems like it might be something important. Wonder what exactly the lady has to say?"

"I'll not let you invade the lady's private writings." Slim's face warmed. He became surprised at the sheer heat of the ire growing within him. It welled, filling him, and threatened to spill over.

"Awww, don't be that way, Slim. We're only teasing ya'." Hank moved toward where Slim and Junior stood, holding out the letter.

Slim stepped back, straightening himself, looking between the two men.

As Hank came near, Slim opened his hand for the precious piece of mail. But no sooner did it graze his fingertips than Hand snatched it back.

"Maybe just a peek." He ripped at the flap.

Something overcame Slim in that moment. He gave Junior an elbow to the gut and charged after Hank.

Focused on the envelope, Hank didn't see Slim coming until he was on top of Hank. It ended almost as quickly as it started. Hank covered his head with his arms and yelled his surrender.

Slim paused.

Hank peered out from between his forearms. "You're crazy."

"Give me that letter," he seethed.

Hank held it out.

Slim snatched it and relinquished his hold on the ranch hand. He dusted himself off and turned away from the two men.

Junior leaned against the pump, his hand still on his stomach, muttering something about Slim not able to take a jesting. What did it matter? They had crossed a line. And they didn't even care to understand.

CHAPTER 4

On the Horizon

Slim sat behind the barn in a rare quiet moment. He had taken to writing more of his stories down. Was that for his own sake? Or Ada's? To better share them with her?

They had been exchanging letters for some weeks now, and he could not deny that her compliments made him feel special. Important. Like he was good at something.

And he liked it.

But he'd best not wander too far from there...that didn't have to mean that he liked her. Those thoughts might take him to places he couldn't follow. His smile fell as did his heart at that realization, however. What could that mean? He'd rather not dwell on it.

Turning his attention back to his story, he tried to get his thoughts onto the page. A brave schoolteacher had found her way into this one. Now, that was dangerous. Or was it? She had been so kind. Perhaps, he was just returning the favor.

He continued working. When he paused several moments later to read back over his work, he rolled his eyes. Sheriff Maynard had taken a particular liking to the woman. And why wouldn't he? She was warm and thoughtful. Compassionate and somehow always knew just what to say.

Just like Ada.

Yep. He was in trouble.

He gripped the paper, intending to destroy it as he had so many stories that had gone a direction he didn't care for. But as he went to tear the lines, he couldn't. Something stopped him. Could it be that he enjoyed writing about her? Wanted to continue? If he could never be more than what he was to her, why couldn't he live through his character? Isn't that what imagination and dreaming was all about? Or would that, too, be dangerous?

He thought on it.

Movement from within the barn drew his attention. Did the footfalls come closer?

He held his breath and strained to listen.

They did.

He must hide the papers. But where?

It wasn't the best situation, but he shoved them behind his back. They crinkled, and he grimaced. But he couldn't let anyone discover them. Especially this story and the character based on Ada. What if they knew?

Whoever it was moved about before coming ever closer. Who was it? The footsteps were too heavy and steady to be one of the children. Not rushed enough to be Cook. And no hint of a limp—not Uncle Owen.

Soon enough, the mystery was solved when Brandon popped his head out of the barn's back door.

"There you are. I've been looking all over creation for you."

Slim swallowed. He had not been alone with Brandon since the man had delivered that first letter from Ada. And Slim had been dreading it since Mrs. Miller had brought the second. After all, she had warned him this would be forthcoming. Unable to form words, Slim lifted a hand and waved.

Brandon walked to where Slim sat.

Should he stand and greet his boss? The man would see his papers. Then he might find out Slim had been writing about his sister. That would not help the situation.

Brandon stopped a couple arms' lengths away. And peered out over the hillside. "You sure seem to like it back here."

Slim nodded, not trusting his voice.

Brandon glanced down at him, a curious look on his face. Did he wonder at Slim maintaining his seated position?

Slim's features warmed. How he wished they wouldn't.

Blessedly, Brandon looked away once more. Almost as if he were nervous, too. That couldn't be. "I...have something to say. And I guess I need to get it out. No sense carrying on about the weather and such." Brandon scratched at his forehead.

Here it was... Slim braced himself.

"The thing is...when my sister wrote you, it bothered me."

Slim nodded. His face heated even more. He directed his gaze to the back of the barn. No need to torture himself further by staring at his boss.

"But I didn't know why."

Slim's gaze jerked to Brandon's. Did he truly not know?

"Maybe I was just being protective...not wanting her to get involved."

Slim nodded again. He understood that. Brandon didn't want her getting attached to the likes of him. Someone with little prospects.

"I mean, I didn't know your intentions, and...well...I didn't ask. I just reacted."

What? All of this was because he wanted to know Slim's intentions? He was just being kind. That couldn't be all.

"And, so," Brandon said, releasing a long breath. "I owe you an apology."

How was he to respond to that? He'd felt quite deserving of Brandon's every suspicion, every cross word. Wouldn't he feel the same in his shoes?

But that apparently was not the situation. Brandon only worried that Slim might string Ada along. Or use her ill. And maybe that hurt worse. Did Brandon have so little regard for Slim's character? Did he not know his ranch hand at all? Perhaps, then, they were not as close as he'd thought.

Brandon squatted. "I mean, I had no right to think that. You've never crossed me. And you've never been anything but honorable."

That eased the sting. A little.

"But it's my sister. I hope you can understand."

Slim let that sink in for a moment, trying to see it from Brandon's way of things. And, as he let go of being insulted for a few seconds, he did know why Brandon had reacted that way. So, did this mean there was no longer resistance to Slim if he chose to pursue Ada? Would Ada even be receptive?

Slim gulped. A whole new bundle of nerves tightened in his chest.

"Can you?" Brandon said, his brow furrowed.

Slim caught his gaze. "I-I can, boss. In fact, I think I'd feel the same."

Brandon nodded, his features relaxing. "Thank you." He maneuvered to sit where he had been crouching. So, he meant to stay a while?

"Then, the next question is...what are your intentions?"

Slim shot him a look. Why did his boss put him on the spot? He had only just started being able to consider the possibility. How could he even know what his intentions might be?

Brandon's gaze hardened. The man clearly needed an answer. Now.

"I—I—"

Brandon's eyes narrowed. "Look, I know you two have been exchanging letters for some time now."

"All innocent, boss. I promise. I send her stories. She asks for more."

Brandon's features betrayed his skepticism. "That isn't all."

The heat returned to Slim's features. "There's not much more to tell. We exchange simple pleasantries. She shares a little about what's going on with her classroom, asks me about the ranch..."

The hardness of Brandon's features did not let up.

"Honest, boss."

Brandon sighed, and a softness came to the edges of his face. "Then I guess you'd better decide what your intentions are. And soon."

What could that mean?

Brandon pulled an envelope from his pocket.

Slim's heart beat faster. Another letter from Ada? How was that possible? He had just posted his last letter to her a day ago. But as

Brandon held it out, he saw that the address was not in her handwriting, but in Dan's. What did that mean?

"I'll let you read it for yourself. Then we'll talk." Brandon rose.

Slim watched him, his mind filling with questions. What was in the letter? What could it mean? Was something wrong with Ada? Had she shared something with Dan or Lily? If so, what? His heart raced, and he could hardly slow his thoughts to capture one of them.

"I'll leave you to it. Let's talk after supper."

Slim nodded, a bit numbed by the things bombarding his brain.

Brandon moved off and back into the barn.

Slim had not realized the slight tremor in his hand until he looked down at the envelope. But there it was. Had Brandon noticed? He hoped not.

Tearing at the flap, he released the contents.

Slim,

I hope you're doing well. And finding things to keep you busy. Are the new hands adjusting well to your teasing? I hope so. I hope you all are getting along and downright inseparable by now. Well, not truly inseparable.

Things at the ranch are good, but busy. Finding worthwhile help is more difficult than I'd thought. My most trusted hand got injured and will be down for a few weeks. And I was already short. I really need someone I can rely on.

I've written Brandon and requested your presence in Tombstone for the time my ranch hand is down. I hope he can manage without you. And perhaps your new pals can let you come here for a few weeks.

Would you consider it? It would be great—working with you again. I hate to be desperate, but that's where I am.

I have included enough money for the price of a train ticket to Tombstone because I know you won't leave a friend in need. That's one of your admirable qualities. I just hate to be taking advantage of that.

Sincerely,
Dan

Everything fell into place—Brandon's concerns among them. Did that mean Brandon had as good as given his permission? Slim had to admit, at least to himself, that the thought of meeting Ada in person had crossed his mind at least once as he read the letter. But, as much as he wanted to meet her, he would go even if she weren't there. That would just be sugar in the tea.

Regardless of the reasons, and what order they took in his mind, he was going to Tombstone.

Ada and Mrs. Wilmont stepped into the café. She wasn't sure what made her so uneasy about this encounter, but her stomach was in knots.

She scanned the tables within. Was Stanford already here? Or would they end up waiting on him? There he was—in the corner. He rose as she set eyes on him.

A wide grin graced his handsome features. And she flushed. What was that about? Was she so taken with his fine face? Goodness, she didn't even know the man.

He stepped around the table and waved them over.

Ada touched Mrs. Wilmont's arm. "I found him."

Mrs. Wilmont's gaze followed where she pointed. "Ah, yes. There's my Stanford. Shall we?"

Ada nodded. She couldn't stop the slight tremor that went through her. Excitement? Trepidation? Whatever it was, she decided not to think on it too much. He was a good-looking single man, and she was an unattached lady. There was little reason to feel anything but hopeful about their interactions.

Soon enough, they stood at the table. Stanford pulled out his aunt's chair. Ada was tempted to seat herself. They weren't in the high society of Richmond, after all. But something in his manner gave her pause. He interacted with them as a gentleman. So, she should play the part of a lady.

After pushing Mrs. Wilmont's chair to the table, he came to stand beside Ada. He put a hand to the back of her chair. "Miss Miller, if I may."

She nodded. "Thank you, sir."

He assisted her just as he had his aunt. Then he took his seat between the two ladies, beaming. "I must be the luckiest man in all of Arizona to have such fine dinner companions."

"My, my, Stanford, you do flatter," Mrs. Wilmont chided, raising a brow.

Ada's face warmed. His compliments did put her a bit off-balance.

He turned his full attention to Ada, seeming to ignore his aunt's comment. "How do you find Tombstone, Miss Miller?"

"Oh," she said on a breath, shooting Mrs. Wilmont a look. "I like it quite well. My students and I are getting along, and I find that life here is...every bit the adventure I hoped it would be."

He quirked an eyebrow, and despite his rather blonde hair and mustache, he appeared much like his aunt in that moment. "Is that so? Adventure, you say. It must be so very different from what you're used to. While the town does have some niceties, it cannot provide the culture of Richmond."

Ada considered his words. And how to respond. The culture, as he put it, was not necessarily something she missed. It had been more caging than anything.

"Do you not agree?" His brown eyes flashed as his smile broadened.

"That is true, Mr. Wilmont. There are more...amenities in the city back home."

"Stanford," he said as he looked about the area.

"Pardon?" Did he address himself? That was a bit odd.

His gaze landed on hers once more. "Please, do feel free to call me 'Stanford.' It is, after all, my name. 'Mr. Wilmont' makes me sound dreadfully old."

She peered down at her hands in her lap, needing relief from the intensity of his eyes. "Yes, of course."

"I hope I am not too bold, Miss Miller." He set his hand near her utensils on the table. Did he mean to reach out to her somehow? It was rather bold. "But I would like the privilege of calling you by your Christian name."

Ada looked at Mrs. Wilmont. What must she think of this exchange? But the woman's attention had turned toward the door to the kitchen. Did she no longer mind their conversation?

"I..." She paused. Why? What he asked was not unreasonable. He was one of the only men of her acquaintance in Tombstone. Though it may encourage him to believe her open to his interest. Wasn't she?

His gaze remained on her face, captivated it seemed, by her every move. He did make her feel things. Perhaps, she might be open to his attention.

"I would like that."

He smiled again. And his breathing became deeper. Had he been holding his breath? Was he so concerned she might dismiss his request?

"I am only getting hungrier," Mrs. Wilmont complained. She continued to glance around the café, seeking out the server or at least someone who might assist them.

Stanford shifted his focus. "I can find someone. I'll remind them there are needing customers out here."

Was it Ada's imagination, or was there something of a hard edge to his voice? It must just be in her head. There was little reason to become agitated.

"No," Mrs. Wilmont said, holding up a hand. "That won't be necessary. I can wait. They seem rather busy."

Stanford's features did not soften.

Ada watched him. Was he upset for his aunt's sake? That must be it —ill-tempered because the older woman was uncomfortable. He was a fine, caring nephew.

It was only a few moments more before a harried young woman stopped by their table. "My apologies, folks. We are swamped. And short a waitress. But let me get you something to wet your whistle."

"Short a waitress? I don't see how that—" Stanford started.

"Yes, dear," Mrs. Wilmont interjected. "A glass of lemonade would be good for me. Ada?" The older woman looked across the table at her.

"Yes, lemonade, please."

Ada shifted her focus to Stanford. What had he been trying to say? Was he irritated at the waitress?

"Tea, please." His lips were tight and thin, but he seemed to be all politeness.

Would she now try to read into everything he did, so she could dismiss him as a possible suitor? It would not be the first time. Her father had often pointed out how she made every attempt to disqualify many fine choices. Did she not realize that all of God's creatures were flawed in some respect? That, at least, was her father's argument.

She let out a breath. Perhaps, she should spend a little less time being critical of others and a little more time looking at her own flaws for the sake of bettering herself.

That would be a more worthwhile endeavor.

"Something amiss?" Stanford's words pulled her back to the present.

"Nothing at all." She offered him a smile. "Just thinking."

"And what could our newest addition to Tombstone be thinking about?" He arched his eyebrows. Was this his coy way of flirting? Did he suspect she thought about him? She might be put off, except that he was right...at least in part.

"Just something my father used to say." She could be coy, too.

"Oh? Do share." He lowered his voice as if she held the greatest secret.

She glanced at Mrs. Wilmont. The woman's brows had lowered. Did something concern her? What?

"I...think I'll keep my secrets for now," she said, rearranging her utensils.

"What do you think, Aunt Lottie? How shall we pry this information from her?"

Mrs. Wilmont snorted. "Someday, you'll learn."

They both looked at her.

What could that mean? Ada wondered after Mrs. Wilmont's words. But not for long.

The young waitress arrived then with their drinks. "There. Want to hear the specials?"

Ada tried to focus as the woman talked about the day's menu items, but she couldn't shake the suspicion that there was more going on under the surface here.

Slim had packed his one suitcase. It took little effort and less time. There wasn't much he owned in the world. That had not surprised him. What had shocked him was the amount of space his writings and the letters from Ada took.

He wanted for a few moments to pour over her words once more. But that would not be wise. Not with Hank and Junior lurking around. And after his recent conversation with Brandon, he didn't know if he should do that.

They had indeed met after supper that evening. As much as he wanted to have a clear answer for his boss, he still didn't. After all, he had no idea what was in Ada's mind about their exchanges. It still seemed rather innocent to him. So, he was as honest as he could be with his boss, but he ended up being more vague than Brandon liked. And it was obvious in the man's reaction.

There was nothing for it, though. Brandon couldn't squeeze water from a stone. If it wasn't there to be had, he couldn't pull it out of Slim.

Still, as Slim considered the letters, he couldn't help it. He opened the suitcase and slipped one into his pocket—reading material for the train ride.

Uncle Owen would be taking Slim to the train station tomorrow, early in the morning. He'd catch the train in Tucson and be in Tombstone sometime later in the day.

Then he would see her.

The group had put together a care package for Ada. It seemed everyone had pitched in—Brandon, Amanda, the kids, Cook, and even Uncle Owen. Slim had tried to prepare something for her—he wanted to finish the story he started that had the brave schoolteacher in it. But then...she would know. For certain. And he couldn't imagine that going well. So, he'd best not.

Maybe he could pass on another of his stories. That didn't seem quite as special. Still, he didn't want to show up empty handed.

He stepped out of the bunkhouse and moved toward the barn to check on his horse. That would be the only thing—he sure would miss that animal.

Dan had written to Brandon that he might need Slim for a couple of months. That was longer than Slim had suspected. But it would be fine. He was eager to work with Dan again. It would be familiar. And easy.

Though, he had started to enjoy Eli's company.

As he passed into the barn, he heard sniffling. What could that be? He stilled, listening to figure out which direction the sound came from. Tilting his head this way and that, he decided the noises came from the hay loft.

But who? Should he call out? Or would that spook whoever was up there? The muffled cries sounded child-like. One of the Miller children? Had someone gotten hurt? Or were they hiding from someone or something?

Slim had a pretty good relationship with all of the children that frequented the Miller Ranch. Perhaps he'd best climb to the loft and see what he could do to help.

Stepping to the ladder, he lifted himself up and scaled the moderate rungs with ease. The loft was not the smallest one he'd been in, but he still had to duck his tall, broad frame.

He glanced around. It wasn't so big that a person had many places to conceal themself. So, he didn't have to search long. At the far end of the loft, near the back of the barn structure, was Nisto. When did he get here? Wasn't he supposed to be in town with Cutie and Mariena?

It mattered little at the moment. He had curled his limbs into his core as he sat and buried his face in his knees. The sight tore at Slim. What could have happened? He did not think the boy was injured. Not that he could tell at first glance, at least.

"Hey, Nisto," he said by way of announcement. "Didn't expect to see you today."

The boy quieted but didn't lift his head. Just shifted to turn away from Slim as much as possible. Slim's heart grew heavy at the sight. Something had happened. Something bad.

Slim closed the distance with slow movements. Then, continuing with careful and intentional maneuvers, he lowered himself to sit beside Nisto, about two feet away.

"I sure do like it up here." Slim looked over the barn. It was a great vantage point. "You can see quite a lot."

Nisto sniffled again.

"Not a bad climb. But I can't imagine Uncle Owen making it up here, can you?"

The boy shook his head slightly.

"He did. Few years ago. Billy the Kid and his gang attacked the ranch. Maybe Samuel told you about it. But I wonder if he told you that Uncle Owen and he hid in this hay loft. And they were never discovered."

Nisto's deep brown eyes sought Slim's. They were wide.

"Truly." Slim leaned back, propped up on his extended arms. "Somehow, Uncle Owen managed to get up here. Took three men to get him down, though. What a chore that was!"

Nisto's lips curled slightly. "Uncle Owen is brave."

"Yes. That he is."

The boy shifted and looked out over the barn again. "I wish I could be brave."

Slim furrowed his brow. "Who says you're not brave?"

Nisto shrugged.

"There aren't many people who've been through what you have. Much less can survive it and still be able to see good in life. Or laugh at my stories."

Nisto didn't crack a smile. Whatever had happened had wounded him.

Slim softened his voice. "You don't have to talk about it, but I'll listen if you want to."

The boy peered at him with a sideways glance.

"I mean, you're always listening to my stories. Seems right I listen to yours."

Nisto studied him. "But your stories are made up. And they have happy endings."

"And yours doesn't?"

The young lad seamed his lips.

Slim waited for a few moments as the silence dragged on. After some time, he drew in a deep breath and let it out. "I don't want to push. If you ever do want to talk, I'm—"

"I wish I was more like Samuel." The words came out in a rush.

Slim jerked toward Nisto. An anchor weighed in his stomach. He wished to heaven he hadn't heard those words. But, as much as he wanted to say something, he held back.

"Nobody wants me around." The boy buried his head in the pocket between his knees and his chest again and sobbed.

"Who, Nisto? Who doesn't want you around?"

Nisto pulled his head up but didn't look at Slim. "The kids at school. They said... and then they..."

Slim frowned. His heart squeezed. He understood, perhaps more than Nisto would ever know. And he also knew that, right now, it was difficult for Nisto to form the words. Maybe couldn't say them out loud —that would give them too much power.

How would he best comfort the boy? Reassure him that he was worth something? To his family? To the Millers? Even to Samuel? All the words that came to mind sounded pitiful and hollow.

He set a hand on Nisto's back. "It's not right."

Nisto shook his head.

And Slim sat with him for a long time, letting him cry. If Slim did speak, it was to agree with the boy that the pain was real, and the situation difficult. What else could he offer? Because his own heart was being torn open. And his own wounds were as fresh as ever.

The world was a hard place for people who were different. He had no fine words to change all that. No matter how he wished it.

Ada walked to the telegraph office. She needed to send the letter she had written to Mother yesterday. While her mother's letter had been filled with questions for Ada, it contained little about her own situation. How did Mother fare? Was she well? Did she still bemoan Ada taking hold of the opportunity to come west and chase her dream?

Even so, that did not mean Ada couldn't share her adventures with Mother. Maybe, just maybe, they would help her see what a difference her daughter made out here. And how important it was that Ada took the chance.

When it was her turn at the window, Ada handed over the letter and waited for her mail. A couple of envelopes were handed back. She glanced over the fronts—one from Amanda Miller and one from Slim. As much as she wanted to hear from her brother's wife and take in news of the ranch, her brother, and her niece and nephews, she turned her attention to Slim's letter.

There wasn't really an explanation for why she was so drawn to his. Other than her eagerness for the next story. She enjoyed their correspondence, for certain, but that couldn't be the reason she put Amanda's to the side. Except...hadn't she just received one from him not two days ago? Was all not well?

Her pulse raced as she moved to a bench and urged the envelope to open. Soon enough, she held the papers from within securely in her grasp. The writing was hurried and the note short. What could that mean? Was he so rushed? Had he not the desire to attend to the letter properly? That bothered her...perhaps more than it should. But she unfolded the papers and read:

Ada,

    This will be quick. I have news. And I best just say it. I am coming to Tombstone.

Slim was coming here? What for? To meet her? That seemed odd. Did he think more of their exchanges? They were pleasant and friendly, to be sure. But it surprised her that he would go so far as to make the trip. What must Brandon think of it?

    She took a breath. Don't get ahead of yourself, she chided. It would be best to hear him out.

Dan has written and asked for my help. One of his ranch hands is down

with an injury, and he needs someone he can trust. It will be good to work with him again.

She paused. And was surprised at the pang that hit through her chest. Was she now disappointed that he came for Dan's sake and not to meet her?

Did she even understand her own feelings in the moment? Slim had become a good friend and a great help with his stories. That was all. He had never once made an overture otherwise. And she best not read into things that weren't there. Besides, hadn't she just decided to entertain Stanford Wilmont's attentions?

I am sorry. I don't have the time to get a story ready for you this time. There is much to prepare. I should arrive on Thursday's train.

Thursday? It was Tuesday! He would be here in two days? How could she prepare herself for their meeting? She took a breath. It would be fine. He was her brother's ranch hand and Dan's friend. This would be fine.

I do hope you will allow me to visit you once I arrive.
    Your friend,
    Slim

She held the letter together in her lap. Two days. And she'd had no idea. None. Not from Brandon. Not from Lily. No one.

How was she to manage this?

CHAPTER 5

Arrival

Slim stepped off the train, relishing the solidity of the platform. He could live a hundred years and never need to board another. It had not been to his liking—the jolt of leaving the station, the loud clacking of the locomotive on the track, and the screeching of the heavy machine coming to a stop. It wasn't natural. It wasn't right. Give him a stagecoach any day. Though, he was amazed to have made it to Tombstone with such speed.

"Slim," a voice called from off to his right.

He turned in that direction, giving himself a moment to let his vision settle. Was it possible that he was so disoriented from the ride?

Dan moved toward him, beaming.

Slim smiled in spite of the strangeness in his head. He stepped to his friend, lifting a hand to grab ahold of Dan's already raised one.

Dan gripped Slim's hand, pulling him closer for a quick hug, and smacking him on the back. "Been a while."

"Yes." Slim reined in his emotion as he moved back.

"How was your trip?"

Slim looked back at the train. "I..." What could he say?

Dan quirked a brow.

"It was different."

Dan laughed and gave Slim's shoulder a good slap. "Let's get your things. Lily is excited to see you." His friend maneuvered him toward the station, where he spotted Dan's wife.

She was every bit as pretty as Slim remembered. Perhaps even more so, now that she held herself with an air of confidence. Being with Dan had changed her. Being loved had changed her.

"It is so good of you to come," she said.

Slim did not doubt she meant it. Sincerity shone in her eyes. Was she so concerned after her husband? What had Dan not shared with Brandon? Glancing at Dan, who now moved off to gather Slim's cargo, Slim wondered about the state of his friend's budding ranch.

"I do hope you had a good trip." Lily's voice drew his attention back to her.

"Yes, well, I..." Again, he was caught. "It was fine."

She tilted her head as if to question him. Then she smiled. "You're here, now. And we aim to make you as comfortable as possible."

"I appreciate that. But I'm here to help. To work."

She nodded, her smile communicating her gratitude.

Dan came back with the crate bearing Ada's things from the family. "This seems to be everything. Did they misplace something?" He eyed the one bag Slim carried.

"No." Slim's face warmed. Did Dan expect him to have a trunk? Should he have more?

Dan's features smoothed. "Very well, then. I'll load this, and we'll be on our way."

Slim nodded and watched as Lily took up step beside her husband, and they made their way to a waiting wagon.

Dan set the crate in the back and held out a hand. What did he want? He moved his hand more pointedly in the direction of Slim's suitcase. Should he give it up? Slim had kept it close to his person the entire trip. After all, it contained such personal things—his stories and the letters from Ada.

But Dan wasn't asking to go through his things, only to load them in the wagon bed. So, Slim handed it over...though with some hesitation.

Then they all climbed onto the benches. With nothing further to delay them, they were off.

As they moved through the town, Slim was amazed at the size of Tombstone—much bigger than Wharton City. But so was Tucson. Still, for whatever reason, he had not anticipated the size of the town. There were stores, saloons, and other places of business lining the main stretch. And so many people milling about. As they passed through, a small group of men, all with red strips of cloth tied around their waists, glared at them.

"What's that about?" Slim muttered, just loud enough for Dan to hear.

Dan half turned. Did he intend to keep the conversation level low? Was that so necessary? "They are members of the Cowboy Gang."

"Gang?"

"They're nothing but trouble—rustlers, thieves, outlaws. You name it, they've done it."

"And that's common knowledge?"

Dan nodded.

Lily seemed to pale a bit but straightened her spine. Was she, too, afraid?

"Why aren't they locked up?"

"There are too many of them. And even the law is afraid of them, I guess."

Slim furrowed his brow. What kind of town was this? The lawmen afraid of the lawbreakers? That couldn't be a good thing. His dear friends appeared unnerved and perhaps even a bit fearful of the situation. What did that mean for him? Or more...for Ada?

"And Sheriff Maynard, once again, slept well, knowing that the town of Dayton City was safe and at peace." Ada finished the story and lowered the papers.

The children cheered.

"More!" one of the girls in the second row called out.

"That's the only one I have," Ada said, laughing. "You know, Mr. Dagley sends me one at a time.

"Read us one of the other ones again," a younger lad piped up.

She gave him a kind look then swept her gaze over the entire class. Their faces appeared eager and hopeful. So much, she wished she could oblige. "I think you are all hoping I will forget your arithmetic for the day."

A few groans followed.

"We aren't," the same girl insisted. "Honest."

Ada touched the girl's desk. "I know. But we need to attend to it all the same. Let's pull out our slates, children."

There was a rustle of movement as the students obeyed.

Ada stepped to her desk and set the papers containing the story on a pile with the others. She let her fingers linger on the pages for a moment. Slim had given her a great gift these past few weeks. And to her students. They looked forward to his stories—a rare treat. She must find a way to thank him. But how?

Pulling herself from her reverie, she turned to face the class. They sat at the ready. "Where were we? Yes, our subtraction facts..."

For the next half hour, she explained and then quizzed the students on the properties of subtraction and how they related to addition. The students did well, with only a few of them needing extra attention.

Soon enough, they were gathering their things as she dismissed them. All too soon, the classroom was empty. And she was alone.

This was the part of the day she both loathed and loved—the quiet of the cavernous space and a time to collect her thoughts. She made short work of clearing her myriad of tasks and working through the stacks on her desk. Then she erased and cleaned the board. Now, home.

She peered down at the watch pinned near her collar. It gave her pause. How had she not realized? Slim's train would have arrived an hour ago.

Not that she could have met him at such a point in the school day. Nor was she certain that would have been appropriate. And he had not mentioned when they would meet. Would it be days? Or perhaps tomorrow? She did not know.

What were his thoughts on their exchanges? Did he think more of them than she? Or less?

This was madness. She needn't scrutinize everything so closely. Nothing would come of it. That conversation would happen when it did. There would be no use worrying over it now.

Gathering her things and pinning her hat back on, she moved to the door and after securing the building, closed the schoolhouse and headed home.

Slim maneuvered the horse and cart through Tombstone. He remembered the path Dan had earlier taken rather well. It helped that Slim was good with directions. And that Dan was good with giving them.

Now, where was that schoolhouse? Dan had said Ada was staying with a widow, Mrs. Wilmont, who lived not one mile from the schoolhouse.

As he neared the edge of the main stretch, he spotted the brown building Dan had pointed out before.

Slim's heart began to beat harder. She was near. So near.

He followed the path marked out by many wagons traveling this way. And he prayed—about this meeting, about the Lord's will for him, about his nervousness, about other things.

Soon enough, he noticed a homestead to the left side of an upcoming hill. That must be it.

His pulse raced. Was he so out of his element?

Slowing the horse, he tried to calm his breathing. Would that ease the pounding of his heart? He feared the sound could be heard by anyone who came near. But it didn't matter. There was the door to the homestead—the only remaining barrier. All the letters, all the words between them—now they would be able to speak in person. What would he say? What could he say?

Maybe this was a bad idea. Perhaps he should have written first or asked Lily to call on Ada and set up a meeting. Or even met her at church come Sunday. But he knew better. He couldn't put it off. Not then and not now.

He had come all this way. And he wanted to lay eyes on her and talk with her, see if she was truly what he thought. So, he dropped off the bench and stepped around to grab the care package from the back of the cart. Then he took the few steps to the front door.

This was it.

He raised a hand. Then took a deep breath. And knocked.

There were some moments of silence. Was no one home? He hadn't considered that.

But then he heard footsteps nearing. The door handle clanged.

Then he was face-to-face with her. And not for the first time.

Ada's fine smooth face, kind brown eyes, and full lips drew him in. Her hair was pulled up, and a hat covered most of it. But that, too, was familiar. He had seen her before. And from the look in her eyes, she was attempting to place him as well.

"The train platform," he said.

"Tucson," she sputtered at the same time. Her features became rosy at her words.

He smiled. How was this possible?

The edges of her lips tugged upward. "How did you find me? What are you doing here? Who are you?"

What did she mean? And he realized she had no idea who he was. He hadn't introduced himself. "It's me. Slim."

"Slim?" She appeared truly confused. "That can't be. Y-you were in Tucson."

He nodded, slowly. "On an errand. For your brother." Yes, for Brandon. Her brother...and his boss. No matter how drawn in he was, he needed to keep that in mind. Her brother was his boss, his friend, and a man he greatly respected.

The color in her cheeks deepened. "I...I can't begin to thank you for your assistance that day." Was she stumbling over her words? Could it be that she was nervous?

He pulled his hat off his head and fumbled with the brim as he averted his gaze. "I'm only glad I was there."

They stood for a few moments. In silence. Awkward silence. Why did he have to be so awkward?

"Who is at the door, Ada?" a voice called from within.

Slim startled. Was that the widow, Mrs. Wilmont?

Ada, likewise, seemed jarred from her thoughts. "Do you...want to come in?"

He nodded, stepping forward and putting his hat back on his head. Then, remembering why he had come, moved back to the porch and picked up the crate he had set to the side. "I come bearing gifts."

"Oh?" There was a lilt to her voice. Did she think that he alone was giving her all these things? Heat crept up his neck.

"Your brother and his family, also Cook, Uncle Owen...everyone it seems...wanted to send you something," he said as he brought the box to the table.

An older woman swept in from the direction of the kitchen. "Hello, sir." She looked at Ada.

"Mrs. Wilmont," Ada said, somewhat exasperated. With herself? "This is Slim Dagley."

There was no other explanation given. Had she spoken with the widow about him? That filled his chest with warmth. He looked at the older woman.

"Slim, this is Mrs. Wilmont." Ada motioned toward the woman.

"Glad to meet you." Slim nodded, removing his hat once more. "Fine house you have here."

"Thank you, Mr. Dagley. It is good to finally meet you, as well. I have heard so much about you." Her smile was genuine and pleasant.

Ada shot her a look.

Slim couldn't help but grin. Perhaps, there was more reason to hope than he'd thought.

"Mr. Dagley," Mrs. Wilmont said, ignoring Ada's stare. "Are you able to stay for dinner?"

"I would like that." He turned his gaze back to Ada. "Very much."

She looked down, the color returning to her face.

Had he been too forward? How could he salvage his blunder? "I... don't have to. My friends—"

"Oh, I insist," Mrs. Wilmont cut in.

Ada had set her eyes on his again. "It would be nice," she said. Her voice clear and sincere. "To catch up."

"Good. It's settled then." Mrs. Wilmont clapped. Then she drifted back toward the kitchen. "Ada, why don't you freshen up?" Mrs. Wilmont turned her focus to Slim. "She only just returned home herself."

Slim nodded. That must be why she still had her hat on.

"Thank you." Ada gave Slim one last look. "If you'll excuse me."

She moved off to the open door at the far side of the great room. Slim could not tear his eyes away until she was well out of sight.

He realized he was already a bit more invested than he'd ever planned to be. But he didn't regret it. Not one bit.

Ada touched her hair one last time. It wasn't perfect, but it was the best it could be. She hadn't expected company this evening. And the hat hadn't done her any favors. It had flattened any fullness left in the top of her hair. Pins could only do so much. Oh, well.

She ran a hand down her skirt and moved to the door. As she stepped out, she didn't spot Slim where she had left him by the table. Or in the great room. Where had he gone?

Voices in the kitchen drew her in that direction. And there he was—helping Mrs. Wilmont brush the tops of biscuits. How did she cajole him to assist with dinner? She had not seen a man so ready to jump into an apron...ever. Yet there they were, baking and chatting about who knew what. It took her aback. In a good way.

She cleared her throat.

Both turned in her direction.

Slim's features broke into a smile.

"We were just getting the finishing touches on the meal, dear." Mrs. Wilmont patted Slim's hand. "Thank you. I can manage, now."

He nodded and with some hesitation, moved away from the stove, pulled off the apron, and stepped to Ada. "Did you look in your care package, yet?"

"No. I think I might save it for after dinner."

When she looked back at him, he seemed to be staring at her hair. And his features had gone slack.

She put a hand to her pinned curls. "Is something amiss?"

He shook his head, but the look on his face did not change. Something was not right.

"Are you well?" she asked, lowering her voice a little.

He glanced away. "No. You just...look so pretty." His eyes fell to her face again. But his color had paled slightly.

She wished they were alone or that they were close enough she could inquire about his shift in mood. But they weren't, and she couldn't. If he didn't wish to volunteer the information, she didn't think it appropriate for her to pry. So they were back in that awkward silence. Only this time, he avoided looking at her. And he appeared as if he'd seen a ghost.

It bothered her. Maybe more than it should.

"Please, have a seat," she offered, holding an arm out toward the large room to the side. "I'll...set the table."

He did not argue but stepped off in that direction with nothing further.

Though when she returned to the table with the plates, she noted that he did not sit but stared out the window with that same haunted expression. What had happened?

It wasn't long before the table was set and the food had been placed, but Ada remained distracted by Slim's reaction and continued distant expression. Though, when Mrs. Wilmont called for him to come over for supper, he seemed much more pulled together. He even offered Ada a smile—a small one albeit—but a smile all the same.

They settled, and Mrs. Wilmont returned grace. Then they dug into the food.

Mrs. Wilmont inquired after Slim's life in Wharton City, for which Ada was grateful. She hadn't known quite how to proceed after his reaction. But her heart ached to know how.

When did she start to care so much? Had she not just earlier today worried that she was overanalyzing this whole thing? And now, her heart had somehow become more involved than she would have guessed.

A loud knock on the door sounded.

Mrs. Wilmont and Ada stared at each other.

"Y'all expecting someone else?" Slim asked, concern written on his features.

"No," Mrs. Wilmont said, rising. "But people do drop in from time to time."

Ada's chest tightened. That wasn't really true. At least, not in the time she had lived here. There had not been unannounced, unexpected visitors. Then again, she reasoned, she hadn't been here all that long.

Slim stood as Mrs. Wilmont reached the door and opened it.

Stanford greeted the older woman. "Good evening, Aunt Lottie!"

Ada breathed her relief. Then paused. What would Stanford think of Slim being here? Would Slim think Stanford was her beau? What did she want them to think of each other?

Stanford stepped in, still talking. "I was nearby and thought I might drop in on the two loveliest ladies in all of Arizo—" he paused as his gaze landed on Slim. He glanced between Ada and Mrs. Wilmont. "I apologize." His confusion was easy to read on his face. "I didn't realize you had a caller."

"It's not that I..." Ada started. But wasn't sure how to finish that sentence. She didn't want to offend either man. She looked at Slim.

His gaze was on Stanford. And he stepped toward the man. "I am a friend of Ada's brother. Everybody calls me Slim," he said, sticking his hand out.

She breathed her relief at his interjection. With any luck, it would ease the tension.

"Stanford A. Wilmont, III," Stanford said, shaking Slim's hand.

"Good to meet you, Stan."

"Stanford A. Wilmont, III," Stanford corrected.

Slim nodded. But did not seem to catch the hint in Stanford's tone.

"You from Tombstone?" Slim moved back toward his seat.

"I am not, Mr..."

"Dagley. But everyone calls me Slim."

"I don't know that I will be 'everyone,' in this case." Stanford smiled, but it didn't seem genuine. What did she expect? This must be terribly awkward for him.

"And you, Mr. Dagley? Have you lived in Arizona your entire life?"

Slim looked as if he wished to sit, but he refrained. Perhaps because Stanford did not. Would not Mrs. Wilmont invite her nephew to remain for dinner?

"No. My parents came from New York and settled in Wharton City."

"I see." Stanford moved to stand behind Ada.

Slim glanced between the two of them. He appeared somewhat uneasy with Stanford's move.

As was Ada. Did Stanford mean to stake some sort of claim on her? She wasn't certain she appreciated that. But what could she do? Anything she attempted might be an outright affront to Stanford's pride.

Mrs. Wilmont came to stand by Ada as well. Bless the woman for trying to dial down the tension, but the space did become a little claustrophobic.

"Why don't we all sit and continue our conversation over supper?" the widow said.

At last! Ada let out a breath. Would this make things easier or more difficult?

"That is too kind, Aunt Lottie," Stanford said. "However, I fear I must decline." He set a hand on the back of Ada's chair.

Ada didn't so much as breathe.

"I do not wish to impose. And, unfortunately, I have business in town."

"That's too bad," Mrs. Wilmont said, ushering her nephew to the door.

Slim retained his standing position, watching Stanford as he paced ahead of Mrs. Wilmont. "It was nice to meet you, Stan."

Stanford had set a hand to the door latch but paused. He drew in a breath and muttered, "Stanford A. Wilmont, III." But it was said so low, and Slim had sat, already turning his attention back to his plate. Ada doubted Slim had heard.

But Ada did.

Stanford did not sound happy. He opened the door and shut it more firmly than necessary.

She let out a breath but was not able to free her mind of this new dilemma the remainder of the evening.

CHAPTER 6
Doubts

Slim smiled at Lily as she set steaming food on the table—eggs, ham, potatoes, and biscuits. How did Dan luck out with a woman with such skill in the kitchen? Everything smelled just as good as if Cook had made it.

Dan winked at his wife as she sat, then he turned his attention to the others at the table. He made quick eye contact with both Slim and Tom before bowing his head and launching into a brief prayer of gratitude for the meal and for Slim's safe arrival.

Why did he have to do that? It wasn't Slim's preference to be the focus of anyone's prayer or thanks...not even for a moment. Something about it made him feel antsy inside.

As the prayer ended, Slim kept his eyes on his plate. Perhaps the other ranch hand wouldn't think anything of it. However, just as soon as everyone opened their eyes, dishing out food seemed to be the priority. So, Slim put his plate forth and got his portion.

He was pleased to find that everything tasted as wonderful as it smelled. Lily could give Cook a run for it. Not that he'd ever share such with Cook. That is, not if he planned on eating from her vittles anymore.

"How was Miss Miller?" Dan's voice cut through the silence.

Slim waited for Lily to answer, eager to discover her thoughts on Ada. But it became apparent soon enough that she didn't plan to answer. Glancing up, Slim found that both Lily and Dan watched him. Did they wait for his response? He swallowed the bite in his mouth and stared at his friend. "She—ah—"

"Didn't you visit her over at Widow Wilmont's yesterday?"

Slim glanced at the other ranch hand, whose focus was on his plate. "I did."

"And? Was she not well?" Dan's brow furrowed.

"No." Slim was quick to say. "I mean...yes. She was. Very well."

Dan's eyebrows arched, and he exchanged a look with Lily.

"That is, she seemed well enough. To me." Oh, he was going about this all wrong!

Dan took a swig of his coffee, then ventured, "That so?"

Slim narrowed his eyes but slightly. He'd heard the hint of a tease in Dan's voice. He knew it well. "Yes."

"Is that why you stayed for dinner?"

If only Slim could knock the smirk off his friend's face. Dan took his tease too far. Slim pushed back from the table a little and crossed his arms over his chest. "I stayed because Mrs. Wilmont asked me to. I'm sure, she was only being kind."

Dan shrugged and turned his attention to his food, his features returning to a more neutral expression.

Slim's shoulders relaxed. Had he become so defensive? Why? Perhaps he should change the subject. "How, um, is the herd faring this year?"

Dan glanced at Lily again, then at the other ranch hand.

Tom pushed his plate forward and stood. "I'd best be back at it."

Should Slim find that curious? Cause he did. Was there something more to the man's quick departure than the need to return to his chores? Still, Slim only nodded as the man excused himself and moved off toward the door.

Dan, likewise, watched Tom leave and turned back to Slim. "That's a complicated question."

"Oh?"

"Let me warm your coffees." Lily stood and stepped to the stove.

"We have a strong herd. Good stock. But we've had some...challenging interactions."

"With a neighboring pasture? Rustlers?" Why didn't Dan continue?

"With the Cowboys."

Slim leaned back. He thinned his lips. "The ones that don't follow the law?"

Dan sucked in a breath through clenched teeth. "It isn't that simple."

Slim took a long sip of his coffee. "I don't understand. How 'complicated' can it be?"

Dan's eyes deepened. Slim saw real fear in them. And it gave him pause. It wasn't like Dan to be afraid.

"People who don't take them seriously...well, it doesn't end well for them." Dan looked at Lily. "Or their families."

And Slim knew...Dan feared for Lily's sake. This whole situation would be different if he weren't responsible for her.

Slim hated that he understood. But he did...all too well. In that moment, Slim was pulled back in time...to a day he was loathed to remember...

He and his sister always walked home from school together. And, on this one day he recalled, the usual boys taunted him along the first leg of their journey. But that's where it typically ended. Until that day. Was it because Slim pretended it didn't bother him? Because he ignored them? Perhaps. Either way, he should have done more.

The red hair. It had been because of the confounded red hair.

They called Slim the usual names. But he had numbed to that. Then they turned on Anne. She didn't deserve it. And she didn't know how to respond. Their words made her cry. And that only made them try harder.

It was then that Slim realized the bullies had stayed with them far beyond the schoolyard. And so he had gripped Anne's arm and hurried her along. Not that it mattered. The boys could run circles around them. Those ruffians pulled at her pigtails, jerking at her head. That was the beginning of the end.

Slim shut his eyes as if he could close his mind off to the memory. Still, it moved in front of him, uncaring of his willing it to stop. One of the boys had pulled out a pocketknife. Anne had been so scared. Slim had tried to fight them. But there were too many, and they were too big. They held him down while two others cut off Anne's hair...her deeply red hair.

Thankfully, that was where it ended. They had run off after, hooting as they went. Slim had never been able to shake the sick feeling weighing in his stomach. It remained with him to this day.

Never. Never would he be so helpless again. And never would he chance passing on that red hair. It was too great a risk.

His heart tightened, and his chest felt heavy. When Ada had removed her hat last night, he saw that the blonde was tinged with red.

Impossible. Things that had started to become possible became impossible in an instant. He had to do what he could to protect his heart from something that would never, could never be.

Ada watched for her friend. It had been too long since she had spent time with Lily. The lag had not been her intention. But between school, preparations for class, and Stanford's attentions...there hadn't been many available moments. It was only a few minutes before she spotted her friend entering the eatery, and she waved her over to the table she had procured.

"Thank you for meeting me," Lily said, settling in the available chair.

"My pleasure." Ada smiled. "I only regret it's been so long."

"I don't think a couple of weeks is so long." Lily set a hand over Ada's on the table. "Don't worry yourself so."

Were things so different? Social gatherings back east kept Ada and her circle in contact rather frequently. And here, a couple of weeks was not much time? It had seemed forever to her.

Ada only nodded. "All the same, I thank you for understanding."

The server stopped by the table, took Lily's drink request, and listed off the specials before moving on to give the women a moment.

"So," Lily said, lowering her voice as if they were conspirators. "Tell me about your meeting with Slim."

Ada swallowed her sip of water and fought to keep her features in check. Her own emotions were still a jumble. What should she share? What could she, in truth, say about it? She had yet to sort it all out for herself. And perhaps, then, there was nothing to tell.

"It was...fine. He was pleasant and...as he should be."

Lily gave her a quizzical look. "What is that supposed to mean?"

Ada sighed. She wasn't doing this very well at all. "He was quite as he presented himself in his letters. Every bit as I expected—warm, friendly, open. Only..."

Silence filled the space between them for a moment.

"Only what?" Lily broke in.

"I don't know. Something happened that set him at odds for part of the evening. I'm not sure what."

"There's no way to know with Slim." Lily straightened her place setting. "It could have been anything...just being in a strange place after such a journey even. Though, I can imagine that would set quite a number of people at odds."

Ada nodded, but she couldn't shake the feeling that there was more to it. The look on Slim's face...it had seemed haunted. Too much so for her to so easily dismiss it.

The server stopped again and took their order. Then they were alone once more.

Lily leaned toward her. "I have heard talk," she said as she peered around them, "that you are being courted by Mr. Stanford Wilmont."

Ada glanced down, her features warming.

"So, it's true?" Lily pressed.

"Not...entirely." Ada laced and unlaced her fingers before setting her attention on her friend. "We have shared company on more than one occasion, that is true. But there is no formal understanding between us."

Lily straightened, but her gaze belied her curiosity at the whole thing.

Ada sighed. "It has happened so fast. I've not had the time to catch my breath and think on it."

"The way the ladies at church are talking, I have no doubt he will make such a request. And soon."

Ada twisted her mouth as her stomach pinched a little at the thought. Why? Was it merely her tendency to fear the worst? Stanford was admired in the town. He was a standup fellow—the kind any woman would want to be pursued by.

"What will you say when he does?" Lily's question was gentle. Did she fear overstepping?

"If he does, I don't know that I have reason to refuse him. He has never been untoward. And his aunt has been good to me."

Lily nodded and shrugged. "That is true. And he is a Wilmont. He has standing and money."

Ada nodded. All the more reason to put her trepidations to rest.

"But I wonder…" Lily tilted her head to the side. She did appear the picture of ponderance.

"Yes?" Ada prompted when Lily's words trailed and did not continue.

"You said you 'didn't have reason to refuse him.' What reason have you to accept his court? Do you admire him? Respect him? Want to know him better?"

Ada remained silent. And, as much as she wished to push forth an affirmative response and move the topic elsewhere, she could not. Why? Was she so unsettled?

And why did her thoughts flit to Slim in that moment? What possible part could he play in all of this? Certainly, none when it came to her. He had made no overtures, voiced no intentions where she was concerned. Nor should he be a reason for her to delay in accepting anyone's suit.

Then why the tug in her heart and the anchor in her gut?

Slim moved toward the schoolhouse. Why had he promised to visit and talk to the children today? He had known better…even at the time. It wouldn't behoove him to continue to see Ada or interact with her if he needed to protect himself. No, rather the opposite. Distance would be his friend. Instead, here he was, walking up the steps to the front door of the building. And he would be face-to-face with her in a few moments.

He steeled himself against the inevitable. What would it be like? Would he feel the same rush of emotion he had when she opened the door at Mrs. Wilmont's house not two days ago? Or would there be more of this sinking feeling deep within?

Reaching up, he prepared to knock. But the door swung open, and Ada all but plowed him over.

He lifted his hands to brace her as she rammed into him. And, in the next moment, she was pressed against him, struggling to maintain her balance. Though Slim steadied her with ease.

"Slim! I apologize for my clumsiness. I never meant to—" Ada started to say at the same time as he said, "Are you all right?"

An awkward pause followed. It had happened in an instant, but the sensations that rushed through him at her nearness flew through him even faster—the feel of her, the smell of her, the warmth of her body against his. It was too much. And yet only a tempting.

"Yes, I am quite well. Thanks to you." She looked down.

As did he. There was no space between them—not for propriety's sake, not for breathing room. And she did not make a move to remedy that. Had she, likewise, been so unnerved?

And though a part of him loathed to do so, he set her away from himself, keeping her balanced as she stood on her own.

Her face had reddened somewhat—a stark contrast to the lightness of her hair. The hair he did not care to look at. So, he met her gaze.

She looked everywhere but at him. "I had, ah, just stepped out to open the door for you." She seemed to fumble through the explanation.

"Oh," he mumbled, pulling his hat off. "I'm sorry, I was in your way."

The color on her features deepened. "It's not your fault." She met his gaze then and looked away. "I should have been more careful."

He chuckled. In spite of his uneasiness, in spite of hers, he couldn't help himself. They were just too awkward.

Her brows fell, coming together in a quizzical look. "I fail to see what is so humorous."

"It's not." He set his hat back on his head. "Not really. But this," he said, motioning between them, "is pretty ridiculous right now."

Her mouth widened, and she giggled.

He liked that he could put her at ease. More, that she could take hold of the levity and let the tension go.

After they let loose all remaining pent up anxiety through a moment of laughter, she let out a long exhale. "Please, come in. The students will be along shortly."

He nodded and followed as she turned back toward the interior of the building. From this angle, the red tint to her hair wasn't as evident, but it was still there. How could he shove past that? For there was something magnetic about her. So much so, he wished he could put the issue with the red hair to rest.

"I haven't told them you are coming. I wanted it to be a surprise. And will they ever be thrilled!"

"Oh?" Why would they be excited to meet him?

"Yes, indeed. They have enjoyed multiple retellings of your stories. I believe even the youngest among them could almost quote your tales word-for-word by now."

Slim's features heated again, and he halted. That couldn't be so. Why would they care so about his stories? They were nothing important. Just a silly pastime.

Ada turned at the front of the classroom. She seemed surprised that Slim had stopped only halfway down the rows of desks. "Something wrong?"

He shook his head. "I don't think so." Forcing his legs to move, he joined her at the front.

"I hope it's not asking too much. If you would...might you share another story with us?" Her eyes were wide on him then, almost pleading.

It made his bones feel a bit softer. He had not prepared anything, but he heard himself say, "Of course."

The smile that broke across her face meant everything to him.

Ada watched her students, smiling to herself as they held to Slim's every word. Did he know how captivating he was? The students traveled with him to fictional Dayton City and adventured with Sheriff Maynard eagerly, wanting for more—leaning forward, poised as if to race after some imaginary foe.

As he circled around and brought the story to a satisfying conclusion, the whole room seemed to let out a large, collective sigh. She couldn't help but notice that she, too, breathed a bit more comfortably, knowing that the sheriff had, once more, brought justice and order to the day.

Slim's gaze was on her then—expectant, hopeful. For what reason? Was there something she was to do? Then his mouth turned down and his brow furrowed.

She glanced about the room. Several other pairs of eyes were on her as well.

How thoughtless! The class was hers to command once more. Stepping forward, she cleared her throat and prayed the heat in her features did not produce as deep a shade of red as she feared.

"Let's thank Mr. Dagley for that marvelous story. And for visiting us." She clapped and nodded toward him.

The students applauded with a level of enthusiasm she had not yet seen in them.

Slim's own face colored. He gave a slight bow but did not say anything, only stepped farther back. As if he did not enjoy the attention.

She offered him a half smile and moved in front of the children once more to rescue him. "I believe," she said, giving the class a look she knew would silence the rumble that had taken hold of them, "it's time to pack your things before dismissal."

The students nodded and a shuffle of books and slates followed.

Ada focused on their movements, fighting the urge to glance at Slim. It surprised her at how difficult it became.

Soon enough, the class calmed.

She smiled. Then checked her expression. There were times she struggled with it. Her love for these children grew daily. But this was a time to be the teacher. "Remember to work on your reports on your chosen President. I will expect those presentations to be ready next week."

Those same wide-eyed gazes stared back at her.

"Now, off with you." She couldn't stop the grin that covered her features then. And she didn't try. What would be so wrong with them knowing she cared?

The students filed out in a mess of movement and noise, several tossing looks over their shoulders at Slim. Indeed, she could not help peer at him herself.

He stood, arms crossed, watching the children leave. Was he bored? Relieved? What was he thinking? Feeling? It was impossible to discern.

As the last student cleared the door, Ada let out a breath and stepped toward her desk, trying to come up with the right words to say to him. Her chest had a strange tight sensation all of a sudden.

"That was amazing." Slim's words hung in the air.

She looked at him.

His gaze remained on the door.

"What do you mean?"

"How you managed those children. How they respected you."

"What about you? Surely, you saw how they were lost to all else but your tall tale."

He shook his head. Another dodge?

She stacked the books on her desk that she had already tidied.

"Thank you, for letting me visit today."

She jerked her head in his direction as she stood. What had he said? Was he thanking her? "It is I who am grateful. It meant so much to them. And to me."

To her? Had she really just said that? She turned away. But she sensed that his gaze stayed on her. This was nonsense. She needed to clean the schoolroom and get on with her day. "I, um, don't mean to keep you, Mr. Dagley."

"Keep me?" There was a hint of injury in his voice.

She grimaced but moved to the chalk board just the same. "I need to straighten things here. Then I'm afraid I have things to attend to at the..."

He was beside her then.

Her hand shook as she moved her cloth over the board. What could he want? She couldn't let him know he had such an effect on her. Did he truly though? Or was she just nervous about being alone with him... unchaperoned?

"Have I offended you? I only meant to—"

She pushed out a breath and turned toward him but didn't raise her gaze to his. "No. I just...have some errands to—"

"Errands," he cut her off. "Then I'll leave you to it." He crossed the front of the classroom, grabbing for his hat.

She shut her eyes. Why did she insist on being so? Did she really feel the need to protect her reputation? Or was there more to it? Something in his manner...or perhaps in his story that bothered?

"Slim," she said as he moved in the direction of the door.

He halted.

"The schoolteacher. In your story..."

His shoulders visibly tightened.

"Is she...? I mean, she seemed familiar."

Slim glanced back over his shoulder.

"I just..." What did she just? What did she feel?

"What?" he said, his voice soft as he shifted to stand in profile, his gaze still on her.

She stepped forward, making slow moves to close the distance between them. "I don't know how—or why—this became so strange. I enjoyed our letters...the exchanges there."

He looked down for a moment then peered up at her again. "So did I."

"What happened to that?"

He shrugged. "I guess I built all this up in my mind. You," he said, indicating her, "me." He gestured to himself. "And I just don't know where it goes from here."

"Why can't we just...be the people in the letters? Get to know each other?"

Slim let out a long sigh. "I'd like that. A lot."

Her lips widened in a smile. "Me, too."

He glanced at the floor, but when he looked at her again, he wore a half grin. It made him even more handsome. And set off a fluttering in her stomach.

She pushed those thoughts out of mind and tried to tamp down those sensations. Instead, she stuck out her hand. "Glad for the chance to know you, Slim."

He took her hand in his. "Same here." His hand enveloped hers. It was warm and firm. Like his embrace had been just earlier when she had fallen into him. Like the heat that suffused her being at the memory.

She pulled her hand back and forced her mouth to keep a smile in place. This would not work if she allowed her storybook fantasies to carry her away.

CHAPTER 7
Hopeful

Ada moved about the planked sidewalk on her way to the General Store. Another school day had come to an end. The children could not stop talking about Slim's visit earlier in the week. In truth, even she could sense that something special lingered in these days after.

Though she could not think on it without remembering the other... happenings of the day. Her collision with him and their interactions after the students had left. What could that indicate? And why did her insides flutter at these thoughts?

She glanced down at her skirt as she walked. And noted that the fabric no longer had a crispness to it. Her dress would have a layer of dirt for certain by the end of the afternoon. Was there any way to keep a garment from being thusly soiled by the dust stirred up from the passersby, carts, and horses on the unpaved street? How did a lady manage?

She chided herself. Such concerns were out of place. Utter nonsense. Besides, hadn't she come here to get away from all of that?

Nodding at a pair of her students walking by with their parents, she hoped they might want to stop and talk with her. However, the woman gripped the hands of her children tighter and with an answering nod, moved by quicker than was necessary. As if she had to avoid Ada at all costs.

That stung. Did the people of Tombstone not think well of her? Whyever not? She searched her memory to seek out what offense she may have committed. Then she wondered on the reasoning in avoiding the schoolteacher. Perhaps, the woman feared a poor report on her children.

Ada attempted to shrug it off as she continued along the sidewalk. Only...it wasn't so easy. How was she to ever make her way in this town if the people avoided her?

A figure emerged from the store several feet ahead. The man had the bearings of Slim...and in profiled silhouette, gave her pause. Was it? Her core warmed at the thought of conversing with him. Or perhaps, it was because of their last encounter and the embarrassment that still lingered.

She hung back. Should she now avoid him? But her eagerness to see him won out, and she stepped closer just as the man turned toward her. His features now evident, she could see it was not Slim. And her excitement waned.

As he passed, the man tipped his hat to her, his eyes searching her face. Why would he do such? Her cheeks warmed. Then she realized... she had been staring.

Shaking off her unease, she stepped within the shop, desperate to move forward with her day and forget her misstep. The interior of the store removed her dress from further risk of dirt stirring up. But it offered nothing further. There were those nearby whose heads tipped up when she entered. But she was quickly dismissed as they went about searching out their wares. She swallowed and lowered her gaze. Why did she think anyone should treat her with any special regard? If she'd wanted pomp at every afternoon stroll, she should have stayed in Richmond.

Stopping in front of the ribbons, she looked over the selection and tried to put the whole thing from her mind. She was no one. In a big town.

"Ah, a pretty for the fair lady," a voice from off to her left disrupted her concentration some moments later.

She turned to see Stanford standing at the end of one of the aisles, his eyes caught on her. Offering him a genuine smile, she shifted to face him. "Stanford. How fortunate to run into you."

"Yes, well," he said, moving closer to where she stood in front of the tabletop covered with spools of brightly colored satin. "Would that all of my trips to the General Store be so graced."

Her grin widened in spite of her nerves. Why did he always put her off slightly? As if they played some game, and she didn't know the rules. But she did. All too well. Lily's words about Stanford's probable forthcoming request to court her echoed in her mind. Did he seek her out today? Would he put forth that question now?

He plucked a bright blue ribbon from among the others scattered about. "Have you made your choice? Although, I think any of these, albeit fine ribbons, only pale in comparison."

"Comparison to what, sir?" Had he thrown her off or did she tease back? Even she wasn't certain. But she kept the smile on her face.

He tilted his head down and gave her a questioning look. Did he think her coy? "Why to your loveliness, Miss Miller."

Her pulse thundered at the base of her throat. Had his comment so disarmed her? "Your words are kind. But you only make it all the more difficult to make a choice. And I must have something to hold my hair back."

His eyes flitted to her blonde locks. "Indeed."

She set down the spool of dark pink satin. "Perhaps, today is not the day for such selections."

His gaze was intense on her face then. "Perhaps, not."

Silence fell between them, but it did not dissuade his glare upon her features.

She cleared her throat. "I, um, that is...the ribbon was my sole reason for coming to the General Store." Looking about him for his goods, she was confused to see nothing that would indicate he planned to make any purchases. "Did you find what you needed?"

He sighed. "Not today. But I have found something better." The smile he shot her was disarming and a bit too sweet.

She looked to the floor, unsure how to respond. Was she so nervous, or was he being too forward with his compliments? Her stomach did a flipflop, and she felt rather out of place.

"Might I," he said as he jutted forth an elbow into the space between them, "escort you to your next stop?"

"Oh, I have only to check the telegraph office for incoming mail."

"Then I would enjoy very much the pleasure of walking you there."

She let her lips lift in a simple smile as she took his proffered arm. Then they moved out of the store and back into the brightness of the day without further ado. But as she followed his lead, she wondered after this strange turn of events. From a dismissed annoyance on the street to the object of such a man's attention. And, in that moment, she enjoyed his attention perhaps more than she should.

Slim said goodbye to the blacksmith and moved across the street, mindful of the many carts and horses passing by. Tombstone was busy —that was for sure. And so much bigger than he was comfortable with. He missed the smaller Wharton City and the peaceful solitude that could be found among the open spaces there. Although, Tombstone had its perks. There was Dan, of course. The two had already fallen into a comfortable working routine. It was as if no time had passed. None at all.

And he couldn't keep his thoughts from Miss Miller. Not only their letters, but their interactions since he arrived. He delved into the few exchanges as if to mine gold. As usual, he found himself smiling more broadly.

A couple sidestepped in front of him. Had he almost knocked them over? He voiced an apology and moved on, more careful to keep his mind on where he was and what he was doing. No matter how difficult that would be. There was one more stop to make before returning to the ranch—he had been charged with sending Brandon a telegram.

Nearing the stores, a couple walking in that direction gave him pause. Perhaps, he should let them pass, to avoid another awkward near-miss. But as they neared, he was better able to distinguish that it was Ada on the arm of Stanford A. Wilmont, III.

Slim's heart seemed to halt pumping for a moment. What were they doing together? And why was she on his arm? Did the two have an understanding? They certainly had all appearance of a courting couple. Had he...misunderstood something in his interaction with Ada? Was Stan her beau? He searched back through their conversations—both written and verbal—but could not find any reason to think such.

Still, nothing could erase the image in front of him. Or what it did to his heart. A pang shot right through his chest. It surprised him, though, that it would bother so much, affect him so. After all, he and Ada had no such understanding, either. She was free to entertain any man's court. Even if not for the red in her hair and what that meant for him, he held no claim to her. Did he even want to?

He was not so involved yet, not so entangled that it truly injured him. Still, he best take heed and guard his heart from further engagement here. If such a thing were even possible. He just couldn't... wouldn't risk it.

Ada laughed lightly at Stanford's comment. He had a good sense of humor. And she found him rather entertaining. Wasn't that a good sign? She didn't want to court a dull man.

As they walked on, in the following moments of silence, he tugged her closer. But she gently pulled back, keeping an appropriate distance between them. When she chanced a glance at him, he looked opposite. Had she offended him?

She gave his arm a little squeeze, hoping that might communicate better how she felt. It was not her intention to put him off, only to retain some firm boundaries. How could she let him know she was not trying to set him aside? They continued on their way, and he said nothing further in the minutes that proceeded, putting her at a loss. Setting her free hand also on his arm, she could not avoid it bringing her a little closer to him. Though still a comfortable distance remained between them.

He turned back toward her, his eyes shining. Was that...happiness? She smiled back.

The wails of a small child nearby stole her attention.

"What is it?" Stanford asked, his eyes full of concern.

She held up a hand to halt their progress. "Do you not hear that?"

"What?" He looked around, as if to spot some source of danger.

She gripped his arm, urging him to face her again. "That crying."

The lines on his features relaxed. "It's probably nothing."

"Don't you think we should make sure?"

The look that crossed his face was difficult to discern. But she couldn't worry with that right now; she had to locate the child. Tugging back her hand, she couldn't stop her frustration at Stanford's unwillingness to release her.

She moved forward, Stanford in tow, trying to determine the location of the distressed child. They moved in a circle at first, as she scanned the immediate area. But the cries came from further ahead. So, that's where she went—further down the sidewalk. As they walked on, the cries became louder and then quieter. Had they passed the child? Turning, she finally discovered a small girl huddled, concealed by a barrel, next to a storefront.

When she attempted to pull free once more, Stanford put a firm hand to her arm. "What are you doing?" His eyes became wider.

"I have to help this child. She seems lost. Maybe hurt."

Stanford looked at the pitiful small girl, his features taut. From concern for the child? Or something else? She didn't have time to discern right now.

"I don't think you should get any closer. What if the child has lice? Or is carrying something else?"

What was he saying? The girl needed their help. Needed Ada's help. And she wasn't about to entertain a stubborn streak right now. She had one of her own. Finally jerking free, she took careful, slow steps toward the girl.

"Ada..." Stanford seethed.

The girl's wails let up as her eyes caught on Ada's. Her gaze widened. She was truly afraid. Then, suddenly, the tears intensified.

"I'm not going to hurt you, little one. I'd like to help."

The girl wailed again, shutting her eyes and letting the tears run.

Now, Ada was right in front of her, kneeling. "Please, tell me your name."

The girl watched Ada again, and her crying let up ever so slightly.

Ada reached toward her.

"No," Stanford warned. "Don't touch her."

Ignoring his concern, Ada let her gentle hands communicate what her words were not. She pressed fingers ever so lightly to the girl's hand. "Are you hurt?"

The child stared at Ada's hand on hers. It was difficult to determine if she was more scared by Ada's forwardness or if the touch put her at ease.

"Where's your ma?"

"Mama!" The child jerked away. More words poured out, but they were not anything Ada could understand.

"Heaven help us, she's not even American," Stanford said, a hard undertone in his words.

Ada jerked around. "She needs our help. I don't care where she's from."

"We best let her be. This is not our concern." Stanford reached for Ada. Just as he made contact with her upper arms, he started to pull her away.

She maneuvered to evade him. "You're scaring her."

Stanford pushed out a breath. "Ada, you don't understand how things work—"

"Didn't you hear her?" another voice interjected. "That little girl is terrified. Don't make it worse."

Ada turned to see Slim, standing confident and tall, just as he had been that day on the train platform. So assured of himself and what he said.

Stanford balked when he spotted Slim. "This is no concern of yours."

Slim's gaze narrowed.

"Or ours," Stanford said, his words exasperated as he reached for her again. "Let us go find the sheriff, if that makes you feel better."

Slim stepped toward them, preparing to intervene, by the look of it.

Ada stood and pulled free once more. "Perhaps, you should find the sheriff," she said through clenched teeth. "I intend to help this girl find her mother."

Stanford glanced between Slim and Ada and back again. "Fine. I'll be the one who does what should be done in this manner of situation." His voice was tight and his eyes hard. He then spun and moved off.

All the air seemed to rush from Ada. What had she done? What had she said? Pushing those thoughts to the side, she turned back to the small girl, who continued to wail for her ma. Dropping back to her knees, she tried to speak with the girl. But to no avail.

Ada looked to Slim.

His face twisted in concern as well. But as he noticed her looking at him, the contorted lines smoothed. He stepped closer and said, "We'll get her home."

Ada opened her mouth to ask him just how he planned on doing that, when a woman rushed between them and straight to the girl.

"Mama!" the girl cried as the woman lifted her. Small arms clung to the woman's neck.

Ada stood and stepped back, now beside Slim.

The dark-haired woman spoke long strings of their language, soothing her daughter. Then she set eyes on Ada. She reached for Ada's hand and said, "Spasiba."

Ada wasn't sure how to respond. The woman seemed grateful, but how was she to know for certain what the woman said? So, she nodded.

The woman looked at her daughter once more and moved off.

Ada watched her walk away. "I hope she knew I was trying to help."

"I think she did. She looked as if she appreciated your effort," Slim said, his deeper voice reassuring her. It did soothe her nerves.

She turned. He was closer than she'd thought. It didn't bother Ada, only surprised her. "Thank you."

"For what?" Slim's words came out on a laugh. "I didn't do much to help."

She met his gaze. "For caring."

Their eyes met and held. Something about his demeanor continued to bring the whole situation down. As if there wasn't more to it than it seemed on the surface. She liked that about him—his easiness and warmth.

"I was on my way to check for mail," she started, as he said, "I'm headed off to send a telegram."

They smiled at each other.

"I am headed on to send a telegram to your brother," Slim said, his eyes seeming to dance in the sunlight. "Would you like to come?"

Her brother! Would he let her send a line? "I would."

Slim took her by the elbow, a gesture that made her feel helped and protected, and turned her in the direction they needed to go. As he released his hold, however, she looped a hand through the crook of his arm. When he set a questioning look on her, she grinned. And they moved on toward the telegraph office. Not a thought to Stanford's progress.

"What language do you suppose they were speaking?" Ada wondered out loud as she and Slim moved toward the edge of town, now having finished their errands.

Slim looked on ahead of them, thrown off a bit by her question. Since leaving the telegraph office, they had been talking about the Miller Ranch and life there. All his concerns had melted as his mind traveled back to his home...and took her with him. That last part had more to do with his enjoyment of the moment than he'd like to think.

"I wasn't able to figure it out. But I can't say I know much about different languages and their sounds." She seemed to stop herself. Why? Were things going to become awkward again?

Silence fell between them.

He watched the landscape fade from the harriedness of the town center to the more natural vistas that accompanied her on her daily walk. The silence wasn't uncomfortable. Rather, it was companionable. Like two old friends.

"Russian." His abrupt response surprised even him.

She jerked her gaze toward him. "What?"

"They were Russian." The intonations of the language had indicated such.

"How do you—?"

He shook his head and shrugged off her question. There was no need to get into it. To possibly expose things he'd rather keep to himself.

Her care for the girl had touched him. It didn't seem to matter to

Ada that the girl was an immigrant's child. Or that she wasn't well dressed. Ada cared. Period.

"I am glad you came when you did." Her grip on his arm shifted and tightened.

Warmth filled his core.

"I don't know what got into Stanford." She sounded as if she truly mused the thought. Did she not know? Could she not see? Or did she determine not to see?

"I was...glad to help."

Another moment of silence passed between them.

"What has Sheriff Maynard been doing of late?" Her voice and step seemed to perk with those words.

He glanced at her. "Sheriff Maynard?" She couldn't be serious. Was she at all interested in his stories that way? Or was it for the sake of the schoolchildren?

"Yes. He is quite the dashing hero. I am oh-so-eager for another installment of his exploits."

Slim chuckled.

She gave his arm a little tug. "Don't dismiss me. I really want to know."

He was certain his face had started to color. She had cut off his response with her comment. His intended words were of how she couldn't mean it, her interest in his stories at least. These tales were only good for entertaining children. Was she being kind? Or did she think so much of his imaginings? Of his fictional creations?

"Do you think on the stories ahead of time? Or do they come to you as you tell them?"

Now, she was interested in how he came up with them? She couldn't be. But when he glanced at her, she looked to him expectantly.

"Both. Sometimes I would tell a story to Samuel and Nisto that I just kind of made up on the spot. But the ones I have shared with you and the class...well, those I worked on."

"Have you ever thought to seek publication?"

"No." Now, he was certain his face burned. She sounded like Brandon. Where did this faith in him come from?

"You should." She all but gasped as she said the words. "How many do you have written down? What have you thought up and not penned out yet?"

He held up a hand. "Slow down."

She offered him a sheepish grin. He had to accept the fact that she really did believe in him.

"I have a couple dozen in my head and only the ones I sent you written out."

"Maybe you could make a collection of short stories." Her encouragement moved him.

"I'm not so good at getting them down on paper. The ones I wrote to you took a long time." There. That would dissuade her.

"Then you must let me help. You can dictate them to me. Perhaps, you'll be able to get it out better if you don't have to do the writing."

He didn't relish the idea of sharing all the stories. There would be the risk that she might bore of them or find out they weren't truly as good as she thought. Still, he couldn't find a reason to turn down the opportunity to spend more time with her. More and more, his earlier concerns about her hair lacked the weightiness they first seemed to.

When he looked toward her again, he found her eyes wide and expectant...eager almost. How could he say no to that?

CHAPTER 8
Conflict

Ada and Mrs. Wilmont moved toward the church. Such a fine Sunday. It was a perfect day—temperate and sunny. Enough so that Ada wished a picnic had been planned. But she dismissed it...no hope in wishful thinking.

Her gaze wandered to the people standing about. Many were her students and their parents. All turned away as she neared. None seemed the least bit interested in conversing with her. What was going on?

"Isn't that Slim?" Mrs. Wilmont leaned toward her.

Ada looked in the direction Mrs. Wilmont had indicated. Indeed, it was Slim. He stood off to the right side of the church entrance with the Hayworths. Her stomach did a little flip as she set eyes on him. What was that about? Could she not control herself?

He was handsome—that was true. And sturdy. She knew that well enough. Glancing down, she hoped her features did not betray her as her face warmed yet again at the memory of their previous interaction. He'd caught her and held her fast with those strong, very capable arms. Even now, she could make out the bulk of his muscular arms through his shirt.

His jaw was square and strong, his face well proportioned, and he stood tall and confident. She did wonder at his nickname. For there wasn't much about him that was slim. He didn't carry extra weight, but he was far from lanky.

A movement to the left caught her gaze. Lily must have spotted them, for she waved at Ada, bidding her join them. Dare she?

Slim turned. His eyes were bright as they sought out the source of Lily's attention. As they connected with Ada, they seemed to shine ever more as the corners cinched when he smiled. Was he so glad to see her? Could he be as moved as she?

Ada wanted to turn away from the warmth of his gaze but found herself unable to.

"Don't just stand there, child," Mrs. Wilmont's voice cut into her thoughts. "Go on over."

Ada regarded the widow. "Will you not come along? I don't wish to abandon you—"

"Nonsense. I have my own friends to catch up with." The tender smile on Mrs. Wilmont's face was amused.

How could Ada be so thoughtless? Of course, she would have her own circle to attend to. Hadn't Ada met several of the women last week?

Mrs. Wilmont gave her arm a gentle squeeze and moved off to the opposite side of the church entrance, leaving Ada standing alone in the yard.

She took a step in the direction of her three friends, but someone stepped into her path. A taller man with a mustache and an air of authority.

"Miss Ada Clara Miller?" The man pressed a hand forth.

Ada set her hand into his. "Yes?"

"I'm Mayor John Clum."

"Oh, Mayor Clum, it is good to finally meet you." Ada let her gaze wander over his features. Was there something amiss?

"My apologies for keeping you. I only wanted to introduce myself and apologize that I was unavailable before now."

Ada nodded. "Wholly unnecessary, Mayor. I understand that the matters of the town sometimes take precedence."

He smiled. "All the same. I would have liked to greet you myself and explain about your accommodations. Are you well settled with Mrs. Wilmont?"

"Oh, yes." Ada beamed. "Mrs. Wilmont has been a wonderful hostess."

"Excellent." His attention drifted to somewhere in the distance. And hers was tugged toward her friends. When she met Slim's eyes, his brows creased. Was he worried after the intrusion? She examined him a little more closely, concerned after his unease.

"I am glad to hear it." Mayor Clum jerked his head in a nod. "I won't keep you, but if you need anything, please don't hesitate to visit my office."

Ada barely had time to smile before Mayor Clum had walked off.

"Ada," Lily called, somewhat insistent.

Moving toward her, Ada made an effort to avoid Slim's gaze.

Lily laid her hand on her husband's arm as Ada neared. "Is everything all right?"

"Yes." Ada peered back at the ground. "Mayor Clum only wanted to introduce himself."

A strained silence followed. When she lifted her eyes to Lily's, the woman was smiling. As if she knew some great secret. Did she think Ada's awkward behavior was all because of Slim? That Ada had been caught so off guard by Slim? Or that few words were forthcoming because of his nearness? How Ada wished she could prove Lily wrong. Was there any way to save face?

"Ah. How kind of him. How did your week fare? Any trouble with the children?" Lily inquired, her eyes dancing with contained laughter.

"The past few days have been wonderful." Then she caught herself. "At the school. Things have been going well at the school." She wanted to roll her eyes. This wasn't like her.

Slim's breath caught.

She glanced in his direction. He seemed to be making every effort to stifle laughter. At her expense? The scoundrel. "The children enjoyed Slim's visit. His stories always captivate them. And his delivery made it extra special."

Lily's brows lifted. "And what did you think?"

Ada wanted to disappear. How could her friend not help her out of this? Instead, Lily seemed determined to highlight the awkwardness. "I...liked it as well."

"I enjoyed it very much," Slim said, shifting.

Ada looked at him to find his eyes intent on her, his gaze warm. She turned back toward the Hayworths. "How is life on the ranch? Any..." What might she ask to sound as if she had any clue what occurred on a ranch? Even though her brother ran a successful ranch, she had never bothered to learn much about it. So, she searched for something. "Calves?"

Dan quirked an eyebrow. "We have a small number of younger ones. But our calving season isn't quite here."

Had her question given her away? Was it an odd question to ask?

"But there are a good number of cows due to deliver," Slim added.

She nodded, thankful for the rescue.

"I, for one, commend you on your work with the children," Lily interjected. "Teaching is a gift."

"One that she certainly has." Slim said.

But as Ada looked at him, his gaze on her shot heat through her body. Did he truly admire her so?

Lily made a small noise. When Ada looked toward her, she found the woman stifling a laugh. Ada wasn't certain whether she should be embarrassed or curious.

"There is something else..." The mother's reaction the last time she was in town still bothered her. Maybe her friends would have some thought about it. As it was, Ada couldn't work out any plausible explanation. Other than, perhaps, the townsfolk just weren't open to her coming.

"Yes?" Lily's smile vanished.

"The people don't seem to be very welcoming toward me."

"What people?" Slim asked, concern etching his features.

"The parents of my students, the townspeople...I don't know. Seems it's everyone I come across. Everyone is somewhat...standoffish."

"Standoffish?" Lily exchanged a glance with her husband.

"When you first came, was it the same for you?" Ada asked, hoping her voice didn't betray her desperation to know it wasn't just her.

Lily shook her head. "No. I found quite the opposite to be true. The people here were rather open. It made this place feel like home."

Ada frowned. Why then? Was it something about her?

There was more of a silence than Ada was comfortable with.

Lily spoke up after some moments. "Maybe they just want to make a good impression on you. That can make anyone a little uneasy. After all, you are spending so much time with their children."

Ada considered that. It seemed reasonable. Maybe that was all there was to it.

Dan cleared his throat. "I think it's time to find our seats."

Indeed, several of the townsfolk around them had started making their way into the building.

Ada nodded and followed as Dan and Lily picked up step, moving in that direction as well. Should she find Mrs. Wilmont? But the woman had disappeared. Perhaps, she was already within.

Slim moved easily beside her. "I have...um...been working on another story." He spoke low, perhaps for her ears alone. Was he still so embarrassed about his writing?

"Oh? I think the children would love to hear it."

"Ah...that would be fine." Slim held up an arm, indicating for Ada to precede him into the church.

Had that not been his intention? For her to invite him back? Or was there some other reason he shared?

Ada spotted Mrs. Wilmont among friends in her pew. But Mrs. Wilmont appeared too caught up to think on Ada. So, she followed Lily into a pew about halfway down the aisle. When she sat, she found herself between Lily and Slim.

Slim's arm grazed hers as he settled onto the hard wooden bench. Would he distract her the whole of the service? She prayed not.

He glanced at her. Had he felt her gaze? But instead of questioning her, he offered a smile.

She returned it before he shifted his attention to where the reverend stood at the pulpit. Then she worked to push all else from her mind but Reverend Jones's words.

If she could.

The last strains of the hymn trailed, and Slim let out a breath. The service was over. Without anything further, he stepped into the aisle to let Ada, Lily, and Dan out of the pew. Though, he could not help that his heart beat hard and fast as Ada passed by. In fact, his heart had been playing at such the entire sermon. It had been particularly difficult to concentrate with her near. Was he so lost to her charm?

Lily indicated that he should follow Ada out.

He grimaced and did so. Had Lily caught his frustration? She was being a bit obvious. His desire to get to know Ada better was being hurt by Lily pushing at them. Was Dan's wife so eager for a match here? Why?

Still, Slim moved after Ada, watching her movements as they came to the back of the church.

Reverend Jones shook hands with Ada and then Slim, his eyes dancing between the two of them for a moment.

"Slim Dagley," Slim said, giving the reverend's hand a strong shake.

"Glad to meet you. I have heard much about you."

Slim looked to Ada. Had she been sharing about his stories? With the reverend? Who else had she told? Didn't she know he wished it to remain a secret?

"My son cannot stop talking about your tall tales."

Slim's ire melted into self-recrimination. How had he let himself get carried away? Of course, the children would be sharing with their parents.

"I—thank you, Reverend. I can't say much for the stories. They are only to amuse the children."

"Nonsense," Ada spoke up. "I believe they will be widely read one day."

The heat in his face deepened. Did she have such faith in him?

Reverend Jones's gaze darted between them once more before settling on Slim. "Then I look forward to reading them myself."

Slim wanted to speak, to naysay this line of thinking. But Ada and the reverend bade each other farewell. So he did the same, moving off after Ada.

As they descended the steps, he thought after her words. Widely read? Preposterous.

"Miss Miller," a voice called to them from behind. A voice Slim knew before he turned to meet the man face-to-face—Stanford A. Wilmont, III.

"Stanford. So good to see you." Ada beamed. Was she so taken with the man? Even after his behavior the other day?

Slim made a great effort not to bristle visibly.

"Mr. Dagley," Stanford said in all politeness, before all but dismissing Slim. He took Ada by the elbow and made a move to escort her off.

Blatant rudeness. Slim would not have it. He followed along, not missing Ada's confused stare.

Stanford gave Slim a hard look. "If you will excuse us, I need to speak with Miss Miller privately." Then he turned to Ada, again ignoring Slim and any response he might give.

Ada tugged free of Stanford's grasp. "I think it best we remain where we are." Her voice had an edge to it. Did she feel unsafe?

Stanford threw a pained expression in her direction, glanced at Slim, and then back to Ada as he sighed. "Very well. I only wanted to apologize. For the other day. It was not gentlemanly of me to behave that way. Please, forgive me, I do not know what came over me."

The strained lines on Ada's features smoothed out, and her anger seemed to dissipate as her shoulders relaxed. "All is forgiven."

What? Why the ease of forgiveness? He had not only behaved badly, the situation revealed more about him than what was on the surface. Could Ada not see that?

Stanford's hard stance gave way as well. "I cannot tell you how relieved I am."

Ada nodded.

Stanford glanced toward Slim again. "And how are you this fine day, Mr. Dagley?"

Slim's clenched teeth resisted giving way, but he worked to ease any visible signs of his tension. "I am well, thank you."

"Excellent," the man tossed in his direction before turning back to Ada. "I had hoped, Miss Miller—"

"Please, call me Ada."

"Ada," Stanford said her name as if she were a heavenly being. What

Slim wouldn't give for such a golden tongue and his easy charm. "I had hoped, Ada, that you would permit me to call on you this afternoon."

Call on her? What exactly were his intentions? Not that Slim could do anything to stop her from accepting. The situation wasn't even such that he could interject. He prayed Ada would find some excuse to turn him away. She couldn't be interested in his attentions after what had occurred with the small girl two days past.

"That will be fine," she said, giving him a little smile.

Slim worked to control his frustrated response that almost erupted into something near anger. It couldn't be that this woman would entertain someone like Stanford and someone like Slim. They were of two different worlds. If she would consider Stanford, how could she be interested in Slim...especially considering all that man had to offer?

"I'd best get back to the Hayworths'. I think we had plans for lunch."

Ada's gaze met his. She did not appear pleased. Did she seek more from him? He wasn't sure he wanted to compete with Stanford for her regard. That would put him—his heart—at considerable risk of being crushed.

But could he leave her here with Stanford? Would Stanford take a leap and move toward a more formal understanding between them? Slim couldn't stomach that. So, he remained glued to the spot.

Stanford's brows rose. "Didn't you need to find the Hayworths? Mr. Hayworth is just over there." The man tilted his head forward.

Slim turned. Sure enough, Dan stood chatting with another man, not ten feet away.

What could he say to that? Had Stanford cornered him to show him up? Or for some other reason?

"I—" Slim started, rather unsure how to proceed.

"Stanford," an older female voice interjected into the conversation.

"Aunt Lottie." Stanford offered a wide smile. Something about it seemed forced. Like how it didn't show in his eyes.

"I need to steal Miss Miller for a moment." Mrs. Wilmont glanced between the two men. "There is someone I would like to introduce her to."

"Of course," Stanford said, all smiles and graciousness.

Ada looked at Slim, however, with an apologetic shrug as she followed Mrs. Wilmont, leaving him and Stanford facing each other.

As much as Slim wished to ignore the man, he dared not let Stanford think him weak. So, he glared openly at him.

Stanford put a hand in his pocket. "I will bid you good day, Mr. Dagley. There are things I must attend to as well."

Slim nodded. "Good day, Mr. Wilmont." But he remained rooted as Stanford walked off. If only he could keep that man in his sights. For there was something about him Slim didn't trust.

After Stanford helped Ada up into her seat in the cart, he moved off with a wave and a tip of his hat. Ever the gentleman, ever the charmer. What could she do?

Turning, she smiled at Mrs. Wilmont as the woman urged the horse forward. Their normal routine dictated that Mrs. Wilmont strike up a discussion, but today she remained silent. And Ada was too distracted by her thoughts to initiate a conversation of any merit.

Her earlier exchange with Slim and Stanford still plagued her. She hadn't wanted to forgive Stanford, but that was not for her. God had forgiven her, wasn't it for her to forgive others? But all was well. Perhaps, it was just as Stanford had said—something unlike himself had taken hold of him. Perhaps, some fear or nervousness? There were many innocent reasons people reacted certain ways.

But there was the look upon Slim when Stanford appeared and then again when she declared him forgiven. Had she vexed him so? Was it her attentions toward Stanford or her relieving the man of his guilt? Either way, it bothered her. More than it probably should. She was not beholden to Slim. Nor should she care such for his opinion. They two were in no way linked.

Still, she had a pang of regret when Stanford had asked to call on her. Slim had not said anything either way. And he had not made any offer similar to Stanford's. How was it, then, that she felt so strained at her actions and words?

"You're awfully quiet," Mrs. Wilmont offered as she continued to focus on the path.

But her words disrupted Ada's thinking. "As are you."

Mrs. Wilmont again fell silent. What Ada wouldn't give for a peek inside her head.

"I...was just thinking," Ada admitted.

"Oh?" The older woman's prompt for something further left words nearly spilling from Ada.

But she held them back. Could she share confused thoughts about the woman's nephew with her? Would Mrs. Wilmont not champion the man? Of course, she would.

"I...only consider things that were discussed before," Ada said.

"I did notice you spoke with Stanford and Slim. Was that..." The woman's voice trailed for a moment. Did she search for the right words? "...a good chat?"

Ada peered at the woman, who continued to fix her gaze ahead. "It...was," she said with only a moment's hesitation. She needed to push down this trepidation. Hadn't she forgiven Stanford? Then she needed to act like it. "In fact," she said, taking in a breath and easing it out, "Stanford plans to call later."

Mrs. Wilmont lifted a brow. "Call?"

"Yes." It would be good. Everything was fine.

"Today?"

Ada nodded but seamed her lips. There were too many emotions within to trust herself further.

"That will be..." There was that pause again. "...good."

"Yes. Yes, it will."

As they rounded another bend, the house appeared. Perhaps, Ada could retreat to her room and pray. That's what she needed—clarity and guidance.

Mrs. Wilmont slowed the horse as they approached.

Ada lowered herself from the bench and moved around to help with the horse.

By the time Mrs. Wilmont made it to the horse, Ada had been nuzzled. Too much of Ada sneaking carrots to the mare led to that behavior. She was certain of it.

Mrs. Wilmont led the horse and Ada toward the barn. And together they unhitched the animal, put her to stall, fed, and refreshed her.

Only then did Ada turn and move toward the house. But Mrs. Wilmont held back.

Ada shifted to look at the woman.

"These decisions...these choices...ought not be made lightly." Mrs. Wilmont rubbed hands down the front of her skirt.

Furrowing her brows, Ada wondered at the words. What was she trying to say? Did Ada err in permitting Stanford's call? "I don't understand, I—"

Mrs. Wilmont waved a hand in front of her face. "I do not mean to overstep, Miss Miller."

Why did she call her such? They were well past being on a first name basis.

"I only wish to be what I imagine your mother would be for you. What any mother would be."

That did not help Ada's confusion. Was the woman trying to communicate that Ada had been too bold? "Do you think I should—"

Again, that hand came gently up. "I do not mean to say you should or shouldn't do anything. I only want you to be cautious and careful. Mindful. Of what could be, what is, and where your heart is leading you."

Ada nodded. What an enigma the woman was today. How she wished for a straight answer from Mrs. Wilmont.

"Shall we?" Mrs. Wilmont stepped toward the barn's exit, indicating that Ada might join her.

"Of course." Ada fell into step with the older woman, following her lead as they left the barn and went into the house.

Mrs. Wilmont moved toward the kitchen as she removed her hat. "What shall we have for lunch?"

And just like that, the conversation turned. Even as Ada offered Mrs. Wilmont a smile as she tried to come up with a response, she could not shake the sense that there was more to the woman's words.

"You've been awful quiet." Dan's voice distracted Slim from the chatter about the sermon.

Slim glanced up to see his friend looking straight at him. Had his lack of enthusiasm in the interchange been so noticeable?

All eyes fell on him then.

"I was...just thinking about that scripture in Colossians."

Dan shared a look with Lily. "What scripture in Colossians? The reverend spoke about the feeding of the five thousand."

Slim shut his eyes. How could he have been so dim? They had been discussing the sermon for near an hour. It wasn't difficult to guess they had followed along quite well. At least well enough to remember the reference.

"I guess, I'm just distracted."

Dan shot Lily another look. "I'd say so."

Lily stood. "Let me grab these dishes and let you two keep talking." She made short work of gathering their plates and utensils.

Slim made a move to stand and assist, but another curious look from Dan brought him back into his chair.

After Lily walked off, Dan leaned forward. "She's been more tired than usual these days."

Slim nodded.

Dan's gaze was intent on him.

Should Dan's statement mean something to him? Was Dan indicating she lost sleep for some reason? Slim certainly didn't want to be thinking about that.

"And she's not felt well much."

"Is she sick?" Slim wondered out loud. It seemed that was the right thing to ask. What did Dan hint at?

Dan chuckled. "Nothing that can't be cured in a few months."

A sickness that took months to recover from. She must be really ill indeed. "Then you have seen the doctor?"

Dan nodded, eyes bright. Why would he appear so happy at this news? It seemed a bit off. "Come on, Slim. She'll be better in a few months."

His friend was hinting at something pretty hard. But Slim had not a clue. It was probably best to respond to his words instead of guessing.

"I'm sorry to hear that. Maybe it's not so bad. Maybe it won't take so long for her to be back on her feet."

Dan's smile spread. "No. It'll for sure be a few months."

Slim started to feel as if there were a big secret he was supposed to know. "We can hope and pray that—"

"Ah, Slim, she's pregnant!"

Slim jerked back a little. Pregnant? Is this what Dan had been hinting at so hard? Did he now seem daft to his friend?

"Say something," Dan entreated. He did appear distressed.

At last, Slim found his wits and said, "I...I'm thrilled for you!"

Dan nodded. "I can't quite believe it. I'm going to be a father."

Slim smiled. "It'll be great."

"But...then again, I'm going to be a father." His smile fell.

Slim was confused once more. "That's also true." His friend seemed so distressed that he didn't think it would be good to point out that he just restated himself.

"I mean...I'll have a baby—a son...or daughter. And I'll have to teach him all kinds of things. What if I forget something? Something important."

Slim reached over and slapped his friend on the shoulder. "You've got a good head about you. And you have Lily. Y'all are partners, after all. I have no doubt you'll make a great team."

Dan's face had paled. He seemed to be coming around to himself though. "I suppose."

"You won't be alone in this." Slim leaned toward him. "You've got friends. Really helpful ones...like me."

Dan managed a small smile. "I guess."

"You guess?"

"I mean, yeah. I know. And you're a great friend. But what do you know about babies?" Dan appeared stricken then.

"What did Brandon know? Or Cutie? I mean, think...Cutie has a baby girl. What on earth could he possibly know about it?"

That did not alleviate Dan's distress.

"And yet, he's doing it."

Dan nodded slowly.

"So, you can do it." Slim meant it. He believed in Dan. "Besides, you have a few months to get used to the idea. Don't be so hard on yourself."

Dan remained silent.

"Now, don't you worry yourself with a half-wit ranch hand right now. Go spend time with your wife." Slim looked in the direction of the kitchen. The sounds of clanging dishes had just stopped.

Dan met his gaze finally. His features firmed, and the light returned to his eyes. "Thanks."

Slim nodded. "Go."

Dan rose and walked into the kitchen.

Slim was tempted to sneak a peek at the two, but he didn't dare. Such moments were for them alone. And his own spirit had started to fall. Would he ever know such happiness? Without fearing what may become of his children? That they would be tormented like he was? Between these thoughts and his earlier disappointment as Ada accepted Stan's step forward in their relationship, a shadow fell over Slim's thoughts. And the day became that much more difficult.

CHAPTER 9
Disappointment

Ada worked a pair of knitting needles together, looping the rough yarn as she did so. She rather enjoyed working with her hands this way. But as much as she tried to concentrate on the movement of the yarn against the metal, she couldn't help thinking about Mrs. Wilmont's earlier words.

What could she have meant when she said there was more going on? With Stanford? Ada could reasonably guess that the man was interested in more than a casual acquaintance. But was she? Stanford seemed every bit the kind of match her father would have wanted for her—gentlemanly, intelligent, witty, charming, and well established financially.

But was that so important to her? She had grown up very sound in that regard, but what had it ever gotten her? It wasn't the key to happiness.

Her mind drifted to Slim. She found his livelihood rather appealing—working with his body and managing the cattle. His muscular frame had been evident to her when they had collided. He was strong, and his arms quite capable. Not only to steady her and keep her upright, but to bring quite the reaction in her. Her faced burned, and she glanced in Mrs. Wilmont's direction to ensure the woman hadn't noticed. Ada decided she'd best push such thoughts to the side. It couldn't be a good idea to dwell on that.

Yes, Slim was gentle, kind, and sweet. But she couldn't escape that he lived day-to-day. Was there any stability in that? Could she be content with that kind of life? She told herself she wanted adventure, but that didn't mean she was ready for that level of risk. Yes, she had to admit that while she knew money had its place, it had supported a lifestyle she had become accustomed to.

She paused and admired her progress. But something wasn't right. The piece didn't look like Mrs. Wilmont's. Not in the least.

"What is the matter, dear?" Mrs. Wilmont looked over the rims of her spectacles.

"I don't know." Her growing washcloth seemed mangled and had unplanned holes in it. "Why does mine look so different from yours?"

Mrs. Wilmont smiled. "It's only your first piece. Be patient with yourself."

"But is it supposed to be so...open?" Ada slid a finger through one of the holes.

"That is where you missed a stitch."

Ada smoothed out the piece and tried to pull at the yarn around the biggest hole. "Is there any way to fix it?"

Mrs. Wilmont chuckled softly and shook her head. "I'm afraid not. It's there for good."

"Oohh," Ada grunted in frustration as she noted the numerous holes. It did indeed make her work look rather haphazard. "Is it even worth it?"

"Of course. There's no other way to learn."

Ada hadn't realized she'd spoken aloud. A little flustered from her obvious outburst, she set the needles and yarn to the side.

"Don't be discouraged. I have faith," Mrs. Wilmont said with another smile before she refocused on her own yarn.

Ada watched her work the shawl. She was almost done with it. And she moved her hands so expertly...and so fast. Would Ada ever be able to do so?

A knock on the door caused her to jump.

"That will be Stanford," Ada said. Him calling this afternoon had been far from her mind.

Mrs. Wilmont set her things to the side and rose. "I'll get it."

The woman didn't look in Ada's direction again. Was she pleased at this intrusion? Or bothered?

Ada watched her move to the front door and open it. There was Stanford, standing in all his finery with a small box and a handful of flowers. Had he changed his clothing since church? For what reason?

"Good afternoon, Aunt Lottie."

"To what do I owe this pleasure?" Mrs. Wilmont said, as if Ada hadn't just told her. Why would she do that?

"I have come to see..." he started, glancing around the space. He set his gaze on Ada and smiled. "Ah, Miss Miller, there you are."

Ada rose and offered him a smile. She hoped it didn't betray just how tired she was. The last thing she truly wanted was to entertain Stanford. Charming as he was, she had wished for an afternoon with less activity—a time to settle in and just be.

"I'm here to call on Miss Miller." Stanford looked back to his aunt.

"Very well. Are those for me?" Mrs. Wilmont tortured him. She reached for the flowers.

He pulled them back a little bit. "They are for Miss Miller."

"Oh?" Would Mrs. Wilmont make this all the more awkward?

Ada stepped forward. "They are lovely."

Stanford moved toward her but stopped.

Mrs. Wilmont still partially blocked the doorway.

"Excuse me, Aunt Lottie, may I...?"

Mrs. Wilmont moved to the side. "Of course."

Stanford breezed past her and strode to Ada. As if he had but one thing on his mind. He pressed the flowers toward her.

She received them, their fragrant blooms filling her senses. "I thank you. I hardly expected them."

"Then you must entertain me more often. I know how to treat a lady."

The door shut with a loud thud.

"Excuse me." Mrs. Wilmont had a hand on her chest. "I did not mean to make such a ruckus."

Stanford turned back to Ada. "I also brought you some chocolates. My favorite—coconut filled."

"Oh." How could she tell him she wasn't fond of the stuff? Something about the texture of coconut did not agree with her.

He opened the box and held it out to her. "Take one."

"Perhaps later, I—"

"Just one?" His brows lifted. He became the picture of vulnerability.

Would she not take the offer and put him out of his misery? She swallowed, not relishing the idea of the grainy stuff in her mouth. "Really, Stanford, I'd rather not, I just—"

"Not even one? For me?" There was a lilt to his voice.

Would he pressure her so? Perhaps, he only wished to see her enjoy one. He had made such an effort on her behalf. Could she not indulge his kindness?

"All right." She reached into the box and lifted the smallest one she could find. "Shall we sit?"

"Not until I see you taste this delectable sweet. I just know you will love it as much as I."

She swallowed again; this time her mouth was quite dry. Still, she lifted the chocolate to her lips, closed her eyes, and popped it onto her tongue. The chocolate was indeed delicious, but soon enough, she had naught but coconut in her mouth. And she struggled to maintain a neutral face.

His eyes were intent on her.

She pressed a smile onto her lips. "It is rather...unique."

Stanford touched her hand. "I knew you would like them. And think, you have so many more to enjoy."

She nodded, suddenly feeling a little nauseated. All the more so as he continued to hold the box out to her. "I had best get these flowers in some water." Then she moved off to the kitchen to settle the flowers.

Stanford watched after her. She sensed his gaze on her. Could she not have two seconds to spit out this horribleness? So, she closed her eyes and swallowed, nearly gagging in the process.

Mrs. Wilmont appeared beside her with a vase.

She smiled her thanks toward the woman and maneuvered the stems into the fine glass container.

Mrs. Wilmont then took the vase and headed toward the water pump in the sink. "You go on, dear, and mind Stanford. I'll be along shortly."

Ada moved back to the great room to find a beaming Stanford.

He stepped closer, as if to intercept her. Would he try to touch her hand again? Or be even more forward than that?

She forced her lips to turn upward even as a sinking feeling filled her gut.

He glanced toward the kitchen and then moved until his mouth was near her ear. "I am very glad you like my gifts."

The heat of his breath on her ear made her a little uncomfortable. Why would he be so bold?

She stepped back and then moved around him to the chair she had earlier vacated. "Yes. I appreciate your kindness."

His gaze stayed with her. At least, it seemed she could feel his eyes following her every move. How long would he linger? She felt even more weary than she had before.

He settled onto a nearby chair and stared at her. "Do you know how breathtaking you are?"

She fidgeted with her hands then reached for the yarn and needles. That would be something to disguise her anxious thoughts. "I thank you."

A thud to the right drew Ada's attention. Mrs. Wilmont had set the vase on the dining table. Then she moved to where she had sat before. But she did not pick up her knitting, rather plucked a small book from the side table.

Ada was relieved the woman would chaperone. But one look at Stanford's grimace made her think he would rather his aunt not be there. Now, that would be highly inappropriate—a man calling, giving suit to a lady without a chaperone. Just what was he about?

They sat in silence for several moments. But that didn't keep Stanford from staring at her. Though she focused on her working hands, she still sensed it.

At length, Stanford sighed. "I had hoped, dear Miss Miller, to invite you to supper with me tomorrow night."

She looked up at him. He seemed genuine and so eager for her attention. Should she accept? After all, he was a highly sought after bachelor in Tombstone. "I...would like that."

"Splendid! I shall collect you at six."

She nodded.

Some more moments passed in silence. It became increasingly awkward.

"I'd...ah...best not overstay my welcome." He rose.

Ada stood as well. "So soon?" What was she saying? She was tired, ready for some space from the pained politeness.

His eyes seemed to sparkle despite their intensity. "I prefer to leave my companions wanting in anticipation for our next meeting. Lingering will only diminish that."

"A wise standard." Ada nodded.

He leaned toward her. Would he attempt to whisper in her ear again? But he glanced at his aunt and backed away. Then he took her hand and led her to the door.

She didn't care to be led, but she should walk him to the door.

He paused, lifting her hand to his lips. "Until tomorrow."

She almost pulled her hand away. He was forward indeed. But she did not wish to create tension between them or embarrass him in front of his relation. "Until then."

He let her hand fall. Then he turned and exited.

She let out a long breath. It had been painful, their interaction. Did Mrs. Wilmont think the same? Would she be offended at Ada's lack of warmth toward her nephew?

Ada did not wish to refuse his efforts, but there was nothing about their interaction that increased her favor. Could Ada discourage his suit without damaging her relationship with Mrs. Wilmont? What was she to do?

The main stretch of Tombstone was quite a sight in the late afternoon. Different businesses were more active. The General Store, Telegraph Office, bank, and such had closed down. While the saloons and gambling halls were just getting their first wave of patrons. As Slim looked around, he noticed that fewer families were about, more men traipsing around alone. And rougher men...but not all. Some of them were well-dressed. Clearly upper crust.

But he did rather enjoy the coolness that the evening brought. He had walked down the planked sidewalk on one side of the main street, and now back again. But he still didn't see anything that would entice him. He wasn't interested in many of the establishments that were active right now.

However, there was the Birdcage Theater across the street. And it was busy indeed. What would it be like to see a play? A story lived out on a stage. Slim couldn't imagine how that would go, what it would look like, or even the experience. Perhaps, he would have that opportunity while in Tombstone.

It would still be the better part of an hour before Dan's horse was ready at the livery. Reshoeing wasn't the problem. That didn't take so long. But the man working this afternoon had said there were some things he had to do first. And of the hour he needed to waste, Slim had filled about ten minutes.

He rolled his eyes. How would he manage all that time?

The aroma of roasted beef wafted out of the nearby café. Should he go ahead and sup here? It was likely the dinner hour would be well past before he returned to the Hayworths'. And that pot roast did smell rather good.

He closed the remaining distance to the café and stepped within. Scanning the room, he spotted a table near the window. But something else caught his eye—a couple on the other side of the dining space. The woman looked like Ada. Though Slim couldn't quite make out her companion, as the man's back faced him. But he would wager almost anything it was Stanford.

Ada let out a laugh, genuine and musical—a very pleasant sound amongst the clanging of dishes. Did she find Stanford's company so enjoyable? But as he watched, he could not account for her behavior any other way. She watched the man, intent on his every word.

Something in his chest tightened. Was he jealous? That didn't seem right. True, Ada had been warm and friendly…and there had been some sparks between them. But he didn't need such entanglements. Certainly, not now. And he wouldn't risk his heart after seeing her gaze at another man the way she did Stanford.

It was probably for the best. They two were well suited. Both came from money. Was that important to Ada? He remembered her interaction with the poor immigrant child and mother. No, she wasn't stuck on wealth.

Then why Stanford? The man was rather off-putting. And Slim couldn't shake that there was more to him than what was on the surface. Something darker. But Slim couldn't put his finger on it. The fact that he didn't know the man all that well may account for that. But Ada hadn't much paused to forgive Stanford his offense. Was she so blind to his faults? To what lingered beneath?

"Sir, did you need a table?"

He turned. A petite woman with brown hair watched him, eager for his answer.

What could he do? The thought of eating in the café, having to watch any interaction between those two, did not appeal. Neither did walking away and not knowing.

"Yes. That is, I would like that table by the window, if that's all right."

The woman nodded. "Yes, sir, it is available."

She ushered him to the table, and he sat, hoping that Ada didn't notice him come in.

He glanced in her direction.

Ada still attended to whatever Stanford was saying.

"What'll you have?" The brunette interrupted his thoughts.

"Ah…the pot roast dinner. And a coffee."

The woman nodded and moved off.

Slim peered at Ada again and strained to hear more than he possibly could. He could only pick up the occasional laughter. And that came more than he'd care for it to. Stanford wasn't that funny. Or that interesting. Right?

He did notice that they were enjoying their cobbler and coffee. Well, Stanford had coffee. Ada didn't appear to have more to drink than a glass of water. How long had they been here? How long would they linger? Did they have other plans for the evening?

The thought of her meandering around Tombstone at this hour on Stanford's arm did not settle well. He'd best push it aside if he hoped to stomach dinner. But he could not tear his gaze away from them. And it gave him pause to wonder what he wanted. Did he want to be with Ada at that table, having her laugh at his jokes?

He imagined what that would be like. It brought warmth to his being. And a bit of a giddy feeling. Could it be? That he did want more than the simple friendship he and Ada enjoyed? Or was that a step too far? He had become determined to guard his heart. Seeing her here with Stanford though, gave him reason to doubt. Perhaps that needed to be his plan— protecting himself. No sense putting himself out there only to be rejected.

Though as he forced his gaze to his own table, he found he could not let it go either. Did he begrudge her being with anyone else? Or just Stanford? Slim decided it truly was that the man hid something. He didn't like the idea of Ada being misled or misused. And he resolved to keep a closer eye on Stanford. He would have to figure out what the man was about and what his intentions with Ada were.

Slim's heart thumped hard in his chest at the prospect of what could happen to her if Stanford were keeping something devious hidden. It could only lead to heartache for her. And Slim couldn't stand for that. No, he cared too much.

Ada took another bite of the blackberry cobbler. It was every bit as good as she had hoped. After all, it was her favorite. The berries were a delicate mix of sweetness and tartness. The breading of the cobbler had been sweetened enough to offset any lack of it in the fruit—a careful balance.

"What do you think?" Stanford asked.

Ada looked up. She had been lost in thought again. How many times had it happened on this outing? Was she so disinterested that she couldn't follow better? It would help if he wasn't droning on about himself so much. Still, she had pardoned her lack of attention enough times this evening. Dare she do so again?

"I...don't know." There. That would likely take care of it.

"No?" His brows rose.

Had she erred? He didn't seem pleased.

She reluctantly pushed the remainder of her cobbler away. "I must apologize," she said, then blotted her mouth with a napkin. "It is getting late."

His features twisted, displaying his confusion. "It isn't quite seven."

Why did she feel so weary then? It didn't matter, she was ready for her bed. "For a teacher, that is plenty late. I have an early morning."

Stanford's brows furrowed. "Just a short stroll. I promise, I'll have you home by seven-thirty."

She sighed. It wasn't a big ask, but could she withstand more of this? Risk embarrassment and offense in her lack of concentration? "I thank you for the offer, but I fear it is time for my rest."

His face fell, his expression replaced by one of dejection.

She didn't like seeing him so put off. But she didn't want to give in, either. Why must he make this so difficult? Her gaze wandered around the café as if the answer would just appear on the wall. Perhaps, she only waited for him to come around to better humor.

A patron at the far window caught her eye. He was somewhat silhouetted by the fading daylight coming in. But somehow, she knew it was Slim. Maybe it was his build. He sat alone at the table. Why was that? And, as she watched him, he turned and met her gaze. She suddenly became charged with energy—something akin to the sparking embers of a fire. Only, he did not seem happy to see her.

"Have I upset you?" Stanford's question pulled her regard back to him.

"No, not at all." She tried to laugh off his insinuation, but it came out stifled.

"You've not said anything for a while."

"Oh." She took a sip of water. "I think I'm just tired." Her gaze darted back to where Slim sat. And when she turned to Stanford once again, she noted that his eyes had followed the path of hers. He now glared at Slim.

Stanford's mouth pulled at one side. What did that mean? His expression was difficult to discern. Abruptly, he faced her. "Are you finished?"

What did he mean? Finished with him? Her heart beat faster. How was she to answer such a bold question?

"With your dessert? Do you need more time to finish?"

Her pulse calmed. "Oh, yes, I have had plenty. Thank you, for dinner."

He had already looked down, perhaps intent on pulling out the money for their meals. Had he even heard her? But he set the money on the table and looked at her once more. And, reaching his hand out, enfolded hers. "The pleasure has been all mine."

Lifting her hand, he pressed a kiss to it before she could pull away.

She peered over in Slim's direction. Had he seen?

Slim's glare told all. How could he appear injured and vexed at once?

She was able to retract her hand after a couple of failed attempts.

Stanford did not seem dissuaded. He set his napkin on the table. But there was something bubbling under the surface. She could sense it.

Ada played with her linen napkin, a bit softer and more worn than the stiff table covering. How had this gone this badly so quickly? Had she now offended Stanford? Perhaps, she wasn't responsible for his reaction. She could only be true to herself and let things land where they did. Even as she told herself this, she knew better. How she proceeded here would make or break her connection with Stanford. Was she ready to throw it away?

"I am sorry if I have upset you," she started. "And I apologize for my distraction this evening."

His gaze was hard as his eyes met hers.

She let out a breath. "I suppose I'm even more tired than I thought."

He maintained a neutral, somewhat drawn expression for several seconds. Then he leaned forward, and his features softened. "I understand. I should get you back to Aunt Lottie's then."

She nodded. "Thank you. I have...had a lovely evening." She prayed her hesitation, whatever it meant, had been imperceptible.

Stanford rose and held out a hand to her. If he did notice, he was ignoring it.

She slid her hand into his and stood as he tugged at her arm.

Once on her feet, she realized how close he stood. It made her more than a little uncomfortable. But her legs were already grazing the chair. There wasn't anywhere for her to politely escape to.

"Shall we?" She indicated the exit, praying he would heed the suggestion and not tarry. This could not look good, and she didn't want to create a scene.

After some tense moments, he nodded and stepped back.

She took in a full breath and let it out. Why must this be so strained? It mattered little; she must focus on maintaining some distance between them for the remainder of the time it would take to get her home. And she prayed it would be easier than she anticipated.

Slim maneuvered down the main street. It wasn't as easy as it had been before. He had a couple of whiskeys to thank for that. Why had he done that? He knew better, but it had seemed logical at the time. Still, he thanked the Lord that he still had much of his wits about himself. Enough to stop drinking. But his head already swam a little. Thankfully, just a little.

He made his way to the livery. With any luck, his horse would be ready, and he could get to the Hayworths' ranch before things got out of control. It was probably best he mind his words—in number as well as what he said. Even a little drink could make him loose tongued.

As he approached, he spotted his mare at the ready. Good thing. His desire to be abed was never so great.

"Just finished up, Mr. Dagley." A voice from just within the entrance spoke.

A man stepped out to greet him. Must be the farrier, he decided.

"Did she give you any trouble?" He attempted to push the words out clearly. Was there any discernable slur to his speech? He prayed not.

The man's brows furrowed, but his expression soon shifted. "Not at all. She's a fine animal."

Slim tipped his head. If he hadn't been holding to a post, he wasn't certain he could keep from stumbling as he did so. Maybe those whiskeys affected him more than he thought. He almost never drank. It just wasn't fitting. Men who made a habit of it tended to go too far, and some ended up giving everything they had to the bottle.

That would not be him. He would not let this happen again. How had he this time? When he considered his actions, Ada's face was on the forefront of his mind. So was his urge to return to the saloon. Did he want so much to forget? To stop thinking about her? Why? She was his friend...maybe even no more than an acquaintance. But he had hoped...

That wouldn't get him anywhere. She had chosen Stanford. Hadn't she? Even as he followed those thoughts, he couldn't convince himself that this was the end of it. Something in the way she had looked at him across the café. There was something in her eyes. Did she feel as drawn to him as he did to her?

"Mr. Dagley?"

Slim focused on the farrier once again. The man's expression belied his confusion.

"You okay?" There was that creased brow again.

"Yeah. Just tired."

"That ain't all." The man watched him.

Nonsense. There was nothing wrong with him. "What do I owe you?"

"I put it on Mr. Hayworth's tab. It is his horse, ain't it?"

Slim nodded and moved around the large man and to the horse. He steeled himself and started to mount.

"You sure you're all right?"

What was with this man? Was he Slim's keeper? "Yeah. I'm fine."

The man shrugged. A gesture of dismissal. "Tell Mr. Hayworth I said, 'hey'."

Slim tipped his hat to the man. "Will do. And thank you for your assistance with the horse."

The man only nodded as he stepped further within the stables.

What did that man know about it? Slim was fine. Nothing that a little sleep couldn't fix. He urged the animal into a trot and directed her away from the main stretch. Though, something weighed on his heart. Something heavy. He tried to push forward and move past it, but it plagued him.

He wanted to see Ada. Tonight.

That was ridiculous. Not only was she probably still out strolling with Stanford, he didn't want anyone—least of all her—to see him like this. But when he came to the edge of town, he found himself steering the horse toward Mrs. Wilmont's cabin.

He couldn't be serious. If Ada was home, she would be more interested in retiring for the night than talking to Slim. It wasn't likely she'd receive him. That was if she was even there.

Still, he did not turn back.

Moments later, he found himself staring at the cabin. What was his plan now? He hadn't one. This was the most nonsensical thing he could have thought to do. But he was here. And his desire to see her pushed him onward.

He slid from the horse, a little more unsteadily than he'd like. Then he walked to the door. But as he raised his hand to knock, he had the first thoughts of how unnerving it might be for the women to hear a knock at this hour. It would be best if he got back on his horse and went home. That's what he should do.

But he knocked. And winced.

Footfalls within made him regret it even more. There was nowhere to hide now.

The door opened to reveal the Widow Wilmont, still fully dressed from the day. Did she not seek her room at this hour? That line of thinking felt fuzzy.

"Slim?" the woman said. "Is everything all right?"

He took his hat off. "Yes, ma'am. I only needed...wanted...to talk to Miss Miller."

Mrs. Wilmont gave him a long, hard look. She clearly did not approve. Of his being here? Of the hour? Or did she discern he had been drinking? Any of those were reason enough to send him on his way.

But her expression softened. "I'll tell her you're here. Would you... like to come in?"

It didn't take a mind reader to sense that she was uneasy with that last part. "No, ma'am. I thank you, but I'll wait here."

She nodded. He did not miss the relief that shone in her face. Then she eased the door closed.

It was only a handful of seconds later when the door opened once more, and Ada stood in front of him. She still wore her dress from the day but had taken her hair down. Did she braid it for bed, or let it fall loose?

He looked away, chastising himself. This was no time for thoughts such as these.

"Slim? Did you need something?" She, too, appeared concerned. And again, he wondered what part bothered her the most. Could she tell he'd had a couple?

"I wanted to talk to you." He felt his control slipping. It was an odd feeling. Like something was sliding the floor out from under him.

"Can it wait until tomorrow? It is awful late." She peered back inside.

He would wager that Mrs. Wilmont sat not far away, just out of view. But Ada was right. It wasn't the best time. For her or for him.

"I'm sorry. It can." His heart dropped. Was he so affected?

"Goodnight, Slim." She turned, pressing on the door.

And suddenly he couldn't let her. He pushed his foot out and stopped the door.

Her wide-eyed gaze caught on him.

"I just...need to understand." The words spilled out of him without a thought. He became torn between his need to know and his desire to let things lie until he had better control of himself.

"Understand?" She blinked. Was it as prominent as it seemed to him?

"Why you went with him."

She swallowed. Her hesitation pained him. "With him?"

Would she play ignorant now? Or did she only wish to push him further?

"Yes, him. Stan." He tried to disguise his exasperation by looking away, but he found he couldn't. His eyes pinned her.

She peered at the floor. "I..." she started but seemed to struggle. "It was dinner."

He crossed his arms. It wasn't just dinner—it was more than that.

But before he could counter, she did. "And I don't know what it matters to you."

He held his ground, though the shock of her words had hit him square in the chest. Making an effort to soften his voice, he continued, "I...he doesn't deserve you."

"Oh?" There was a flash in her eyes then. "What do you know about that?"

His defenses rose in response. "I know what I see. You are kind and good and caring and..." He felt himself start to ramble and let his words fade.

"But none of that means I can't entertain any man's suit that I wish." She shot back, though her voice was gentler than it had been.

"I just...don't want you to..." What? How was he going to finish that sentence?

"Perhaps, it is up to me. You are not my protector, Slim. I appreciate the concern, but it doesn't mean I—"

"He's not right for you. Can't you see that?" His words were harsher than he'd intended.

She shook her head at his tone.

Silence fell between them.

"Again, I'm quite certain it doesn't concern you." Her voice was firm.

How could she be so dismissive? Did she not see that he cared? For her wellbeing, for her future...for her. He threw his hands up. "I can't stop you. But I don't have to watch."

"I'm not asking you to," came her short reply.

He watched her then.

"I think it very odd that you would bother. You, who have made not one attempt to further our friendship. Or seek something beyond that." Her words bit at him.

"Then that's how you see it." He leaned closer. "But I know what I see. And he's not good for you."

She leaned back. Was his closeness so difficult for her stomach? "You've been drinking. Go home and clear you head."

He shrugged. "If you'd prefer I leave. I'll leave." He spun and headed toward his horse.

"Good," her voice carried louder than he'd have expected. It struck him. Right between his shoulder blades.

As much as he wanted to turn and face her again, he forced his feet to keep going. He reached his horse just as he heard the door slam. Gripping the saddle, he set his head on the side of the animal. What had he done?

CHAPTER 10

Closer

Ada cringed as she approached the Hayworth ranch. She was not looking forward to this visit. Oh, she was eager to see Lily. But she dreaded the possibility of bumping into Slim. Their exchange two nights ago had left her strangely hurt.

There was no reason to think Slim would seek her out. Or that he would even come to the house while she was there. He had said his piece, and that may very well be that.

With this encouragement to herself, which felt oddly numbing, she pushed her horse onward. She would have to take a moment this evening and respond to Mother's most recent correspondence. Mother had, as usual, inquired after her well-being. And assured Ada that all was well with her—she was comfortable, and her every need was being attended to.

Mother had also taken the time to offer advice on Ada's circumstances—specifically on the two men she entertained. Though Ada hadn't expounded on the situation, Mother had seemed to read between the lines. She encouraged Ada to follow her heart in matters such as this, but to think about the future as well. Ada took that to mean her mother wished her to think about her financial security and the comforts that came with that. It wasn't as if Ada hadn't spent enough time struggling with that very thing. Maybe after Slim's display that evening past, this could be easier.

The sounds of the nearby homestead drew Ada's attention back to what was in front of her. How had she arrived so quickly?

Even as she approached, there was no denying she scanned the area for Slim. Did she truly want to see him? No. That couldn't be. Not after the way he had talked to her.

She tied her mare to a post and moved to the door, still sneaking glances around the yard. It was nonsense. Slim had to be out in the pasture somewhere. Doing what ranchers do.

A gentle knock was all that was needed to bring her face-to-face with Lily.

"I am so glad to see you!" The woman pulled Ada into an embrace.

Ada hugged her back. "It is good to be here."

Lily moved into the house, indicating that Ada should follow. "Thank you for coming."

"It was not a problem." Ada cringed again at the lie. What was Slim doing to her?

Lily stopped by the dining table and indicated they should sit.

Ada complied. There was something different about Lily. A bounce in her step. And a glow about her person.

Lily beamed as Ada settled into her seat and reached for her glass of water. The woman's face fairly shone.

Taking a sip, Ada pondered again on Lily's altered appearance. Had she done something new with her hair?

No sooner had Ada set the glass down then Lily gripped her hands. "I have something to tell you."

Now, it would come. Did Lily know about her and Slim's awkward exchange? Would Lily want to talk about it? A sinking feeling filled Ada's stomach. But then again, Lily seemed altogether too happy to want to talk on that. She appeared positively giddy.

"Tell me," Ada managed. She clasped her friend's hands.

"Dan and I are...well...the thing is... Oh, I'm no good at this! We're going to have a baby!"

Relief spread through Ada's being. And then the realization of what Lily said followed quickly behind. "A baby? That's so exciting!"

Lily nodded. "I have so wanted to tell you, but I needed to be sure."

Ada waved her off. "That is no matter. I am just so happy for you." As much as she meant those words, they caught in her throat. Was she... jealous? Of her friend's good news? That surprised her.

"I can't quite express all the emotions inside of me. It's all so new... and exciting...and—"

"I can imagine," Ada broke in. "But...are you well? I understand some women have quite a bit of sickness in the early weeks."

Lily nodded. "I certainly have that. But it is nothing much. It could be worse."

"Do you..." How was she to ask this? "...feel any different? I mean... inside."

Lily had not stopped smiling, and her grin deepened then. Surely her lips could not stretch any more. "I do. And I don't. It's...difficult to explain."

Ada nodded. More words would not come. And she could not escape that part of what went on within her was envy. She loved this for her friend, but a part of her...a part she often shoved to the side...wanted it for herself.

"The months ahead stretch on. I don't know how I'll be able to wait so long to meet him." Lily set a hand to her stomach. Did she even know she did so? "It's like waiting for the biggest Christmas ever."

Ada made her lips curve upward. She was happy. She was. "We must celebrate this," she said, praying her words would change her hesitation.

Lily gestured in a dismissive way. "I don't want to make it big news just yet."

"A secret? I will do my best to keep it then." She mock-saluted. "Does anyone else know?"

Lily gulped some water and then looked to her friend again. "Dan, of course." She smiled again. "And he told Slim."

The mention of Slim caused an ache to swell in Ada's chest. Why did she let him affect her so? He didn't seem all that concerned with her feelings anyway.

Lily balked. "What was that?"

"What was what?" Ada asked, somewhat taken aback.

"Your expression. It changed. Is something wrong?" Lily's eyes widened, and her smile disappeared. Did she worry that Ada was not as happy as she made out? Perhaps, it was Ada's reaction to Slim's name. Should she share with Lily? Could she avoid it at this point?

"It is nothing."

Lily tilted her head. Her features displayed her disbelief.

"It isn't anything to concern yourself with. Not when we should be celebrating."

Lily shook her head. "Something is bothering you. And I'm your friend. If you wish to share, I want to hear it."

Ada pulled in a deep breath. Maybe Lily would have some words of wisdom.

The door opened, cutting her off.

She turned to see Dan and Slim walk in. Her eyes caught on Slim's. And a tingle shot down her spine. No, she reminded herself, he didn't get to affect her. Not after...

"Good day, Miss Miller." Dan tipped his hat to her.

"Please...it's Ada."

Dan nodded. Then his expression changed. His brows scrunched, and he frowned. "Are you well?"

"Yes. Of course." She glanced at Lily, whose gaze upon her was just as curious.

"You look a little pale. Are you sure you're all right?" Dan pressed.

Ada wanted to disappear. Was that possible? "I...perhaps, I need some fresh air."

Lily started to rise.

Ada set a hand on hers. "Please, sit. It may be better if I go home and rest."

The lines in Dan's features deepened. He appeared concerned. "I don't know that you should go anywhere. Not until you're feeling more yourself."

"I am fine. Maybe a slight headache." She peered at Slim for a brief moment. Then shifted her gaze back to Lily. "I promise. I am well enough."

Dan did not seem satisfied. "Still, I must insist that you let someone take you home in the wagon. We can hitch your horse to the back."

She wasn't getting out of this. Still, she protested. "I don't wish to take you from your wife."

Dan waved a hand dismissively. "No need. Slim can get you back to Widow Wilmont's cabin. Can't you, Slim?"

He nodded but didn't speak.

Ada's face warmed. That was the last thing she wanted—to force Slim to share company with her. Or to find herself alone with him.

"Yes, please do let Slim help you," Lily spoke up. "Now you are turning feverish."

"Go hitch the wagon," Dan said to Slim.

"But I—" Ada started.

"Nonsense." Dan stepped around the table and stood behind Lily. "It's no trouble. Besides, you're like family."

She sighed. This was not going to be pleasant.

Slim maneuvered the horse and cart toward the front of the Hayworths' cabin. How had he landed in this mess? It was clear Ada did not wish to be escorted. Least of all by him. And he couldn't blame her. He had been the villain in all this, coming at her like he did. Had she shared all with Lily? His face burned. That wouldn't do. Not one bit.

He took some deep breaths, and his features cooled. This would be tricky. But he did not regret the turn of events. There were things he needed to say...wanted to say.

Dan must have seen the wagon through the window. For the door opened and he exited, Ada on his arm. She protested the entire time, but Dan would not hear it. Dan and Lily had both been concerned after Ada's change in demeanor. As well he imagined they might be. They were so caring.

But he was not blind. He could guess that her reaction had more to do with anger that welled within her toward him than any physical ailment. At least, that's what seemed most likely.

As Dan led Ada to the wagon, Slim tied her horse to the cart. By the time he maneuvered back to the front, Ada was seated and ready to go.

Dan met Slim's gaze. "If need be, take her to the doctor."

Slim nodded. He didn't think Ada would need anything but to be free of him. The reality of that weighed heavy in his midsection. This wasn't how he had ever imagined things between them. Still, that was the way it was.

He hoisted himself up beside her, taking care to put what space he could between their bodies. No need to cause her further discomfort. Then he motioned to Dan as he urged the horses onward.

As they began to move, he could almost feel Ada seething beside him. What could he do? What could he say? How could he express his regret?

The cart hit a bump in the road, and the wagon tilted slightly, causing her body to lean into his. She scrambled to right herself. That hurt.

"That's not necessary," he grumbled. He felt more than saw her gaze on him. She could probably wound someone with that glare.

She pushed out a breath and turned her attention to the opposite side of the cart.

"I didn't mean that." He softened his voice.

She didn't turn.

"Look, Ada, I...hate what happened."

Still nothing.

"I hate that I drank. I hate even more that I decided to confront you. I don't know that I can ask you to forgive me, but I am so very sorry." There. He had said it. It was up to her now.

Her shoulders relaxed just a bit. She faced forward, still refusing to look at him. Instead, she seemed rather intent on the boards at her feet.

What else could he say? How could he make this better?

"I...do forgive you."

What? His eyes shot to her. That was a bit unexpected. Maybe there was hope...

"I know you're only trying to look out for me."

Truly? Did she really see his intentions so well? He was grateful.

Their ride continued in silence. But he couldn't not speak further.

After some moments passed, he swallowed and pressed forth an admission. "Something you said struck me. And I can't get it out of my head."

She peered at him. And when their eyes met, she looked away.

"You said that my words the other night were out of place because I had not made one attempt to further our friendship. Or seek something beyond that." He felt her gaze on him again. So, he shifted to meet her eyes. Something filled the space between them. Something heated. "You were right."

One of her brows shot up.

"It was not right of me to criticize when I had made no effort to speak to you. To court you." He pushed the words out. Otherwise they may not come at all.

Her regard fell back to her shoes.

"I had thought..." A lump formed in his throat. He swallowed past it. "I had thought my intentions were plain."

She watched him again. It was unnerving. If only she would not. Was there nowhere else for her eyes to go?

"See, I...do want to spend time with you. I do want to court you." Out of the side of his vision, he noted her mouth agape. "But I guess I missed my chance." The words were strangled. How he hated them.

Silence thickened the small space between them.

"I don't know if that's true." Her voice was small, timid.

He met her gaze. Her eyes were kind. And there was something else there he couldn't quite identify. "But you are entertaining Stan's suit."

"True."

A pause lay heavy in that moment.

"But he and I have no formal understanding. Nothing that would prevent me from receiving another man's call."

He examined her face. There was no hint of jest about her. Would she really let him pursue her after the mess he made of their last conversation?

"In fact..." Her words were measured and careful. "I think I would quite enjoy getting to know you better."

Something swelled in him then, expanding his chest and making his head swim a little. His gaze held hers. Had he imagined it? Or had she dared to be so bold?

His shoulders squared, making room for the growing warmth within him. "Then, Miss Miller, I would like to ask you to join me day after tomorrow. It would be my pleasure to show you the Hayworth property."

She smiled. It was simple. And sweet. "I would like that very much."

Ada had tired of being in the saddle. It wasn't that she didn't enjoy the horse or the ride, it was more that she was not accustomed to such a long time upon the animal.

Slim drew near and slowed. "Shall we stop for a moment?"

She sent up a prayer of thankful relief. Had he heard her thoughts? How?

"I am well enough," she lied. Why? Did she not wish him to think her weak? Surely, other women of his acquaintance could remain astride for hours longer.

"It's for the horses." His voice sounded amused. "They need a break. And water."

"Oh." She looked down as her face heated.

Slim urged the horse to pick up step again and led her to a small stream. He dismounted and turned to assist her.

As she dropped into his arms, she felt a rush in her core. From his closeness? The movement of sensation within her was powerful. Was she so drawn to him? Or was it little more than simple attraction? The kind she would have with any number of men. It was a few moments before she realized she was staring up at him.

His hands still rested on her waist. As she studied him, his gaze shifted to her mouth.

Her breath caught. Would he try to kiss her? Would she let him? Could she not?

She shook her head and stepped back.

He gripped her.

Ada's eyes widened. What was he doing?

"Whoa," he said, looking behind her.

She turned. The mare stood directly at her back. How had she forgotten? The horse had not moved since she left the saddle, putting it inches from her. Ada shifted her attention back to Slim's face. "Thank you."

"Not a problem." His voice was little more than a whisper. His eyes pulled her in further. So much so, it was several seconds before she noticed his thumbs caressed her arms. The movement was slight but intoxicating all the same.

"We should...um..." she started.

"Yeah. The horses." He ducked his head.

She looked down and shook her head.

He moved back.

Her body cooled with the distance created. When she looked up again, he had taken the horses' bits and tugged them to the stream.

She soon followed, patting the mare's neck as she stood alongside Slim.

"What did you think?" His words scattered any thoughts that were forming.

She froze. Was he asking her something so personal? How bold of him...inquiring after her thoughts during the moments they were...they had... "Think?"

"Of the ranch and the property?" His attention was yet again on the animals. "It's a pretty stretch, ain't it?"

"Oh, yes." She tried to cover her initial reaction by moving farther away. "Great views."

He nodded and murmured, "The Hayworths are blessed."

Was he still talking about the land? Or something else? The baby? Ada had not been able to shake the strange jealousy that had taken hold of her. But then again, she had been just as envious of their closeness. Dan adored Lily. Would anyone ever look at her the way he looked upon his wife? Could Slim?

Slim crouched and leaned over. He let water from the stream fill his cupped hands. Then he drank it in.

Staring at his back as his muscles moved under his shirt, she realized yet again how capable he was. And she became all too aware of how dry her mouth had become. Dare she bend down and drink as he did? There didn't seem to be any other way to quench her thirst.

Watching for Slim's reaction, she settled by the flowing stream and thrust her fingers in. The water chilled more than she had imagined. It almost made her retract her hand. But she fought to keep them still. She was all too aware of Slim's gaze on her. Making a small scoop with her hand, she gathered a little bit of the liquid and brought it to her face. But the coolness seeped out of her hand. There was not even a drop when she reached her mouth. Was she so useless?

"You have to make it tight. Like this." Slim put a hand under hers, their skin sealing at the various points of contact. Then, dragging her hand down with his, he filled the makeshift cup and helped lift it to her face. Some of the precious water made it to her lips that time.

What must he think of her? Surely, it wasn't that she was independent. She felt anything but. Still, his presence soothed her worn nerves as much as it set her on edge. Something about him made her feel like she could slow her harried thoughts and just be Ada for a bit. That was a gift. For she had always been Charles Miller's daughter, or Brandon's sister, or, more recently, the schoolteacher. Her identity had been wrapped up in those she was connected to. Did he really see her?

In that moment, she realized he still held her hand. With some reluctance, she pulled it back and set it in her lap. She let her gaze wander over the vistas before them. Rustic. Expansive. Would she ever tire of the open space? Yes, she like this place...room for her to breathe.

"What is it like?" Slim's eyes were on her face. "Back east?"

"Nothing like this. A lot more buildings and a lot less..." She spread her arms. Everything in Richmond was jammed together...at least by comparison.

He nodded. Was he so curious? Because he wanted to see it? Or something else? His gaze traveled beyond the stream. "Do you think about going back?"

"Sure." She watched a bird overhead, perhaps looking for a place to roost.

"Oh?" came his unexpected question.

As she turned, she noticed that Slim's eyes were again intent on her face. "Yes. I think about a great many things."

"Yeah?" His words were soft. "Like what?"

"I don't know if you'd care to hear about my daydreaming." She pulled her gaze away. "My father always said I spent too much time with my books and my imagination."

"I promise you, I do want to hear."

Her eyes met his then. He was all sincerity. "Well, I think about Richmond...my life there. And what it would be like to go back."

He held her gaze. His was steady. Though she was sure she saw his jaw clench.

"I think about life here." She glanced back to continue to take in the view from where they sat. "What would it be like to stay?"

He drew in a deep breath.

"I think about my mother. And Brandon. And Father." She let her words fade.

"I am so sorry about his passing."

"Thank you." His condolences moved her more than she would have thought possible. "He was...a good man."

"He must have been." Slim settled onto the ground, making himself more comfortable.

"What?" She let out a little laugh in spite of herself. What did Slim know of her father?

"I mean...to have raised such fine people. He must have done something right." His features were plain. No hint of jest.

"He could also be a hard man." Why had she said that? She jerked back to see Slim's reaction. There was little, if any, change in his expression. It made it that much easier for her to continue. "I mean to say, he had his preferences. His standards for behavior."

"Was that difficult?" His question was gentle.

"Sometimes." She looked at a butte in the distance. "Sometimes, I felt caged by his expectations." Glancing back at Slim, she saw his eyebrows had risen. "My brother got away from all that."

"Did that make things harder?"

Steeling herself against memories she'd rather not revisit, she continued. "It raised his expectations of me all the more."

"How so?" His voice was so tender. It made her ache—for that understanding, that kind regard. From the man who could no longer give it.

"He wanted me to make a good match." Ada sighed. "With

Brandon choosing against the law firm, I guess he saw me as his last chance to preserve it. And that was so important to him. Only...I didn't. I guess, I failed him." A tear trailed down her face. She wiped at it. Did she really care so much? Yes. This affected her. Deeply. Cutting to her core...and her sense of self-worth. Was she only valuable for the marriage she might make? Was there no merit in just being Ada?

"I'm sorry." His words were simple and soothing.

She looked at him again. "Why? It's not your doing."

His gaze softened even more, and he nodded. "I'm sorry you had to go through it." Reaching toward her, he touched a stray ringlet.

She let out a ragged breath. What was it this man did to her? And why did she both want to give herself over to it and run away? Getting to her feet, she looked down at him. "Maybe we should head back."

He rose. "I think the horses need a few more minutes."

She glanced at the animals now munching on grass not far away. What to do now? Sit back down? She had the urge to move, to go. "I... need to stretch my legs."

He nodded. "All right."

Turning away, she halted. "What about the horses?"

"They'll be fine. Besides, we won't go far."

She offered him a small smile. Then he stepped next to her and indicated she should lead. They walked upstream. And she bit at her lip. The urge to share more was almost overwhelming. But she couldn't do that. Her heart needed protecting. And that was what she planned to do.

Slim's every nerve seemed more alive. He walked next to Ada and just relished her presence, her trust. She had told him some pretty hard things and shared her life with him in a way she had not before. Had she told Stan these things? That thought made him more than a little uneasy. Surely, these things were more difficult to expose. There was no reason to think she had.

Their shoulders brushed. And then again. And again. Was she walking closer to him? He turned to look at her. It did seem she was.

But she also appeared to be far away in her mind. Was she lost in memories? Did she need comfort of some sort? Connection?

But did he wish to put himself forth and be bold? What if she rejected his attempt? If she turned away? He already cared for her so much it was hard to imagine the sting of that.

He pulled in a breath. If she needed him, he would do what he could to be there. No matter the cost. Reaching to the side, he touched her fingers.

She grabbed for his hand, interlacing their fingers. Then she leaned into him.

Was this enough? Not for him. He loosed his fingers and put an arm around her, tucking her close to his side.

She did not resist the effort.

Warmth expanded even more within him, stretching out from his core and filling his whole being. She wanted him to care for her in such a way. He felt purposeful in a way he never had.

"What of you, Slim?" came her soft voice. "Have you always been in Wharton City?"

He let out a breath. It was only fitting for him to share in return. And he wanted to. But his awareness in that moment was so sharp. So... full of her. It became difficult to think. So, he just answered her question. "No. My parents came to Arizona from back east."

"Oh?" There was interest in her voice. How he wished against it. His beginnings were nowhere near as grand as hers.

"My parents lived in New York. That's where they met. And they did everything they could to gather enough money to come west for the opportunities here.

"New York? I had no idea. That must have been quite the adventure."

He frowned. How could he respond to that without baring more than he wished to? "It was a hard life. For them. For us."

Her eyes were on him then. Must he continue? He knew his once very red hair had darkened, but could she not discern?

He swallowed. "My parents...I...we're Irish."

The silence that followed was thick. Because she no longer wished to be near him? He closed his eyes and prayed against that. After all, it had mattered not one bit to Brandon. And she had cared for the immigrant child without a thought. Perhaps, she would see beyond it. See him.

"That must have been...very difficult, indeed." Her words were gentle.

His breath stuttered as he drew it in. "I don't know that many people can imagine it."

She stopped abruptly.

And he paused as well. But he wouldn't look at her, he couldn't. Too many questions, too much emotion warred within him.

Her fingers touched his jaw. It was heaven. With much tenderness, she prodded his face to turn toward her.

He did, sealing his eyes against what must be in hers. How could he handle it if she were to—

Her lips were on his then. Soft. And sweet.

He responded immediately, pulling her closer and pressing into her mouth. But he didn't want his need for her to overwhelm. So, he held back the full force of his affection.

When the contact ended, her eyes were closed. He kissed her lips once more, this time just a touch.

He watched as her dark eyes fluttered open. Then they were on him. Stealing his breath. Could his heart survive this pounding?

His chest swelled with love for her. Dare he speak it? He felt it. Most certainly.

She moved in to lay her head on his chest.

He responded by wrapping his arms around her. What had happened here? What did it mean to her?

It meant everything to him.

CHAPTER 11

Advice

Slim smiled as Ada instructed her class. His affection for her had only grown since their encounter three days ago. He'd not had the opportunity to be with her until now. And he relished this time.

She spoke of math and numbers...things that Slim had not been good at in school. He could manage all right, but the processes of arithmetic had been lost on him. Though she seemed to be bringing the lesson to a close.

"Now, if you will clear your desks, I see our guest has arrived."

The students whirled toward the back of the classroom to see Slim standing there. Eyes widened as did smiles.

It moved him that they cared so much for his stories. And, by extension...him. He beamed back at them.

"Mr. Dagley," she beckoned. "Thank you for joining us today. I can't tell you how eager this class is for another one of your stories."

When his eyes met Ada's, it became difficult to remember why he was there. But she had said it—he was here to tell another tale of Sheriff Maynard. And he had conjured a good one. And it included the school-teacher character. Well, perhaps more featured her. Could he do any less? After their previous exchange, he had thought of little else. It affected his work, his routines...everything.

"Mr. Dagley?"

What had she asked? He had reached the front of the classroom and she looked at him, confusion on her features.

"Excuse me, Miss Miller, I was...lost in thought."

She frowned, but he did note that her cheeks colored. "I only asked what you have in store for us today."

He pulled his gaze away from hers and looked to the class. "A story to end all stories."

The students leaned forward in their desks all the more.

"Please, do indulge us." A smile touched her lips. And that was where his attention was drawn.

But he came here for a reason. And that reason extended beyond seeing her and daydreaming. So, he pulled his gaze from her and set it on the waiting pupils. Then he launched into the story. He felt more into the telling than usual. He even tried different voices for the characters as he moved about the space, filling it as much as he filled the time allotted.

The students gasped, laughed, and appeared tense at all the right moments. Perhaps, Brandon and Ada were right. It seemed the children enjoyed his tales as much as they said—not as a pitiful gesture of kindness to him.

As he brought the story around full circle and brought it to a conclusion, there was complete silence in the room. Then the children clapped and cheered.

He had become lost in the story. And their response pulled him back to reality. He smiled.

"Very well, Mr. Dagley! I thank you," Ada said. Though she seemed a little distant. Was she not happy with the story? "I'm afraid that's all the time we have."

He nodded and moved to the far side of the classroom, not wishing to distract any longer. Was that what had bothered her? Had he gone too long?

She went through the task of reminding the children of their upcoming assignments and then dismissed them.

Several students rushed to him, asking questions and making

comments about the Sheriff. And the teacher character. They were enthralled. A couple of the older students tossed a glance at Ada as they or others asked after the teacher. Did they somehow guess that the character was patterned after her?

Either way, it wasn't long before Ada was shooing them along, reminding them that their parents were expecting them home soon. As the space emptied, he turned toward her.

She gave him a look that was difficult to discern before she moved over to the board to clean it.

"Let me help you." He stepped closer.

She backed away, glancing at the door. Did she worry that a student may be lingering and see them? Was she embarrassed to be with him? "I thank you, but I can manage."

"I know you can. I just wanted to help."

She looked to the floor and then back at him. "Very well." Then she handed him the cloth and moved toward her desk.

What was going on here? Had he upset her somehow? He thought about nothing else as he cleaned the board. Once the task was completed, he stepped to where she sat at her desk, huddled over books.

"Ada?" he prodded. Why wouldn't she look at him? "Ada," he said more firmly when she didn't respond. "Is something wrong?"

"No. Not at all." She glanced at him, but quickly looked away.

"Then why the coldness?"

"Why would you think to take our..." She seemed at a loss for words. "What happened between us at the ranch and lay it out for the children?"

"What?"

"Those interactions between the sheriff and the schoolteacher. They were a bit too familiar for my liking."

Had he taken too much of a liberty with the story? Were the exchanges between his main characters too much like his and Ada's?

"I had no idea," he said, keeping his eyes on her.

"No idea?" She stood, pressing to her full height. Because she felt threatened or because she wished to intimidate? That was certainly not necessary. Her tone did that well enough.

"No. I guess I was more...inspired...than I thought."

She folded her arms across her chest.

He came around the desk. "I can't stop thinking about it. About you." Had he truly just said that? Admitted his distraction?

Her features eased. "I suppose it's bound to happen."

It seemed as if things would smooth out.

Then her tone rose again. "But I don't like the idea of my...of our... of these moments being on display for everyone. I thought it was just ours."

He reached out tentative hands and set them on her arms. "That... moment. It was so..."

"So...what?" Her voice was small again.

"So amazing," he admitted. "I haven't been able to get it out of my mind."

A small smile crept onto her features. "Truly?"

"Yes." How could she think anything different?

She let out a deep sigh. "Me, too."

That thrilled him. So much he wanted to press his lips to hers again. And that's where his attention was drawn—to her mouth.

She let out a small sound.

He leaned closer.

"There you are," a voice broke in.

Slim turned. It was none other than Stanford A. Wilmont, III.

Ada backed out of Slim's reach. What had Stan seen? What did he think?

"Stanford," she greeted him. "Were you looking for me?"

"I—yes." He glanced between her and Slim and back to her again. "I thought I would find you in town."

She was typically on the main stretch before returning home— checking for mail at the telegraph office or perusing at the General Store. "Ah. Glad you found me."

It was impossible to miss Slim's pained expression. What could she do about that? She couldn't exactly tell Stanford to leave so Slim could kiss her. In fact, she found she was rather relieved Stanford didn't seem to think more of how she and Slim were standing when he barged in. Why would that be? Why did she not want him to see her and Slim like that? It would be something she would have to think on. Later.

"We were just cleaning things up here." Ada offered Stanford a smile.

His gaze moved to Slim. As if to question his presence in the classroom.

"Mr. Dagley came by and shared another story with the students."

"What a fine thing." Stanford stepped nearer the front. "That is quite a talent you have there. Too bad we don't all have the opportunity to daydream like that. My mind is far too taxed with my business."

She looked to Slim. His fists clenched at his sides.

"Now then, Ada. Shall I walk you home?" Stanford oozed charm.

"Actually, I need to head into town."

"Allow me—" Stanford said as Slim spoke up, "Could I—"

Did they both wish to escort her? This was rather awkward. "I thank you both, but I may need to go straight home, after all."

The men glared at each other. As if each dared the other to speak first.

"And I aim to go alone." Why had she said that? Did she so loathe these two men at each other's throats?

"Please," Stanford cut in. "If I may, I wanted to ask you to join me on a picnic this Saturday."

Slim bristled.

"That would be lovely." Ada smiled.

Slim's eyes were on her. There was hurt there and confusion. How could she help that? If he cared for her as he seemed to, he obviously wasn't going to like her continuing to entertain Stanford's suit. Yet, she couldn't make herself put an end to it, either. Regardless of what happened between her and Slim. She couldn't turn down a man, who was a perfect match for her in so many ways.

Only...she didn't feel for him the same. Maybe that would come. She would have to wait and see. Still, she couldn't turn him away. Not with all that he had to offer. Besides, after everything, Slim still had not made any move toward making theirs such an arrangement that would prevent her from seeing Stanford.

"Very well. Saturday, then." Stanford said, bowing his head slightly and tipping his hat.

"Saturday."

Stanford shot Slim a look that Ada could not decipher. Then he waited. What for? "Did you have further business with Miss Miller?" Stanford directed toward Slim.

"I...do," Slim challenged.

Stanford met his gaze. "I don't know that it's entirely appropriate for you to remain here."

Was Stanford implying that Slim would make a bold move on Ada? Or was he questioning her reputation? Either way, she wasn't sure she liked it.

"We will be just fine." She spoke up. "He will be on his way shortly."

Stanford seemed only somewhat pleased with that. Still, he stepped to the door, even though hesitant, and exited.

Slim turned on her then. "What was that?"

"What was what?" she muttered, trying to sound put out.

"After the other day, after we..." His voice trailed. "How can you continue to see him?"

"We have no formal agreement that precludes it." How had this gone so badly?

"Is that so?"

"Yes," she countered. "As a matter of fact, it is."

They stood, facing each other down for a handful of seconds.

"Then I suppose I will bid you good day, Miss Miller."

She cringed at his formal address.

He turned away as he set his hat back on his head and moved out the door, slamming it as he did so.

Her heart ached. Why had she done that—accepted Stanford's invitation and spoken thusly to Slim? She cared for Slim. So much. Maybe more than she should, and so soon. But she couldn't just let her heart sway her so much. There was more to a good match than feelings. Wasn't that what her father had always said?

She had more to think about than Slim's heart. Though the thought pained her. It wasn't just his heart, after all. Her own feelings ran deep.

In all of this, she had not considered those. What of her own heart? Would she dismiss it so quickly?

Slim stormed out of the schoolhouse. How could she? How could she continue to let that man—or any other man, for that matter—call on her?

Was he wrong about how they felt toward one another? Apparently so. She couldn't feel the way he did if she would even think about letting another man take her on outings.

Then he was struck with a thought...what if she had also kissed Stanford? That sickened him. The hurt now heavy in his gut. It couldn't be. He couldn't believe that.

But yet, he did.

As he stood, stunned by his realization, just outside the schoolhouse, he looked around. He spotted Stanford not far away. Only then moving off. Slim watched him fade into the distance. Had he been waiting for Slim's exit? As if Slim would hurt Ada. Or take advantage.

Slim burned.

The door shut behind him. Had Ada made her way out of the schoolhouse?

"Slim." Her tone betrayed her surprise.

He turned.

She seemed just as confused as she sounded. "What are you still doing here?"

Dare he tell her? Let it all spill out?

She stepped closer. "Listen, I'm sorry about all of that."

His chest was too tight for him to let her apologize so easily. "Then you won't see him?"

She was quiet for a moment. "I didn't say that."

"You will?"

"Yes."

"Then why are you apologizing?" His words were harsher than he liked, but he couldn't rein himself in.

"I guess it's how things happened that I regret. Everything I said is still true."

Slim swallowed. "Have you...kissed him?"

Her eyes lit. "I don't think that's any of your business."

"So, you won't deny it?"

"I have nothing to say on the matter."

Slim closed his eyes for a moment. When he opened them, she was moving off in the direction of Widow Wilmont's cabin.

"Ada..." he called as he raced after her.

She didn't turn.

He caught up to her and grabbed for her arm.

She spun, jerking her arm away. "What?"

Then he saw. There were tears in her eyes. He longed to step forward and cup her face, wipe away the tears. But he did not think she would welcome that. Swallowing, he worked to gather his own emotions. "Ada...I...I'm sorry. I had no right to ask that."

She lifted her hand and rubbed her cheeks, one after the other, smearing any tears there. "I..." Her voice trailed, and she looked down. Would she leave the word hanging?

He decided to speak into the silence. "I was a jealous fool."

She looked at him once more. Then sucked in a breath. "I just...I... that was hurtful."

"I understand that."

"How can you think that of me?" Her eyes were wide. And she seemed so vulnerable.

What did she mean? Had he accused her of something more?

"That I'm the kind of girl who is so...free with my affection. That what we shared wasn't special to me."

It was as if someone punched him in the stomach. She was right. His words had implied as much.

"That was the first time I ever..." She let her words fade.

What was she saying? That their kiss had been her first? That did surprise him. Though he did not think her one to go around kissing every man she entertained. He had not thought such as she claimed... perhaps because she initiated the tender interaction. He reached tentative hands forward, finally setting them on her arms. "I...didn't know. And I regret my words. So much."

She sniffled.

"They were spoken in anger. And I wish I could take them back."

She nodded.

"I'll try to be less of an idiot in the future."

She offered him a slight smile. "You might just try not being an idiot at all to begin with."

"I'll give that a go." He chuckled. And as he watched her face light up, he knew. He was lost to her.

"I know it must be difficult for you. With Stanford and all. Would an outing to the opera make you feel better?"

His throat thickened. The opera house? He had never been anywhere so fine. He had imagined he might make the time to visit the theater, but the opera?

"Please, tell me you'll join me. I would like it very much."

If that's what she wanted, he would find a way to manage through it. Who knew? He may even enjoy it.

"I will." He softened his words, leaning forward.

She beamed. "Then I shall see you Friday evening."

He nodded, still a bit reluctant. Though he did want to spend time with her.

"Will you walk me home?"

Perhaps, then, he wasn't done spending time with her today. "Of course. It would be my honor."

She shifted to stand at his side and set a hand in the crook of his elbow. And so they moved forward. If only he could forget the earlier exchange. If only he could swallow his jealousy and just let this be what it would be. However, he could not forget that, come Saturday, she would be alone with Stanford.

Ada blotted her mouth with a napkin. Mrs. Wilmont had outdone herself. Yet again. The woman was surely the best cook in all of Tombstone. Even more so than the cook at the café.

"What's on your mind?" Mrs. Wilmont's voice scattered her thoughts.

"I was thinking how fine this meal is."

"Well, I thank you," Mrs. Wilmont said. "But that's not all. You've been quiet all evening."

"Oh." Dare Ada share? What would Mrs. Wilmont think about her interactions with the two men—one of whom was the woman's nephew? "It's nothing."

Mrs. Wilmont's gaze softened. "It's not nothing. You are clearly bothered."

Ada sighed. "You're right. I had an...interesting conversation with Slim..."

"Oh?" the woman's eyes twinkled.

"...and Stanford," she muttered.

"Oh." Mrs. Wilmont seemed concerned. Was she so worried about Ada's relationship with the man? This may not be a good idea. "If you care to, I would be happy to hear what is so concerning."

Ada watched her. The woman seemed genuine in her care after Ada and her challenges. Maybe she could trust the woman to really hear her. Taking in a deep breath, she pressed into it. "You know that Stanford has made overtures. And has asked to call on me."

"Yes." The woman watched Ada, her features radiating her kind consideration.

"And Slim has made the same request. He wishes to spend time with me."

"I see." Mrs. Wilmont let out a breath. "I understand. That can become...rather complicated."

"Yes." Ada stood and gathered her dish and utensils. Then carried them to the sink. "I am not sure that it was wise to entertain two suitors at once."

The woman came up behind Ada at the kitchen sink with her own dishes. "I don't know. I should think limiting your options before you have made a decision would be unwise."

Ada shrugged.

Mrs. Wilmont pumped water into the bucket in the sink. Then set the dinner things into the water. "Let's have some tea and a sit down."

Ada smiled. She appreciated that Mrs. Wilmont did not press coffee on her. Somehow the woman had caught on to Ada's dislike of the stuff.

The widow started the kettle and motioned toward the great room. "It'll be a moment. Let's sit."

Ada made her way to an armchair in front of the fireplace. Mrs. Wilmont took the other one. And Ada wondered, not for the first time, if the chair she sat in had belonged to Mr. Wilmont. But she didn't think she should ask. The woman probably pained every time her late husband was mentioned.

"I'm all ears." Mrs. Wilmont said after she settled and picked up her knitting.

"I just don't know what to think...what to do." Ada feared the anguish came through a bit too strongly.

"Why do you have to do anything?" The woman glanced over before turning her attention back to the piece.

"Slim knows I am also entertaining Stanford's suit. And it bothers him."

"So? That doesn't mean you have to be bothered." Mrs. Wilmont continued to hook and slip the yarn.

"Except..."

"Except what?" the older woman said when Ada didn't continue.

"I'm afraid my heart is too tender to hurt either of these two men."

"How can you prevent that—hurting them? One will be hurt, no matter what you do. If their hearts are both so engaged, that is."

Did she imply that they might not both have the same level of emotion invested? Did she see something Ada didn't? "I'm not sure about that."

"Never mind an old woman's musings." Mrs. Wilmont set her knitting in her lap. "I'm far too talkative when I should be listening."

"No. I appreciate your thoughts. Please, continue."

"What do you think? Do they both seem so drawn in?"

Ada looked to the hearth. "Slim is for certain."

"And Stanford?"

"He is...determined."

"Hmmm..." Mrs. Wilmont's uttering came out rather curious.

The kettle blasted a loud whistle.

"Time for tea." The older woman rose and moved into the kitchen.

Ada remained, deep in thought. What she had said was true—Stanford was determined about their courtship, but she had not seen any sign that his heart was so involved. Did he see this as she did—the sensical thing? That they seemed such a perfect match?

A future with Slim didn't seem smart. He didn't have Stanford's resources or money. But she couldn't help but feel pulled in that direction. He felt for her most certainly, but her heart was also entangled.

Mrs. Wilmont handed her a cup of tea. "Here you are, dear."

Ada nodded in gratitude but was too deep in her thoughts to speak.

"There you go...all lost to the world again."

Ada looked at the woman and smiled. "It is bothersome, this puzzle."

"I imagine so. You are such a sweet young lady. I am sure it's difficult to think of hurting anyone, much less someone you have tender feelings toward."

Ada nodded, sipping her tea. That may be the whole of it. She couldn't fathom hurting Slim. But she also couldn't make herself turn him away for Stanford, a man she only felt a general kindness toward. What was the right path for her?

"I can see you are troubled. And when I am faced with such, I find solace in God."

Yes. Of course. Why hadn't she prayed over this more fervently?

"And, as the Good Book says, He will direct your path."

That was true. Proverbs 3 was one of many places where the Lord said He would guide and light the way. She only needed to trust. Why then, did she still feel so torn?

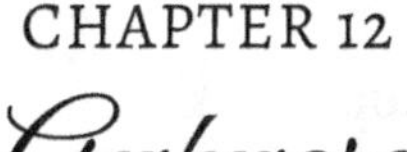

CHAPTER 12

Awkward

"Not like that." Lily protested.

Slim groaned. He was never going to get this right. They had been struggling with his appearance for the better part of an hour. She had informed him that men generally wore fine suits to the opera. He had no such clothing. But Dan had a Sunday jacket he was willing to loan.

Now, they worked with the tie. Slim kept fumbling with the knot. Was he so nervous?

"Let me." Dan stepped in front of him, reaching for the strip of cloth at Slim's neck. Dan maneuvered his hands with confidence and soon enough, Lily's frown lifted into a smile.

"That's much better!" she exclaimed.

Slim looked in the hand mirror. He had slicked his hair back at Lily's insistence. And with this tie and suit jacket, he felt more than a little ridiculous. Was he even himself anymore?

"I don't know about this," he grumbled.

Lily stepped toward him. "Trust me. You look dashing."

"But..."

Lily shook her head. "Just...trust me."

Slim wasn't sure he wanted to present himself as something so foreign. Why couldn't he wear his normal clothing? Be himself? Was this what tonight was all about—making him something else? Was that what Ada wanted?

He furrowed his brows, uncertainty filling him.

"Don't do that," Dan said. "Now, you look mad."

Slim eased his features.

"Much better." Dan clapped him on the shoulder.

"Do you remember everything we talked about?" Lily asked, eyes wide.

His mind whirled with the many instructions she had given on etiquette and propriety in such a setting as the opera house. But he couldn't lay claim to any one of them in that moment.

"Yes," he said. There was the very real fear that she would launch into another lecture if he did otherwise.

From the look that crossed Lily's features, she didn't believe him. But she smiled and said, "Then I think you are ready."

He stepped toward the door.

"Tom is bringing the cart around for you." Dan moved to where his wife stood and put an arm around her.

"I could have—" Slim started.

Dan waved him off. "Nonsense. No need for you to risk getting all dirty in that getup."

Slim groused. He didn't like all this finery. Or being waited on.

"Ah, go on and have a good time." Dan shooed him toward the door.

Slim hesitated. Did he even want to put on this charade?

"Go on," Dan said. "Or you'll be late to collect Ada."

Dan was right. They had dallied long enough trying to make Slim every bit as fancied up as he could be.

Slim nodded and moved to the front door. As he stepped out, he did indeed find Tom checking the straps and harnesses.

"Thanks," Slim said, feeling sheepish.

"Not a problem." Tom's deeper voice almost made Slim feel better about being tended to.

"Be back by midnight," Dan called.

Slim turned, Dan and Lily stood just inside the doorway.

"Midnight?" Slim asked.

"Yeah. Remember...you'll turn into a pumpkin."

Slim wanted to give the guy some words, but he had none. He was too entangled in this mess that would be his evening at the opera. So much so he wasn't really excited about seeing Ada. It was just too much pressure.

Dan's features shifted. He appeared concerned. Because Slim wasn't returning his jest?

"Thanks," Slim said. That was all the thought he could spare.

Slim climbed onto the bench and with a wave, urged the horse onward. He didn't so much as look back at his friends. There wasn't much he could think to say or do. Even in the whole of the ride to Widow Wilmont's cabin. The trip took less time than ever before, and he found himself slowing the horses sooner than he'd have thought. And, as he looked at the cabin, the uneasiness within him only intensified.

He took a deep breath and steeled himself before dropping down from the cart and walking to the door. With a couple of solid knocks, he summoned his companion for the evening. What would she look like? Would she be in such finery as he? Probably more so.

Even though he attempted to prepare himself for Ada's appearance, when the door opened and she stood in the lantern light, he was at a loss. The dress she wore hugged her in all the right places. It was the fanciest gown he had seen in real life. And the open neck allowed him a peek at her fine shoulders and creamy skin. It stole his breath. And his words.

She, too, was taking him in. "My, you look rather handsome this evening."

"And you...I..." He was helpless. There were no words.

She looked to him expectantly.

It didn't matter. Nothing would come.

"Do you...like it?" She ventured. "My dress, that is."

"Like it?" he gasped. "I've never seen anything so beautiful."

"Oh, the dress has been—"

"Not the dress." He cleared his throat. "You. You are...beyond words."

She stared at him. Then her lips slowly spread into a smile. "Thank you."

He could stand and stare at her all night, but he remembered that they had somewhere to be. Somewhere that had a time schedule. He shot his elbow out in her direction. "May I?"

She set a gloved hand to his arm. "Please."

Even as he escorted her to the cart, he couldn't take his eyes off her. Would he ever? Or would he continue to be so tongue-tied and helpless in her presence? He was willing to risk it.

Ada had never found the opera to be more thrilling or more entertaining. She found herself watching Slim just as much, if not more, than the stage production. He seemed so taken, so fascinated with the story put to action. Had he never seen such? Not even a theater show?

His reactions were priceless. He was so enthralled. And she was all too glad to have brought him here and gifted him this experience.

The sound of the last note faded. And Slim stood, applauding loudly.

Her face warmed as she realized everyone watched him, their stares curious and judging. But she couldn't be cross. He had been so invested in the whole thing that he probably couldn't help himself.

She couldn't deny her relief, however, when he sat back down.

The curtain fell and the encore finished. Still, Slim could not contain his continued elation at what he had seen and heard. "It was just...amazing." He looked to her at last.

"Yes, I love the opera."

"It was strange...I couldn't understand what they were saying or singing, but I didn't need to. I felt it."

She nodded. This was one of her favorite things about the opera, as well. No matter how many she saw, she never tired of it. Yet the moment she wanted to hold onto was this one—him looking at her with such appreciation, such awe.

Overcome, she leaned forward and gripped his arm.

He smiled. "Thank you."

All she could do was nod; she was so overwhelmed with emotion in that moment.

"Shall we?" He seemed to notice that everyone was emptying the room.

"Yes." She did not want the evening to end, but she knew it must. Would he ask her to walk with him? Dare she ask him for a cup of tea once they got to the Wilmont cabin? Perhaps Mrs. Wilmont would still be up.

Slim stood and helped her to her feet. Then they strolled to the back of the auditorium and out the doors. In the lobby, others milled about—men in tails and women in gowns. She tried not to notice how they glanced at Slim with their outright curiosity. She was aware that he was underdressed, but she also knew he had dressed in the best he could. And she had no expectations that he meet with anyone else's approval. Still...she did not like the glances.

She spotted Stanford near the exit. What was he doing here? Did he frequent the opera house? She grimaced. Speaking with him was not something she wanted to chance. Her heart was confused enough. But how to avoid it? They would have to pass by him to leave the building.

Tugging on Slim's arm, she halted him. She glanced about for somewhere they might disappear.

"What is it?" His voice was full of concern.

She shook her head. "I just..."

"Miss Miller?" It was Stanford. He had spotted them.

She closed her eyes and groaned. Would Slim see her distress? Would he think it was about him? She prayed not. When she opened her eyes, Stanford had drawn nearer. So, she pressed a smile she didn't feel onto her lips. "Mr. Wilmont, how good to see you."

Slim's hold on her tightened. Was he feeling nervous? Or possessive?

Stanford stopped an arm's length from them. "And, Mr. Dagley," Stanford said, grinning. "It is good to see you in a suit."

Slim's jaw clenched.

"I admit my surprise to find you own one."

Ada's features flushed. Why would he say such a thing? It was rude, to say the least.

Slim remained silent, but every muscle in his body had tensed.

"I think he looks rather handsome," Ada shot at Stanford. What was she doing? The man was only being as polite as he could be—no different than those openly staring at Slim. He was a fish out of water. Still, it was unacceptable.

"Yes, he is that," Stanford continued. "It is a breath of fresh air from the usual attire. Don't you agree?"

She didn't like that Stanford put her on the spot. So she looked opposite, feigning interest in a floral arrangement near the door.

"What did you think of the opera?" Stanford directed at Slim. "Follow along well?" Stanford's smile stretched all the more.

Slim nodded. "I thought it was quite good."

"I am sure you did. After all, you did give them a standing ovation. I, for one, am certain it's only a moderately accomplished production."

Ada wanted to fall through the floor. Her attention was rapt on Stanford, her face red for certain. But was it solely due to her anger? Or was she also embarrassed? Perhaps, it was only embarrassment for Slim. Not of him. She hated that she thought such a thing. Looking up at Slim, she said, "I think it is time we move along. It is rather late."

Stanford grinned. "Yes. And I will have you well rested for our picnic tomorrow."

Everything in her wanted to turn him down right then and there. But they three had already started to draw a crowd. She didn't wish to make more of a scene. So, she only nodded and urged Slim forward.

He resisted at first but then followed her lead. And let her march him outside.

How could she give credence to Stanford's insults? But she found herself unable to find any untruth in his words. Slim was out of place here, in this world. Her world.

She had wanted to show him her favorite form of entertainment, and now she was left with doubts. Only...they were not about Stanford —who she should question. But about Slim.

Slim hurried the horse along. He had a great urge to get out of town. It didn't surprise him that Stanford would take the opportunity to make such jabs, Slim had been surprised at how it affected him. But, why should it? It wasn't anything he didn't know.

Perhaps, it bothered him so because this was Ada's world. She belonged at operas and fine dinners and balls and all of it. And he couldn't give that to her. Not a chance. Never before had the difference in their station been so apparent as this evening.

The fall from the elation of the experience to these depths had been abrupt. And hard.

As well as the realization that Ada did little to naysay Stanford. Slim wasn't expecting her to fight his battles, but she still planned to go on the picnic with Stan. Why? Had this not shown her what kind of man he was? A weasel.

"I'm sorry. About the things Stanford said." Her voice was small.

"Yeah." He felt her eyes on him then. What was she thinking?

"I don't think he realizes what—"

"You don't think he what?" How could she defend Stan? It was incredible.

"I know it wasn't appropriate...what he said. But he's from a different..." She stopped herself.

Slim looked at her. "A different what? Station? Status? Place in society?"

"That's not what I meant." Her words were tight, tense.

"But it's what you said."

Why would he blame her? It wasn't her fault that this was their reality. After all, it only served to show him how little a grasp on it he had. What was he thinking pursuing someone like her?

"Slim, I...don't think that."

"Of course, you do." He pressed out. "Because it's true."

"It's not..." Her words hung. How was she going to finish that sentence?

"It's not what?" he blurted when the silence carried for several seconds.

"It's not like that. Between us." She reached for his arm, putting a hand around his elbow.

He wanted to jerk away. The sting was so great. He couldn't fathom what a future for them would....could look like. Not one in which he wasn't dragging her down. And he loved her too much to do that. She deserved every good thing in life. Even if he wasn't it. "I think we should just..." Could he say the words?

"What?" She looked pained. Did she guess what he was about to say?

"Maybe we shouldn't do this."

"No." Came her simple reply.

"It just...doesn't seem right."

She grabbed for the horse's reins and jerked them to a stop. Then she shifted to face him and tugged his hands until he looked at her, too. She pressed a hand to the side of his face. "You can't do this. You are the one I care about. I won't hear this."

What had she said? She cared about him? His heart ached. If only he could tell her how he felt. But that would just make this harder. So, he looked down for a moment, then met her gaze again, this time with more resolve.

"Please, Slim. Don't do this." She set a hand to her chest. "You're breaking my heart."

She appeared so stricken, so wounded.

He leaned forward and claimed her lips. The kiss filled and emptied him at the same time. For he knew this was his farewell to her.

She gripped his upper arms and leaned into him.

How could he not see her again? How was that possible? He pulled back, tearing his heart apart as he did so. "I'm sorry, I—"

She put a finger to his lips. "Don't apologize. And don't run away."

There was no use arguing with her further. He would take her home. And that would be that. This was the last time he would hold her, kiss her, know the feel of her. And it cut him deeper than he thought possible. So, he soothed his heart for this one moment and embraced her as she rested her head on his shoulder and put her arms around him. He was a cad—knowing she thought all would be well.

It would never be okay. Never again.

Ada couldn't focus on her lunch companion. Not that it mattered. Stanford had been talking about himself for the last hour and a half. And they had only been on the picnic for half that time. Were there no other subjects he would discuss? It was probably for the best. Her thoughts were on the previous evening with Slim. And his words.

Was he done? Had he been too put off by her and the life she was accustomed to? She prayed not. For every time she imagined not being with him again, a hole opened within her. And it sucked every good thing out of her.

"Don't you think?" Stanford's question was insistent.

She shook her head. What had he said? Had he somehow known what she had been thinking about? "Pardon?"

"This is a fine afternoon to be on such an excursion."

"Oh yes. It is. Very fine."

Stanford scooted closer. Only a hand's width of space remained between them. "I must say, Ada, that you are lovely this afternoon. But you always take my breath. You are a vision."

She smiled at him. He certainly could charm and flatter. But was it all to feed his own vanity?

He took her hand. "I know you are allowing Mr. Dagley to pursue you, as well." Where was he going? She became more than a little uneasy. "And I must admit...I am not a good sport about these things."

No surprise there.

"Quite frankly, I am rather frustrated by the prospect." His grip tightened just a tad.

She didn't like that. Jerking back, she attempted to free her hand. But he held on with determination.

"I would like you to think about the possibility of us making a more formal attachment."

What was he saying? Was this his way of asking her to marry him? "Stanford, I don't—"

He shook his head. "Don't answer just yet." Lifting her hand, he brought it to his lips.

She allowed it, all the while wondering at her lack of reaction to Stanford. Slim's very touch had stoked a fire within her. And here... nothing.

"Ada, I...must admit that my feelings, my regard for you, has deepened in these last couple of weeks."

"I have enjoyed our outings as well," she offered, her words careful and measured. "You are a fine gentleman, and—"

"Yes." He seemed rather pleased with himself. "And you are every bit the lady I have prayed about and waited for."

She was becoming more uncomfortable with his forward behavior. And his bold words. It felt as if a proposal would be forthcoming. Soon. "What are you saying?"

"I am trying, so delicately, to point out that we are alike, you and I. We enjoy life with the upper crust. And you are destined for such. I could provide that and more. If you will let me."

She wanted to balk at his insinuation. But he was not wrong. At least, not completely.

He stared down into her face, his eyes so intense.

Her unease grew.

Moving forward, he pressed his lips to hers.

Her first instinct was to pull back. But soon enough, he did so, a smile spreading.

Why had she let that happen? She felt untrue to Slim. But was that so? Still, she couldn't escape it...for in her heart she knew...she belonged to him.

Then what was she doing with Stanford? She needed to find Slim. Tell him.

"I'm afraid I have neglected the time." She made a show of looking at her timepiece. "I must get back. Mrs. Wilmont will worry after me."

"Nonsense. My aunt trusts me implicitly."

Ada offered a small smile. "Still, I must insist we return."

He sighed. "Very well. But think about what I said."

She nodded. Though she knew she would do no such thing. Not with her heart beating hard with thoughts of Slim. How could she have thought of Stanford in the least?

They gathered the picnic blanket and leftover foodstuffs. Then headed back to his fine carriage. She made every effort to limit their interactions, and he helped her up and drove them back into Tombstone.

Would her heart take it? This fervent desire for Slim. How long could she stand it?

Soon enough, they arrived at Mrs. Wilmont's cabin.

"I thank you for the fine afternoon." She maneuvered toward the side of the bench. Could she drop down on her own?

"Let me assist you," he said, his brow furrowed. Had he sensed her desire to end their connection?

He helped her down and then took her hand as he walked her toward the cabin.

Once they reached the front door, she looked to him. Now, she just had to bid him farewell.

"I think I shall come in and see to my aunt for a moment."

She looked to the door and grimaced. How long would he linger? But there was nothing she could do as he reached forth and opened the door, ushering her in and following close behind.

"Aunt Lottie?" he called.

No answer.

Ada froze. Were they alone? That would not be good.

Stanford looked at her. The expression on his face told that he was not likewise concerned.

"Mrs. Wilmont!" Ada yelled, perhaps louder than she needed to. Maybe the woman was in her bedroom sleeping.

"Coming, dear." The voice came from the back room.

And Ada could not decide what was more deflating: the fact that Stanford would remain for a time or that it would delay her departure? Either way, she could do nothing but close the cabin door and wait, trying to make nice with the man. It was going to be a task indeed.

CHAPTER 13
Refusal

Slim moved toward the small bunkhouse. Dinner had been more difficult than he'd expected. Seeing Dan with his Lily was trying. It made Slim think of the possibilities...of what could have been. Yet never would be. He ached. The wound was still too fresh.

All afternoon long, he'd thought about Ada...out with Stan—him talking to her, holding her attention, touching her. It sickened Slim. But he would have to get used to it. She wasn't his and would never be. Wasn't that the decision he made?

Settling onto his cot, he stared at the ceiling. His thoughts continued to wander back to Ada. Over and over. This would not do!

Pulling out paper, he tried to work on his next story. This, too, frustrated him, as Ada was supposed to help him get his stories written down. But that would not be the case anymore. The task now fell to him. He would not have the pleasure of her company—not today, not ever. It had to be this way. His heart could not take anything more.

As he worked, his efforts to move his story along troubled him. He kept coming back to Ada. His thoughts would not leave her well enough alone.

This was impossible!

The door to the bunkhouse creaked. It would be Tom. The man

would want to bed down for the night. He usually did retire early. Slim could either go outside and sit by the lantern light or turn in. Neither appealed.

But when the door opened, it was Dan who entered. "Slim, you in here?"

"Yeah?"

"You have a visitor," he said, smiling.

"Who is it?" But Slim knew it was Ada. Had something happened on her picnic? Had Stanford been too forward? Or even...forceful? Slim jerked upright.

"It's Ada."

"Is she all right?" His heart raced.

"Yes," Dan said, curiosity filling his features. "She's fine. Just wants to see you."

"Oh." Relief poured through him. He eased back onto the cot. "I'm...afraid I'm too tired."

Dan crossed his arms. "Tired?"

"Yes, tired," Slim shot back.

Moving closer, Dan's gaze hardened. "There is a lady here to see you, and you won't see her?"

Slim looked away, nodding.

"What's gotten into you?" Dan appeared incredulous.

Slim could understand. This wasn't like him. And he would be a fool to think that Dan hadn't seen how he cared for Ada. Or how much this refusal to see her tore at him.

"I just...don't want to see her, all right?" He managed to get out.

Dan watched him. "I will respect that. And I don't want to keep her waiting. But you and I will talk about this." His features were set.

There was no escaping that conversation. Still, Slim could breathe easier knowing he wouldn't have to face Ada tonight. But then why was his chest so tight? It was no matter. He only did what was best for her. And he would continue to do so. For her.

The door opened once more, and Slim leaned up, preparing himself to speak with Dan and defend his actions. But it was only Tom.

As the man walked in, he yawned. "I'm beat."

Slim forced a yawn. "Me, too. Been a long day."

Tom tossed him a look that said he didn't believe Slim. "Why ain't you headed over to the house to see that pretty schoolteacher?"

Slim made work of tucking his paper away. "I'm...not in a seeing sort of way."

Tom nodded. "I tell you what...if I had a fine lady like that wanting to see me, nothing would stop me. No tiredness...or worry over anything. I'd be there."

What did Tom know about it? He couldn't understand. Nor was Slim apt to tell him. Maybe if he did, Tom would agree with Slim. Maybe not. Slim wasn't about to find out.

"Want me to douse the lantern?" Slim reached for knob.

Tom gave Slim a long look. "If the lady is so warm to ranch hands, maybe I should make an effort to get to know her better."

Slim cringed and shot Tom a hard look.

"I mean, if you're not interested. Don't mean a fella can't step in, does it?"

What could Slim say? He didn't want Tom—or anyone, for that matter—pursuing Ada. But it would happen regardless of his rathers. Who knew? She might be coming to tell Slim that she and Stanford had made things official. He didn't know...didn't want to know.

"I just want to get some shut eye," Slim said, turning onto his side and facing the wall.

"All right."

He heard Tom shuffling around and moving to his cot. Soon enough, the light was snuffed, and all was dark. But try as he might, Slim had great difficulty finding sleep. And when he did, he was plagued with visions of Ada and Stanford.

Ada was without words. Slim wouldn't see her? How was that possible?

But she knew. Should have known. During their previous interaction, something deep within her had whispered that all was not settled. Still, she had chosen to believe it was. For the sake of her heart.

What was she to do now? Everything had changed. And nothing would be well with her. Not for a long time, perhaps not ever.

She looked at Lily. The woman looked at her in the way she should —as if Ada were pitiful.

"He has had a long day. Lots of work out in the pasture," Lily offered.

Ada wanted to cling to that hope. To think it was only a product of his exhaustion. But she would be fooling herself. And that would not do.

She must figure out a way to move past his rejection. It was either that or convince Slim he was making a mistake. Could she find a way to tell him how she felt? Or would that make things more difficult for them both?

Lily laid a hand on Ada's arm. "Would you like something to drink? We can sit and talk for a while."

Ada looked outside. It had grown much darker in the last half hour. "I had best head back to the cabin."

Lily's gaze followed Ada's. "Not a chance. Dan will take you back."

That was kind, but she didn't wish to take husband from wife at this hour. But perhaps it wasn't safe for her to venture out in the night alone.

She met Lily's eyes again. "I would hate to take Dan away. Perhaps I can sleep here for the evening?"

"Would Mrs. Wilmont not worry herself over you?"

"Yes," Ada said. She had no desire to concern her older friend so.

"Please, just let Dan take you. I will be fine. Besides, I can rouse Tom or..." Her voice faded. Was she so worried about mentioning Slim? Ada wasn't so fragile.

"Or Slim." She finished for Lily.

Her friend nodded.

"I guess, he would come to help you even if he won't come here for me." Why was Ada making this more difficult?

"I'm sorry," Lily soothed. "It's not like that. I'm sure of it."

Ada hung her head. If only Lily knew the half of it.

"Let's get you back before the widow has the sheriff roused." Dan crossed to the door.

Ada followed. It wasn't long before they were in the cart and on their way to Ada's home. They rode in silence, though there were many times Ada wanted to speak up and ask Dan if Slim was well. Or about Slim's reaction when Dan had gone to collect him. But she and Dan's interactions were not such that she felt she could broach such.

In a matter of a half hour or so, they reached the cabin.

Ada moved to drop down, but a hand on her wrist gave her pause. She turned toward Dan.

"Don't give up on Slim."

She dropped her regard to the floorboard of the driver's box. "I don't know that I have a choice. If he won't see me, then I—"

"He's not had it easy. In some ways, he's damaged."

Watching Dan's expression, she hoped to discern his meaning. Slim had told her about his Irish heritage and that it had been difficult. Perhaps she couldn't imagine how much so. Or even begin to understand.

"I see." That was all she had to offer Dan.

Dan's mouth became a thin line. Did he think her so dismissive?

"I won't let him go so easily," she said, her voice not much more than a whisper.

Dan's expression eased, though the concern remained.

He slid over and helped her down. And while there were no other words, she knew he watched until she was safely inside.

Slim awoke to another day. And life seemed a shade duller than it had yesterday. How could he have sent her away? But then, though each time might be hard, perhaps it would get easier. If only a little. He had to start somewhere.

He went through the motions of his morning chores and tasks with little effort at concentrating. What good was that? He couldn't focus anyway. Not on anything but the mistakes he had made. And how his heart suffered because of it.

Would he see her at church? He was fooling himself if he doubted it. If he went, she would be there. Dare he venture out then? It was nearly time to leave...if he was going.

Dan entered the barn. Was he coming to let Slim know it was that time? Or hadn't he figured it out yet? "You plan to avoid her for the next four weeks?"

Slim shrugged. That was his plan, at least.

"That's ridiculous on the face of it."

Slim gave him a stern look. "What's it to you?"

"It may be none of my business, but you're my friend. And you deserve to be happy."

"Do I?"

"Of course, you do."

"And what if I don't think she's it?"

"I could always write to Brandon and see what he thinks about the state his sister is in and your refusal to see her."

"You wouldn't." Slim's eyes narrowed slightly.

"Try me." There was no hint of jest among Dan's features.

The silence was thick between them.

Dan broke it. "Just...talk to her. It isn't right to leave her in the lurch."

Slim examined the dirt for a moment. Dan was right. But he dared not take him up on that. "Maybe you should write Brandon. Let him know I'll be home in the next two weeks."

"What?"

"Jack is getting back on his feet. He'll be ready to get back to it within that time. And you have that new hand starting next week. You don't need me here." Slim met his gaze. "It's time I went home."

Dan was quiet for a time. Then he let out a long breath. "If that's what you want."

Slim nodded. "It is."

"Then I can't stop you." Dan shifted his stance. "But know this—you won't ever get her out of your head."

Slim widened his eyes. Dan didn't know. How could he? This was the only way to get her out of his head. He couldn't live with himself any other way.

Dan shuffled his feet. "I gotta get Lily to church." He moved toward the barn door.

"Need help with the rig?"

"No. I got it." He turned to look at Slim once more. "You've got enough to worry about."

Slim refocused on his task as Dan and Lily drove off. But Slim ignored it, pouring himself into his work.

It seemed like mere minutes before he heard the cart once more in the distance. Were Dan and Lily back from church? So soon? Slim glanced at where the sun was in the sky. It was, in fact, well past noon. What had caused them to linger? That was a useless question. For Slim knew that Lily would have wanted to chat with Ada.

Did the Hayworths now know the whole of it? Did he care if they did? He shouldn't. Could he just avoid them altogether? Not if he wanted lunch. He sighed, wishing he could release the tension that had built in his shoulders.

Was there no hope for him? No solace? Perhaps, he would have found some in the sermon. Hearing God's word always brought him a measure of peace. And he realized—he had not once prayed over this situation. But he should.

Gathering himself, he stepped beyond the barn and moved off a piece to a quiet spot. It took some time to still his thoughts. But quieting his heart was another issue altogether. Though God did not need him to be any certain way. At least in this, he could just be Slim. So, he turned his mind toward heaven and beseeched the Lord.

Ada stared at her students. But she was staring through them more than anything. The day had been a blur. What was happening to her? Her thoughts had been several miles away at the Hayworth ranch. With Slim.

She couldn't help but wonder why he had pushed her aside. Why wouldn't he see her? He wouldn't even talk to her. Was there anything else she could do? If so, it wasn't coming to her. All that was left was for her to ponder on it. So she moped. And stared.

One of the smaller girls in the front row looked up at her. She offered the child a smile and indicated that she should get back to her test. The examination offered Ada some respite from continuing to make a fool of herself in front of the class. At least for the next several minutes she could escape into her thoughts.

What was she to do about Slim? The wrenching of her heart revealed just how much she had come to care for him. It twisted and ached within her chest. Badly. How had she come to have such deep feelings and not realize? Yet it was so. And she feared she would never be whole again.

Tears stung her eyes. That was the problem with indulging her thought trails—the leaking of her emotion. She blinked away the coming torrent and refocused on her students.

A quick glance at her timepiece brought her back to reality. She announced the last ten minutes of the exam. Then she made an effort to look at each child in each row. They, too, had come to mean so much to her. But she still had not made headway with the parents. Why was that? Mothers rushed by her with no acknowledgement, and fathers completely ignored her. Was it because she was an outsider? Or was there more to it?

Knock, knock, knock.

The student she had been watching, a boy in the middle of her class of about ten years, jumped in his seat. In truth, her own nerves were rattled by the unexpected intrusion.

She rose, facing the many sets of curious eyes. "Back to your slates. You don't have long to finish."

Then, satisfied that the children had returned to their work, she moved toward the door. Who would disrupt her class at this hour? Had something happened in town?

More knocking followed as she made her way to the back of the class. For goodness sakes, give me a minute!

She opened the thick door and found herself face-to-face with Stanford. He grinned and thrust a large bouquet of flowers at her. For several seconds, she couldn't find her words. What was he...? Why would he...? And how was she to manage this?

"Ada, I had to see you."

"I'm a bit occupied at the moment." She glanced back at her students, most of whom had abandoned their math problems and stared openly at Stanford.

He pushed past her and into the classroom. "I wanted to surprise you. And give you these."

The flowers were again in her face. She laid a hand on his and moved the buds farther from herself. "That is kind. But I'm quite in the middle of—"

"I'm glad you like them. I was worried I had upset you when we were—"

"Stanford!" She hissed. Why would he not listen? She had little desire to have the details of their courtship out for these little ears.

He appeared stricken. "What's the matter?" This time, he truly seemed concerned.

She took in a quick breath. "The matter is that you came here in the middle of the school day and disturbed my class."

He moved to the side and glanced around her. "Everything looks in order. Bravo, Ada, you have tamed the children."

Her face heated. The sound of slates moving was audible. What were they doing? She dared not turn.

"Bessie," she called to one of the older girls in the class—her most trustworthy student. Turning slightly to catch Bessie's eye she continued, "Have you finished your test?"

"Yes, Miss Miller."

"Good. Can you monitor the others for the next five minutes?"

"Yes, ma'am." Bessie stood and moved to the head of the class, taking up position near the teacher's desk.

Ada shifted her focus back to Stanford. "Outside."

"I don't understand why I—"

"Outside," she said through clenched teeth, putting pressure on his arm and urging him to step out the door.

He moved then, going down the few stairs just outside the schoolhouse.

Ada made great effort not to slam the door. No need to make more of a scene. What was in this man's head? Soon enough, she stood toe-to-toe with Stanford several feet from the entrance. Then she met his gaze.

"Why are you so cross?" His tone seemed rather frustrated. "I came with a peace offering. And this is how you treat me?"

"Stanford," she started, pausing to take in a full breath and push it out slowly. "I understand that this is a gesture of kindness. And it is not that I don't appreciate it, but—"

"It certainly seems that way. I made all the effort to—"

She held up a hand.

His eyes widened, but he stopped talking.

"When school is in session, I am focused on my students."

"But you didn't seem so engaged at the moment," he argued, his voice becoming heavier.

Was he mad at her? No. That was all wrong. "It doesn't matter that I wasn't giving instruction at the moment. I very well could have been. And you come in here as if I have nothing better to do than wait on you."

He looked to the ground. His shoulders were visibly tense, and his breaths came in heaves. "It's not like that."

It almost seemed as if he didn't believe his own words, they came out so weak.

"How is it then?"

He glared at her, his eyes like steel. "I didn't hear you dressing down Mr. Dagley when he came here."

Now, they came to the rub of it. She counted to ten in her head, hoping her words wouldn't be so sharp. "Mr. Dagley was invited to be part of the lesson."

"And you've never extended such an invitation to me."

She pinched the bridge of her nose. How was she having this conversation? And right now? "Stanford," she pressed out as calmly as possible. "This is not the time for this discussion. I have to get back to my students."

"Are the children so helpless?"

She reminded herself that he didn't mean to be so obstinate. It did not make this interaction any easier, though. "It is my duty to mind them. I have made a commitment to this town."

"Maybe you don't need to worry with that anymore."

What was he saying? She stopped herself. It didn't matter. This was not the time. "Please," she said on an exhale. "Go. We will discuss this later."

His jaw muscles twitched. And for a moment, she expected more words—harsh words—to come at her. But they didn't.

Stanford straightened his lapels and turned.

She closed her eyes. What in the world was happening here? Looking up, she watched as he spun back toward her. What now?

"I will give you a chance to apologize later."

"A-ap-," she sputtered. But she bit her tongue.

He had turned once more and was moving off.

She told herself that it truly was not the time to hash this out—she needed him gone so she could return to the class. But she would need a moment more away from the curious stares to still her limbs from shaking.

CHAPTER 14

Confession

The afternoon sun was now overhead. Slim was almost done with Dan's errand. The man had indeed become reluctant to leave Lily...even for a short jaunt into Tombstone. But perhaps the distraction would do Slim good. He moved through the town streets, numb to everything. But it was no use. He saw Ada everywhere. There were whispers of her outside the café, by the telegraph office, moving down the street. And she was always smiling at him, taunting him, inviting him.

How could he deny his heart? There were no two ways about it—he loved her. Truly, deeply loved her. That settled into his being. And stirred his heart once again. How could he face a future without her?

He swallowed. He would because he had to. For her.

This was best for her. He had to give her the best advantage he could. She deserved all the good things life had to offer. And he couldn't provide all that. Not as a simple ranch hand. He'd been fooling himself to think she could ever consign herself to a life with him.

He bumped into something solid.

"Watch where you're going," a man's voice shot forth.

"Sorry, sir, I just..." He wanted to excuse himself. Why couldn't he just control his thoughts and focus on what was around him? As he looked up toward the man's face, he caught the flash of metal—a badge. Then he met the man's hard gaze.

"You just what?" the man said, frustration evident in his tone.

"I was distracted."

The man stepped closer. "You need to be more mindful. Otherwise, you might run into someone who won't take too kindly to your thoughtlessness."

Slim shot a glance to the side. A group of the red-sashed Cowboys watched them from farther away. He knew the deputy was right. It could have been much worse. "I'll take more care from now on."

"See that you do. I'd hate to clean you up off the ground."

"Yes, thank you, Deputy—"

"Earp. Wyatt Earp." The man stuck out a hand.

Slim shook it. "Thank you, Deputy Earp. And, again, I'm sorry for almost running you over."

The man cocked a half grin at him. "I've had worse."

Slim nodded, hoping that the man would just move along.

"You looking for something? You can come in here for a drink." Earp indicated the building behind himself—the place he must have just exited. "Let off some steam at the poker table."

Eyeing the man, Slim wondered if what everyone said was true— that the Earps took a large cut from the establishment.

It mattered not to him. In general, he cared neither for whiskey nor cards. He pictured himself giving in. Yes, wouldn't that just be perfect? Knock himself down a few pegs while he was already so low.

"No, sir, I gotta get back to it." Slim hoped he wasn't upsetting the man. "Got a lot of work to do."

"Maybe next time."

Slim nodded. But he was determined he would not engage in such frivolity. He watched as the man walked on to wherever he had been headed. Picking up step once more, Slim headed toward the livery.

"What was that about?" a gruff voice said from off to the left.

Not again. Looking in that direction, Slim saw one of the men with the telltale red sashes standing—arms folded in front of himself, glaring at Slim. What? Slim could not be less interested. Or more eager to move on.

"Nothing." Slim strode forward.

The man moved into his path. "Didn't look like nothing."

"Just a misunderstanding." Slim wasn't sure whether he should make an effort to move around the man or face off with him. Neither seemed like a good option.

"Oh, we know about having 'misunderstandings' with those Earps, don't we?" The man gestured to two others of the Gang that were even then closing in.

Slim bit his tongue. How was he going to get out of this?

"We've been watching you," one of the others said.

"Oh?" Slim worked to keep his tone neutral.

"We thought you might be interested in making some money. Turn the head of that pretty schoolteacher." The first man's smile widened.

Ada? What had they seen? What did they know? Slim stared at the man, finding a new boldness. "I don't know what you mean."

"These womenfolk sometimes get all caught up. Think they need a lot of...fine things." The man exchanged a look with his comrades. "We could help you get her those fine things. Maybe get a leg up on Mr. Wilmont. That is, if you want her to pick you."

Slim looked from one man to the next. How did they know so much about him? Though that mattered less than their obvious careful attention to Ada.

Still, it was hardly enough to entice him. But dare he turn them down? How was he to do so without causing a scene or creating trouble for himself?

"You boys disrupting the peace?" Earp's voice cut through Slim's moment of indecision.

There he stood, a few feet away. Had he turned? Or was he coming back to the gambling hall just beyond Slim?

"We ain't doing no such thing," the first man shot toward Earp. "We was just talking with this here fella. Nothing illegal about that."

"Seems this man isn't interested in what you're offering."

"So, you speak for the common folk, now?" the second man inserted.

Should he let this deputy fight his battle? He couldn't be such a coward. It was only right he step in. "No. I speak for myself. And I ain't interested."

The man's eyebrows rose. "No? You sure? You might want to give that a little more thought."

"You heard him," the deputy said. "Now, move along."

The first man fairly snarled at Earp. Then he gave Slim a hard look.

This was not over.

Ada breathed a sigh of relief as the last child exited the school house. What a day! First, she'd had no ability to focus the entirety of the day, then Stanford...

What was the man thinking? Was he so empty-headed? So self-focused? But she knew the answer—he was. Had not her previous interactions with him taught her that much? Still, she grimaced at the thought that she would have to have yet another conversation with him. Would he be just as bull-headed then?

Stacking her books on the desk, she then grabbed for the broom. A quick sweep of the room and she would go home. Perhaps, she might talk to Mrs. Wilmont. In previous chats, the woman seemed to be somewhat impartial when it came to Stanford. Ada could at least try. She desperately needed a listening ear and some sound advice.

Ada distracted herself by humming a tune as she finished her task, setting the classroom aright. As she set the broom back in its place, she let out a breath. There. At least she could tidy up. If only her life could be so easy to put back in place. But that was not possible. Some things... often the important things in life...took a bit more effort.

And she would tend to it. Come what may, she would find a way.

She gathered her few things and left the small building. Now, it was the matter of the short walk to the cabin. It proved to be another opportunity for her mind to wander. As she strolled, she did her best to take in her surroundings, finding solace for her thoughts in those things. No need to dwell on what she couldn't fix...at least not right now.

Before long, she arrived at the cabin. And just outside, stood Stanford. Her heart deflated. Must she face off with him so soon?

He did not look pleased. But as his eyes met hers, his features softened somewhat.

"Hello," she offered, keeping the word even. "I had not expected to find you here."

He nodded. "That is obvious. I've been here, waiting, for some time."

"I...had to clean the classroom." She neared the door. Was Mrs. Wilmont here? This was not good for him to be here without a chaperone.

"That is a task that is beneath you." He seemed all too genuine in his delivery. That was what concerned her. Is that what he thought of her job?

Her face must have displayed her feelings, for he cut in again. "You are meant for so much more."

"I appreciate that, Stanford. But I am quite content with what I'm doing."

The look on his face betrayed his emotions as well—incredulous. That's what she would call it. "That cannot be so. You were born for more. Surely, your father would not have allowed you to stoop so."

Her father? What did he know of her father? Anger bubbled within, but she closed her eyes and forced it down. "I do not know quite what my father would say."

That was a lie. She knew Stanford was right. Her father would not like her taking on such work.

How could she make Stanford see? She loved what she did—expanding young minds, opening up worlds for them, and giving them opportunities that only education afforded.

Stanford closed the distance between them and set his hands on her arms. "Ada, I only want to take care of you. The way you need to be. The way you deserve to be."

"I—"

He shook his head. "There is something I need to say."

Apparently, this was one of those times she wasn't going to get a word in.

"I have come to admire you greatly. You have stirred my heart in such a way that—"

The sound of a cart in the distance distracted Ada. A lone figure rode upon the wagon's bench—a woman. It must be Mrs. Wilmont.

Ada turned back to Stanford.

His eyes closed, and his mouth became a thin line. "Not now."

But Ada couldn't be more relieved. She was certain she wasn't ready to hear what he was about to say. Not today. Not after their earlier confrontation. Not after Slim's rejection. Her emotions were raw. Too raw. And there was no way to know what might be forthcoming.

Stanford backed away a full step and turned toward the approaching cart.

Mrs. Wilmont halted the horse just short of the cabin. "Stanford," she said, her feelings difficult to discern. "I did not expect to see you here."

"That's one of the fun things about me. You never know where I'll show up." He peered at Ada.

That, she had come to find, was the truth. He could appear anywhere, regardless of boundaries. Whatever was on her features did not make him happy. And it showed.

"Be a good boy and help your aunt down."

Stanford moved to the side of the cart and assisted her dismount.

"I have a few things in the back that I might need—"

"I actually have to be going," he interrupted her. Then he turned to Ada. "I shall see you later."

Before Ada could ask when and where he would pop up next, he gripped his horse's saddle. She watched as he pulled himself up and with a tip of his hat, headed off.

"Guess I'll get these things in myself." Mrs. Wilmont stepped around the cart.

"Let me help you."

"You have your hands full." Mrs. Wilmont sounded confused.

Ada realized she still had her things from the day in her arms. "I meant—let me put these down and then I'll help you."

Mrs. Wilmont nodded then shifted her focus to the contents of the wagon.

Ada slipped inside the house, dropped off her few things, and headed back out.

Mrs. Wilmont was busy moving things around, repacking them into a couple of crates.

"What did Stanford want?" Her words seemed innocent enough. But Ada wondered what was underneath.

"He...just wanted to talk." Ada didn't want to get into it.

"Oh? Looked like a bit more than that to me."

"I..." Should she just tell the woman? Share her frustration? "We had a misunderstanding."

"Misunderstanding?" Mrs. Wilmont's kind expression melted into concern.

Ada picked up one of the crates. It was heavy, but not so much she couldn't carry it.

The older woman grabbed the other, and they headed for the door.

"He...brought me flowers...earlier."

"When?" Mrs. Wilmont looked confused. "At the schoolhouse?"

"Yes." Perhaps Ada was being too quick to judge Stanford. His heart had been in the right place.

"That must have been an interruption. I hope it didn't take you from your students."

"It was fine. I managed."

"Hmmm..." Mrs. Wilmont moved into the house and set her burden on the dining table.

Ada did the same. "It really wasn't so bad."

"I'll be honest, sometimes I wish that man had a better handle on himself. He's often oblivious to what's going on around him."

That sounded reasonable. Maybe Ada shouldn't be so cross.

"But that don't make things any easier on anybody." Mrs. Wilmont shot her a look.

Ada shrugged.

A smile tugged at Mrs. Wilmont's lips. "What's the story with Slim these days?"

What was she about? Changing the subject, was she? Why? Did she want to direct Ada's attention toward Slim or away from Stanford's shortcomings?

"Oh...I don't know that I'll be seeing him anymore."

"No?" The woman nearly dropped the apples she had gathered in her arms. "Whyever not?"

Ada carried the sack of vegetables to the kitchen. "He won't see me."

"Won't see you? That can't be so."

It was Ada's turn to be confused. She looked at Mrs. Wilmont's determined features while she puzzled on the woman's words.

"That man...now, he's got his head on straight. And it's turned right at you."

Ada's face warmed. Was it so obvious? "Even so, he turned me away when I went to the ranch to see him two nights ago."

Mrs. Wilmont offered Ada a kind smile. "I know these things can often get more complicated than they need to be."

Ada nodded. Her insides did feel as if they were knotted up. Even more so now that they were discussing Slim.

"Then it's up to you to un-complicate them."

"What?" How was that even possible?

"Just get to the heart of it. That's where you will find common ground. And resolution. No matter the challenge."

Ada mused. The woman made it sound so easy. Could it be, though? The thought tempted her. Maybe it could be. But unless Slim would see her, how could she even know? A stirring within gave her new determination. She would find a way. She just had to. Her heart depended on it.

Slim struggled to keep his thoughts together after his encounter in Tombstone. First, running into the legendary lawman. And then his confrontation with the three members of the Cowboy Gang. His nerves still came to life as he thought on it...on how they mentioned Ada so casually. Then again, he knew there was nothing casual about it—it was intentional. Did they truly mean only to seduce him to their side? Or was it meant to blindside him?

Either way, he didn't like it. Perhaps, it was a good thing they had parted ways, Ada and him. But he needed to put the issue to rest for now. It was time for supper. His distracted thoughts would only bother Dan and worry Lily.

Tom brought his horse alongside Slim's. "How was Tombstone today?"

Great. There went his determination not to think on it. "Same as ever."

Tom frowned. What did he expect from Slim?

"Need to talk about anything?" Tom asked.

Where was this coming from? Did Tom know something? "Why? Do you have something you need to talk about?"

Tom shook his head. "Nothing."

Slim didn't have a second to respond before Tom put his heels to his horse's flanks and hurried the animal along.

When Slim reached the barn, Tom had dismounted and started removing the saddle. Should he inquire further about Tom's words? It wasn't as if Slim wanted to have a discussion. He'd best just let it go.

They put the horses in their stalls and made quick work of feeding them. Then the two ranch hands headed toward the homestead. Slim would be grateful for something else to talk about. Maybe he should think up some questions to spark conversation. It was unlikely that dead silence would help his wandering thoughts.

Slim stepped onto the small porch and reached for the door latch, Tom just behind him. They moved inside, and Slim's breath caught in his throat.

Ada stood at the dining table, setting out bowls.

What was she doing here? How long had she been at the ranch?

He opened his mouth to venture one of these questions, but his throat was tight. Too tight to get anything through. He coughed to clear it. That did not seem to help.

Her gaze met his, the moment he entered. The soft brown eyes were hard to read. They widened, giving Ada a look of innocence about her. But was she? Had she come at Lily's behest? Or was this her plan to break past his silence? Either way, he did not appreciate it.

"You okay?" Tom's voice sounded as if he were miles away.

Slim pulled his eyes away from Ada's. Then he faced Tom.

"I'm fine." His words were rather curt—unintentionally so. If he couldn't respond to a simple question, how was he to manage the entire dinner?

Tom jerked back at Slim's biting words. "Sorry I asked."

If only he could take back his tone and his words. But he could hardly put two thoughts together, much less communicate an apology.

"How are you boys this evening?" Lily came alongside Ada, who had stalled in her task. Did he affect her at all? Certainly, not near as much as she did him.

"Well, I, for one, am real hungry," Tom said, moving away from the door and toward the table. "Hello, Miss Miller. Good to see you."

She offered a small nod. "Thank you, Tom." Then she looked at the table. To avoid Slim? What did it even matter?

Still, he had to know. His gaze connected with hers again. He cleared his throat and ventured forth. "What brings you out here?"

"I...came to help Lily."

Slim did not miss the look Lily shot at her. Perhaps, then, Ada stretched the truth. So, she did come to see him. Should he be angry? He felt more confused than anything. But he couldn't deny the stirring in the center of his chest. This would only make his resolve weaker, his distancing from her harder.

"You about finished?" Lily asked Ada.

"Oh!" Ada jerked back from her friend, only then seeming to notice that she still held several of the bowls she needed to distribute. Making quick work of doing so, she then escaped to the kitchen.

Lily watched after her until she moved to the stovetop. "What are you—?"

Ada's pleading look silenced Lily.

Turning back to the two ranch hands, Lily said, "I think the stew is nearly ready."

Tom nodded. "Smells delicious." Then he glared at Slim. What was he trying to communicate? Was this as awkward for everyone else in the room as it was for him?

Right then, the door opened, and Dan came into the house. "Hope I didn't miss anything."

All eyes were on him then.

His movements slowed as he closed the door. "Did I?"

Lily managed a tight smile. "Not a thing. We were just waiting on you."

"Well then, let's dig in." He gave Slim a long look before he moved to his wife and embraced her.

Had Dan been a part of this charade? He would disown the man if Dan so much as knew about it.

Dan pressed a kiss to the side of Lily's face. Then stepped to his chair. "What are we waiting on now?"

Lily shrugged. Then she joined Ada at the large pot, looking in on the bubbling concoction.

Tom took his seat and watched Slim. What for? Was this so amusing for him?

Slim swallowed and crossed the room to sit as well.

Soon enough, they were all at their places around the table, and Dan returned grace.

Slim's thoughts were scrambled. The normally extra seat beside Lily, across from him, had been filled by Ada. How would he avoid her, now? Every time he looked up—there she was.

How could she do this to him? Put him in such a position? But as much as he worked to restrain his anger, he couldn't. Or was the anger a mask for something else? Tender feelings filled him at a mere glance in her direction. And even more so because of her nearness. Was he so hopeless? This was going to be interesting.

Ada watched Slim across the table. Was he upset with her for coming? She had known this was a risk—one she had been willing to take. To be close to him again. For the opportunity to have one more conversation, one more smile, one more...chance to express how she felt.

This dinner got her part of the way there. But she couldn't iterate her feelings in front of everyone. She had to find a way to be alone with him. If even for a moment. Though how that was to happen was beyond her. He might not let her catch him alone. There was little choice but to sit across from her at the meal, but there were any number of excuses he might conjure to avoid her once dinner was done.

Lord, make a way.

Slim was particularly silent during the meal. Though, there were moments she caught him staring at her. Was that a good sign? Perhaps, there was hope.

As the bowls emptied and the meal came to a close, Slim stood. "Thank you for the wonderful meal."

He directed his statement to Lily. Was it the first thing he had said since sitting? It seemed so.

"Surely, you aren't off so quickly." Dan spoke up, a knowing look on his face. "We do have a guest, after all."

Ada groaned inwardly. She didn't need the Hayworths' help this much. It only made things worse. Dan pushing Slim on her was not the ideal way to handle this.

Slim glanced at her, ever so briefly. "I...need to catch up on some work."

Dan eyed him. The silence thickened in that moment.

Why had she done this again? Had she truly expected anything different?

Slim turned to her once more. "Miss Miller, I apologize for excusing myself so early, but I do, indeed, have things to attend to."

His eyes held hers. And there did not appear to be anything but frank dismissal in them. Had she been so wrong? Was he so indifferent? It stung. More than she would have thought possible.

He turned then and moved to the door.

"Perhaps, Tom would escort you home." Dan's voice carried in the space.

She didn't relish the idea of leaving without spending at least a few moments with Slim, but it seemed to be what he wanted. Foolishness. Her plan had been foolish and thoughtless. This could not have gone any other way.

Slim paused at the door. Why?

The moment was tense. But she couldn't make herself look at him. She had done enough to make his day that much harder.

"I didn't mean to say I couldn't take Miss Miller home," Slim said without turning.

What was that? Did he wish, then, to spend that time with her?

What changed his mind? His gaze was on her. But his features were hard.

"I...would like that," she said, twisting her napkin a little too tightly around her fingers. They started to throb.

"When, um, did you wish to return?" Slim held her eyes still. Could she not look away? The intensity of his regard pulled at her heart.

"I would like to help Mrs. Hayworth with—"

"Nonsense," Lily said, cutting Ada off. "I can manage."

Did Ada's face betray how exasperated she had become? She hoped not.

"Besides," Dan added, "we don't wish to keep you out too late."

Ada fought to keep her hands in her lap. She wanted to fold them over her chest and give these two a piece of her mind. It was enough already.

"Then now it is," Slim interjected. "I'll get the cart ready." With that, he jerked at the door and exited.

Ada opened her mouth to tell her friends how much their meddling had frustrated her. But as she did so, she spotted Tom in her periphery. And closed her mouth.

"Let me get you a wrap," Lily said, rising. "The evenings have become rather chilly."

Ada grimaced. Could she handle any more coddling? Her friends meant well for certain, but they were ruining everything. Perhaps, she shouldn't have chosen this to be where she faced down Slim. But then, where? No, it had to be here and now. Her heart could not have endured one more night without speaking with him.

But then, how would she start? What would she say? How did one share their heart without putting it out so far as to make it vulnerable? Or did she even care? For she knew she would risk it—for him.

Slim watched as Ada said her farewells to Lily. Why had he pressed into this task? But he knew. He didn't like the idea—rather, couldn't abide the thought—of her alone with Tom for an evening ride through the countryside. And now he was stuck. Maybe it was for the best. Perhaps, he might be able to make her understand. Then that would be the end of it.

Ada stepped off the porch and approached, her movements slowing as she did so. "I am...ready, if you are."

He nodded and walked around to her side of the wagon to help her up. This brought him in much closer contact than he would have liked. It was too tempting—these touches. But they could not mean anything to him. It wouldn't work.

The small sound she made as he laid his hands on her waist did not help matters. He released her as soon as possible. But his hands had warmed at the contact. And that he couldn't erase.

He came back to the other side, pulled himself up onto the bench, and urged the horse forward with nothing further. As the next moments passed in silence, he prayed that it might be so awkward she wouldn't venture conversation.

The more the minutes ticked by, the more confident he became. And the more disappointed. What was that about? But there was no mistaking his need to have words with her.

"Slim," she said at last. "I..." Her words trailed as her breathing became ragged.

It tugged at his heart. How could he sit here and let her suffer? It pained him too much. He opened his mouth. "Ada, I—"

"Why did you refuse to see me?" she asked, her words somewhat sputtered.

How was he to answer that without giving all away? Dare he share so much of himself? "I...thought it best."

"You thought it best?" she said after a moment.

He felt her gaze on him, seeking, wanting.

"How could it be best?" she challenged.

He jerked the reins, bringing the horse to a halt.

"I'm...just not good for you." There. He had said it. Now, it hung between them and with it, his vulnerability. What would she do with that?

Silence followed. Until he couldn't stand it anymore. He looked at her.

It seemed as if she fought a war within. What was she thinking? Feeling? He needed to know. So much. And without warning, her hands flew to either side of his face and in the next moment, her lips were on his.

He wanted to pull back, but that was not possible. His need for her was too great. So he kissed her back, claiming ground that had been lost. And then some.

When they broke apart, her hands still on his face, she leaned back just slightly.

He drew in a breath. What had he done? What had he let happen?

She moved toward him again.

He put his hands to her wrists and tugged her arms down.

She looked at him, a question in her eyes. And hurt.

"Ada, I...I can't."

Her lower lip trembled.

"I want to—I can't deny that. But I...we can't."

"What is happening here?" she protested. "Slim, the way I feel about you, I just—"

"Stop." The word was spoken softly. He let out a long exhale. "Please, stop."

She reached for him again.

He blocked her attempt, pulling back as well.

Tears brimmed her eyes, and she sniffed. Would she cry? Was she so disheartened? Did she feel so for him? That made this much worse.

"Please, take me home." The words were whispered. She turned toward the horse. Would she now avoid him? Perhaps, that was best.

He urged the mare to resume her pace. The torture would be over soon. And he could hope that his resistant behavior would prevent any other attempts on her part.

He could hope. Because there was only so much strength left in him.

CHAPTER 15
Trouble

Ada had not slept much the previous evening. And it was very telling in her inability to manage her class. What had she been thinking? How could the exchange with Slim have gone any differently? She had pushed him. Too hard. And now, any future with him was a long shot at best. Most likely, not in the cards.

The ache within her was too great. She did not think she would ever be whole again. Had she, in fact, given part of herself to Slim? Only to have him shove it back at her—torn, tattered, beyond repair?

The day dragged on. And it was only Wednesday. There was little chance she could make it. So, she called the class to order. Something had to be done. "Children, I have a treat for you today. Because of your excellent behavior and wonderful performance on your mathematics examination, we will dismiss class a little early today."

The students cheered. At least something came from her inability to stand up front anymore.

"So, if you'll gather your—"

Books and such were being shuffled, some things dropped, as she tried to speak. There was no need for her to ask them to get their things and move out. They already prepared themselves.

"See you all bright and early tomorrow," she called as they began to rise and move toward the door.

But the admonition was more for her. How was she to gather herself for another day...let alone two before she had some time and space for respite?

In minutes, the room had emptied. There. She had some peace before it would refill tomorrow. It would be wise to make the most of it.

Falling into her chair, she took inventory of what she needed to do before making her way home. There was more than she cared for. Though it would not go away, nor would it get done with her wishing it to be so. Garnering her strength, she pushed up and away from the desk. Why hadn't she asked the students to help with these things?

Either way, she had the time to think.

Slim was in Tombstone for the afternoon. Why had he volunteered to gather the few items from the General Store that Lily needed? He had first thought it would be a great way to keep his mind off Ada. Now, he feared he might see her.

And the painful memories of their last interaction still filled his mind. Why had he allowed such tenderness? Such exchanges and touches? He had been powerless, it seemed. But he had, eventually, taken hold of himself and done what needed to be done.

Still, she had nearly said words that he was certain would break him. And forever lose him to her. He had to tell himself it wasn't so. She couldn't have started to say what he'd thought. She didn't feel that way. She couldn't.

He had finished selecting the items Lily needed and loaded them in the wagon. Would he make it out of town without being spotted? But as he scanned the street, he saw her—several yards away—walking down the planked sidewalk. He needed to go. And fast. He doubted he would survive another encounter with his heart intact.

As he reached for the bench, something concerning caught his eye. The Earp brothers and the man, something Holliday, were walking down the main stretch. He'd heard talk in the General Store that they'd had run-ins earlier in the day with some of the members of the Cowboy Gang.

Slim did not want to be a party to whatever was going down. Indeed, men were escorting their wives and children off the street and into buildings. Something ominous was in the air. What was about to happen?

He looked down the main stretch and noticed a few members of the Cowboy Gang moving toward the vacant lot behind the OK Corral. Was that where the Earps and Holliday were headed? It seemed so. But for what purpose? This could not be good.

Slim's gaze then moved to Ada. She was still walking, oblivious to everything. Her regard was on the boards beneath her feet.

Look up! he silently beseeched her. *Get to cover!*

She continued to stroll forward. If she didn't stop, she'd walk directly in the path of the Earps and Holliday. He had to do something!

He moved in her direction, his steps quick. All the while, he watched as the Earps and Holliday closed in. This would not end well. He could feel it in his bones.

So, he pushed his feet to move faster. He was so close.

As he drew nearer, she did look up. Confusion passed on her features, but he would not be deterred. He grabbed her arm and pulled her back in the direction she had come from. In a moment, she was safe once more. Or, as safe as any of them were.

The Earps and Holliday still moved toward Fremont Street. Soon enough, they would find themselves in the empty lot with the Cowboys. Then it was anyone's guess what would happen.

Perhaps, he could get her inside one of the businesses.

"Slim, I—" she started.

"Shhh!" he demanded.

Then the world changed. A shot rang out. Dare he turn toward it? He pushed Ada against a wall.

She glared at him, her lips moving as if to speak.

Then the sound of gunfire filled the air.

He covered her with his body. Would they make it out alive? No matter their odds, he was determined that he would do what it took to ensure she did.

What had happened? Gunshots pierced the peaceful quiet of Tombstone. Slim's arms surrounded her, but she was still filled with fear. What if a stray bullet were to hit Slim? Or her? She clung to him as a wave of dread consumed her. With her thoughts and emotions swirling, it became overwhelming. Her legs gave out, and she dropped into a crouch.

Slim followed, covering her. Did he mean to sacrifice himself?

And then, just as quickly as it started, it was over. And all was still and silent once more.

Then the cries of wounded men assaulted her senses. What was this? She became paralyzed. There was movement around them. What would happen next?

Slim gripped her upper arm and pulled her to her feet, then tugged her back down the main stretch, away from the deafening sounds.

She tried to speak, but the rush of fear overcame any attempt to do so. And so, she let Slim lead her wherever he intended to go. For she knew he would protect her, would keep her safe. At all costs.

An opening appeared in the wall to the left, and he pushed her that way. Down an alley? It didn't seem safest. It didn't matter. She trusted him.

After several paces, he set her against the outer wall to the right. But instead of covering her again, he held himself back and looked her over, a silent question in his gaze.

She shook her head. "No. I'm not hurt."

He gathered her to himself. "Thank God!"

She relished the feel of his arms, his chest, his body against hers. Perhaps, more than she should. But they had just survived being exposed during a shootout. What more could life throw at them?

"Are you...?" She tried to speak but found it difficult. "Are you injured?"

He shook his head against her hair.

She closed her eyes and thanked the Lord for His provision and protection.

"What...what was that?" she managed.

"It's not important." His words were strong, sure. He jerked back, and then she was looking into his eyes—clear, certain, knowing. "I don't know what I...if something had happened to you..."

She set a hand to the side of his face. "Me, too."

He pulled her into his embrace once more.

And as much as the world had immediately become a place of terror for her, in this moment she had never felt so secure.

Slim ushered Ada into Mrs. Wilmont's cabin. They were well and safe at last. He could relax. A bit.

At some point between the shootout and here, Ada had begun to shake. It tore at his heart. She trembled uncontrollably.

He led her farther within and sat her down.

She continued to stare ahead. Was she unaware of her convulsions?

"Ada," he said, touching the side of her face. "Ada..."

She didn't respond.

"Ada darling." He couldn't get through to her. Was she reliving the moment? Or just so troubled by what happened that she couldn't focus?

He pulled her into his arms again. That seemed to have been the only thing that soothed her. It worked before. Would it now? Tugging her closer, he held her with a firm embrace.

She tucked her head under his chin and grabbed onto him, her fingers harder and stronger than he'd have thought.

He rubbed a hand down the side of her face, her hair, her back. "It's all right," he said, hoping she could hear him. "You're safe. We're safe. It's over."

After some moments, her shaking subsided, and she stilled. But he couldn't make himself let go of her or even ease his hold. Was he, too, more affected than he'd thought?

The scene played out as if a vision. Only this time, he hadn't made it to Ada in time. She was caught in the crossfire. And fell, lifeless. His heart lurched, and his stomach cinched.

He held her tightly, assuring himself that she was there and real and well.

"Slim?" Her voice sounded so small.

"Hmmm?" he managed. The reality of their situation flooded his mind. Here they were...again. Hadn't he been determined to distance himself from her? Yet, he could not pull himself away in that moment. Not for anything in the world.

"What will happen, now?" Ada pushed out. Was she talking about them? Or the happenings in town?

"I don't know." That was all he had for her. He wasn't sure what the fallout would be of the shootout. And he could not say where things lay between them.

"I don't want..." she started but stopped herself.

"What?" He kept his tone soft, his words soothing.

"Don't push me away."

He closed his eyes. No matter what he tried, he couldn't put distance between them. Should he then give in? As he held her, the thought felt foreign. Impossible.

Yet, he couldn't forsake his intentions to give her the best chance possible. She deserved that. Deserved more than he could offer her.

"What did I do? Why did you pull away?" Her words were measured and hesitant. Was she worried about breaking this moment?

He pressed a kiss to the top of her head. "It's not like that."

She struggled against him.

He loosened his hold a bit, and she stared at him. "Then why?"

Dare he bare himself to her? Tell her how things were? How could she not understand? "Ada, I..."

"I want the truth."

He searched her eyes and knew that she deserved that, too. Bracing himself, he swallowed and sent up a prayer for strength. "You should have everything that life has to offer."

Her gaze didn't waver. But confusion furrowed her brow.

"And I can't give you that." He looked away. How could he watch her reaction? Watch her judge him.

"What if you are what I want?" Fingers grazed his jaw, drawing his focus back to her face.

"Don't say that. There is more to life than—"

"Than love?" She had said the word. And it hung between them. But she couldn't know what she was talking about. She didn't love him.

"Surely, you must see that someone like Stanford—"

"He is not the one I want."

As much as his heart soared to hear it, he couldn't let himself get caught up. He had reasons. They were good reasons. But in this moment, all that existed was her. And the depth of his love for her. He leaned closer, intent on her lips.

And the door jerked open.

"Ada! Slim!"

He pulled back, letting his arms fall to his sides. Would they be found to be inappropriately close? What would that mean for Ada's reputation? Turning toward the sound, he was strangely relieved to see Mrs. Wilmont standing just within the entrance to the cabin.

"I was so worried," she exclaimed, moving to them. She gripped Ada's now free hands. "Praise the Lord!"

"Who knows what would have happened to me if not for Slim." Ada's eyes misted anew.

Mrs. Wilmont faced him. "Such a gallant young man. Thank you, Slim, for protecting her."

"I don't think I—"

"Of course, you did," Ada said, her gaze hard on him. "You saved my life."

He didn't care for this kind of attention. It seemed too...focused. Too daunting. Didn't she know who he was? What he was?

Slim rose. "I am...glad you are home, Mrs. Wilmont. I need to excuse myself and make sure all is well at the Hayworth ranch." Suddenly, he was all too aware that he didn't know how they fared. Or if they had heard and were worried after him.

Ada looked up, searching his features. "Can you not stay a little longer?"

How he wanted to say he would. And assure her that he would never leave her side. But neither would behoove him. He couldn't promise those things. "I need to let the Hayworths know I am well. They expected me back long before now."

She looked down but nodded.

Mrs. Wilmont put a hand on his arm, drawing his attention away from Ada. "Please, don't try to go through Tombstone. It is madness there."

"Thank you, ma'am, I won't." He looked at Ada once again.

She met his gaze.

And there were things he tried not to let her see. She knew more of him than he wished. But how was he to hide from her when she had secured his heart so effortlessly? He did tear himself away then and moved to the door. Still, he looked back at her. "I'll see you soon."

She nodded, and the faintest hint of a smile graced her lips.

He stepped outside and drew in a ragged breath. How was he going to keep that promise and save his heart?

CHAPTER 16

Escape

Two days. It had been two days since Ada had seen or heard from Slim. What was going on? Perhaps, he was busy. The town had been thrown into quite the upheaval. And everyone seemed to be lying low. Everyone, that was, except the Cowboy Gang. They made it quite plainly known how they felt about the shootout. There was little doubt in anyone's mind that they would seek vengeance.

Mrs. Wilmont encouraged Ada to stay close to the cabin. There was nothing worth venturing into town for. The woman stressed that quite well enough.

But Slim's silence still bothered. Where was he? Why had he been thusly absent?

A knock on the door drew her from her thoughts. Was it Slim? Had he finally come around?

She maneuvered through the cabin to answer the summon. Checking herself, she put on her brightest smile and opened the door. And found herself facing Stanford.

He rushed in. "Ada, I've been so concerned."

She stepped back to prevent a collision. Or had he intended to embrace her? Why had it taken so long for him to check on her if he was so concerned?

"I came as soon as it seemed safe."

Seemed safe? Slim had risked his life, and here Stanford couldn't be bothered to ensure she was well until he was certain it was safe enough for him.

"There is much that needs to be said." Stanford came around and stopped at the dining table. Then he turned.

What could he mean? Trepidation filled her as she watched him. Did he mean to say things that couldn't be unsaid? Things that might involve her?

"Stanford, before you say anything else, I need to tell you something." She took in a breath, steeling herself against his possible reaction.

"Ada," he said, coming toward her and taking her hands once more. "Facing mortality makes a man consider things."

"I really think I need to—"

"And I have—thought, considered things."

"Stanford, I don't—"

"I have come to see how much I truly care for you. Love you. And want to be joined and never parted from you."

He was about to say things. She was sure of it. But how to stop it? Everything seemed to slow.

"And so," he said, dropping to one knee, "Ada Clara Miller, will you do me the great honor of becoming my wife?"

"Please," she said, tugging on his hands to urge him to stand. "We need to talk."

"Of course, my sweet." He drew near. "But that can all wait. We have so much to celebrate."

Did he miss that she hadn't answered?

His lips came down on hers.

She pushed against him, finally succeeding in creating distance between them.

His gaze landed on something behind her. "What is he doing here?"

She turned. There, just outside the still open door, was Slim.

"Just what are you doing here?" Stanford all but demanded.

"I needed to drop off something," Slim countered, lifting his hand, which bore a covered basket.

"Stanford," Ada started. What could she say? She didn't wish to dismiss him this way. But dare she let Slim think she would entertain Stanford's affection?

"What's all this commotion?" Mrs. Wilmont stepped out of her room.

Stanford appeared stricken. Did he not consider that his aunt might be home? Had he counted on such?

As Mrs. Wilmont came into the great room and laid eyes on the three of them, a knowing look passed over her features. "Are we to entertain the whole town?"

"Of course, not." Stanford laughed. It sounded rather uncomfortable. "In fact, I need to be off to check something at the—er—mine."

"But I—" Ada became desperate to speak to his proposal. To clear up everything between them.

"No need." Stanford took her hand once more. "I shall return, and we can start making our plans." He slid out past Slim without looking back.

She met Slim's gaze. He was not happy. Did he not notice that Stanford refused to let her get a word in?

"I need to check the garden," Mrs. Wilmont said after a few awkward moments. "I wanted to add tomatoes to our table tonight." The woman stepped around Ada and Slim, giving Ada a wry look. Then she was outside and out of view.

After what seemed like an eternity, Slim spoke. "He proposed?"

Ada nodded and stepped closer to him. "But I didn't say, yes."

He cocked his head to the side. "Did you say, 'no'?"

"Not exactly." She frowned.

Slim fairly seethed.

"He wouldn't let me speak. Surely, you saw that."

Slim was a statue. No hint of emotion shown on his face.

"Believe me, I have no intention of marrying him. Ever." She became desperate to make him understand.

Sighing, Slim came back to life. "I suppose I know that."

She let out a breath. The world had color again.

"But I'm not sure it isn't best for you."

Not this again. "I think you need to let me decide what's best for me." She came within an arm's length, close enough to touch him.

"You think it's fine, now." He let out a breath. "But I don't know if down the road you won't resent me because I can't provide the things he could."

"Would you hear me? I have no need for those fine things. I've had them my whole life and I can tell you, it's not—"

"Exactly. You have had them your whole life. How do you know that you can live without them? How do I know?"

He had become quite frustrating. She threw up her hands. "You'll just have to trust me."

The look he gave her was one of disbelief. That pained her more than anything he could say.

"Maybe I have had a life of privilege, and maybe my father did provide fancy things for me. But that doesn't mean that I... need those things." She laid a hand to the side of his face. "None of that would matter without love."

Even as she spoke, she watched his emotions play over his features. How could he not trust her? How could he doubt her? Her ability to push through was nearing its end.

"Either this is worth the effort...worth trying for...or it's not." There. She had said it. Had laid it out.

He seemed to look through her in that moment. What did he see? "I...don't know if I can."

It was as if the floor fell away. Was he not willing to see her? To see who she truly was? He would hold onto this idea, this impression of who he had decided she was.

"Go." It was all that was left in her.

He lowered his head and nodded. Moving to the table, he set the basket down and then turned and walked out.

And in the quiet, she shattered.

"Are you sure you won't change your mind?" Dan's gaze held steady on Slim. The sounds of people bustling and moving about surrounded them on the train platform.

"You know, I can't. It's time I get back to Wharton City. Brandon is probably full up to his ears with trouble...especially knowing those two hands he hired this year."

"I wish things could have turned out different."

Slim nodded. "But that's where I belong."

"I mean...I wish things had turned out differently with Ada."

Slim's heart fell. How much did he wish that, too. How would he ever live with himself? Without her?

"Lily packed some food for your travels." Dan handed over a lunch pail. "She truly regrets your leaving. You've saved us...the ranch...two times over."

Slim nodded. "Any time."

The conductor called for the departure of the train.

"I'd best get after it, then," Slim said, looking toward the locomotive. There was no sense in prolonging this good-bye.

Dan dipped his head. "Take care. And if you ever need anything, just let me know. Anything."

Slim smiled at his friend. He sure would miss him. Being at Dan's ranch and spending time with him had been a breath of fresh air. And it sustained him through the harder things he'd faced here.

Putting out a hand, Slim looked to his friend.

Dan gripped it and shook it firmly.

Then, with nothing further, Slim turned and moved toward the train cars. It was a simple matter to board and get settled. He was fortunate to find a seat by the window. That would lessen his unease with the movement of the train.

Turning to look out the window, he scanned the platform for Dan. There. Right where they had parted. Only...he wasn't alone.

A woman spoke with him. She appeared to be rather animated. And the color of her hair...was that Ada? What was Dan saying to her? His face appeared grim and set. He shook his head.

Ada dropped her face into her hands. Her obvious pain pulled at

Slim's heart. It took his breath for a moment. As he watched, Dan put a hand on her shoulder and made an attempt to soothe her.

Why would she not look toward the train? He was desperate to see her face, pour over her features...if only once more. The train whistle blasted. That stirred her to turn. And he regretted his wish. The raw pain was plain. Her eyes were puffy, and her mouth quivered.

He pressed against the glass as if he could reach for her. Indeed, he wanted to. But that would be a mistake.

She shook her head and spun, rushing from the platform.

How could he not go to her? But dare he? Hadn't he made his decision? Yes, and he must give her this. No matter what he wanted, her future comfort and happiness meant more to him than his momentary need to go after her. So, he forced himself to remain seated and set his hands on his knees. Yet, he couldn't turn away. Not even when she had disappeared.

The train pulled into the station at Tucson with a burst of steam. Slim couldn't be more relieved. He had played out the scene with Ada over in his mind. Each display gave him a punch in the gut. He was a cad. How could he have played with her emotions and brought her to this point? It was clear she cared for him. Maybe she did, indeed, love him. That thought only deepened his regret. How had he let their emotions become so entangled? He hated it. Not only for his struggle, but more for hers.

Movement around him alerted that it was time to disembark. He rose and grabbed his saddle bags. His writings were within—the stories that had initially connected him and Ada. At first, he'd thought of abandoning them all together, but something stopped him. He couldn't eliminate their connection or the memories regardless. And these tales were a part of him.

As his feet hit the train platform, he looked over the waiting crowd. Where was Eli? He'd been told that the man would be coming to collect him. Surely, the ranch hand was nearby. But Slim's eyes caught—not on Eli, but on Brandon.

All the heat seemed to seep out of Slim. He hadn't been prepared to face the man quite yet. What did Brandon know of Slim and Ada's interactions? Could he know that Slim had left the man's sister in a world of hurt?

Brandon approached.

Slim couldn't even force a smile onto his face. He was too uneasy.

The man slapped a hand on Slim's shoulder. "It's good to have you back."

"I'm glad to be back." He wanted to avoid the man's gaze, but he felt pinned by it.

Brandon's features were a mask. What was he thinking? What was Slim to do?

"You all right?" Brandon asked, shifting his weight. "You seem a bit...distant."

Slim swallowed. Dare he speak the truth? "I'm just tired...from the trip."

That did not alleviate his boss's curious gaze. Did the man suspect his falsehood? After a few moments, Brandon said, "Let's get your things."

Slim nodded and followed his boss to the other end of the station. They waited until his bag was unloaded. Slim reached for it, but Brandon got it first. He offered Slim a small smile and indicated they should head out.

Slim was all too happy to do so.

As they moved past the train, Slim spotted Brandon's mare and cart. What would this ride to Wharton City bring? Was his boss waiting to talk until Slim had no escape? But he couldn't avoid it either way. Not if he intended to continue working for the man. So, he settled his saddlebags in the back and lifted himself onto the bench.

They rode for some time in silence. Brandon seemed at ease, but there was a hint of tension in the air. Or was that just Slim's imaginings?

"How was your time in Tombstone?" Brandon finally asked.

"It was good to work with Dan again. But there were...other things that were hard. I'm glad to be home."

"Difficult?" Brandon's brows furrowed. "How so?"

Now Slim had walked into it. He opted for another path. "Did you hear about the shootout?"

Brandon's features were unreadable. Had he, or hadn't he?

"Then there was the ever-present, ever-looming Cowboy Gang."

Brandon's eyebrows rose.

"These men...rustlers and outlaws are above the law, it seems. They instilled fear in the people and at least while I was there, never had to answer for any of their crimes."

"That must make ranching difficult."

"Yes. It does." Slim saw no reason not to be honest with Brandon about that. "But Dan is more concerned after Lily. He doesn't want to find himself on the wrong side of those criminals. The Gang finds vengeance an acceptable currency."

Brandon gave Slim another look that was difficult to decipher. "I'm surprised you came home so soon. Sounds like he needs you. At least, until the baby comes."

So, Dan or Lily had written the Millers to let them know about the pregnancy. Brandon was right—perhaps Slim should have stayed. For Dan's sake. But he couldn't escape that his heart would be damaged beyond repair if he had tried. He just couldn't. Yes, he had made the right choice.

"You think you should have stayed?"

"No," Slim said. "Dan hired another ranch hand, and his injured man was well enough to start back. I would have been dead weight."

Brandon shook his head and chuckled.

"What?"

"The things you think. Dead weight. You've never been dead weight."

Slim quieted. Was that so? Was he more valuable to his friends than he thought? They cared, to be sure. But he didn't think he was any more on the ranch than a placeholder.

"Don't you dare breathe a word to the others, but you are the most adept ranch hand I've ever had."

That struck Slim. Perhaps it should have made him proud. Instead, it gave him pause. Could he be so coveted a worker? He only ever did what he knew to do. To the best of his ability. Same as everyone else.

"Don't believe me? Why do you think Dan wanted you so badly? He could have hired another hand easily enough. No, he needed you. You're worth two men."

Slim couldn't speak. These words from his boss overwhelmed him. All his life—he had been unwanted, an outcast among his peers. And he had come to appreciate these friends he now enjoyed, but did he never really believe they cared? He searched his thoughts. No, he had always assumed they had been stuck with him.

"I sure did miss your capable work hands while you were gone. I wouldn't have loaned you to Dan if I didn't expect to get you back. I just didn't expect it so soon."

Slim frowned. His heart dropped. Had he abandoned Dan when the man needed him? Surely, his friend would have said as much.

After some moments in silence passed, Brandon spoke again. "How is my sister?"

Slim jerked his head toward his boss. And wondered again what the man knew.

"Come on, Slim. One of us had to bring her up."

Slim focused on his hands.

"I understand she has become quite fond of you." Brandon's words were measured. Even a little tight. Did his boss not appreciate Slim spending time with Ada? Just one more regret to pile on.

Still, he kept his lips sealed.

"We have to talk about it some time." Brandon's tone was firm. "You know, we do."

Slim nodded. "I...we...spent a bit of time together."

"That's not all."

Slim hung his head. "No, it's not."

"She wrote me a couple of times. But nothing in the last two weeks. What happened between you two?" The man's voice was edged and hard. Now, he would stop Slim from thinking a future between him and Ada were possible. Brandon, of all people, would understand. Slim just wasn't fit for Ada. He could never make her happy.

"We...had a falling out." Slim said at last.

"I see." Again, Brandon's words were pushed out. "Did you hurt my sister?"

The question hung between them. Brandon's gaze dared Slim to speak to his actions.

"Yes." Slim might as well fess up. Ada was sure to write her brother and fill him in on everything.

The muscles in Brandon's jaw twitched as he looked ahead. Would he not look at Slim anymore? "Does she love you?"

Slim closed his eyes. Could he deny this truth? He had been, but it didn't seem right anymore. "Yes."

Brandon jerked his head toward Slim. His features were hard, but his eyes softened...if only slightly. "And you left her?"

Pushing out a breath, Slim steeled himself for what was to come. "I had to. I'm not good for her. She deserves so much more—a life that I can't possibly give her. She's accustomed to comfort and finery. I'm a man who works every day to make life possible."

Brandon pushed out a breath. It was not a pleasant sound. "I don't understand why you're so hard on yourself."

What? Where were the harsh words and the command to never see Ada again?

"You can't seem to understand...you deserve good things in life. You deserve to have the love of a good woman. And to take hold of every opportunity in front of you."

This was wholly unexpected. Shouldn't Brandon be more upset about how Slim treated his sister? But Slim could not escape his words. Was there any truth to them? If there was, then he had made a terrible mistake.

CHAPTER 17
Concern

Ada was glum. The days were dark. In more ways than one. Things had grayed considerably since Slim had left. It seemed the light had just been snuffed out. And there had been a murder in town. One of the Earp brothers had died by a bullet from one of the Cowboy Gang's guns. Everything was in an upheaval. How would the other Earps react? That one, who was well known for his work with the law, Wyatt, seemed especially unresolved.

For her part, Ada steered clear of anything related to the Earps or the Cowboys. As much as possible. The whole thing felt as if it surrounded her and pervaded everything about the town and its people. Indeed, some of her students had not returned since the shootout.

As she wrapped up the day, setting the broom in its spot, she prepared for yet another long evening. Was she so hopeless? Pining after Slim. Refusing to be consoled. It was like a character right out of one of those novels she used to read. So pitiful. Oh well.

She gathered her things and moved toward the back of the room. But as she reached for the door, it jerked open. And Stanford stood in the opening.

"Ada!" He reached for her.

She remained rooted to the spot, not at all interested in being held by him—not even for a second. Or for him to be so close. Unable to pull her toward himself, his hands rubbed her arms instead.

"Why have you been avoiding me?" He seemed hurt.

"I'm sorry, Stanford. I've just been...busy."

He appeared to consider her words. "I daresay you might be even busier once we set a date."

Once they what? Did he truly not understand? She had not answered him before. But he'd not really given her a chance. Perhaps, now was the time to remedy that. She set her things on a student desk nearby. "Stanford, we need to talk."

"I know. There are many details to be considered. So much to decide. Of course, I want to give you a grand wedding. The wedding of your dreams."

Strange. When she had thought on what kind of wedding she would want, it always appeared simpler. Family and friends around her, yes. But in a small church. With a few flowers and a dress of the prettiest violet.

"Day dreaming, are we?" Stanford smiled as he managed to pull her closer. "The wedding will be the event of the year. The good Lord knows this town could use something to celebrate after all this unpleasantness."

She resisted his tug on her person. "I need you to listen, Stanford."

"Of course, sweetheart. Whatever you need to tell me. I'm here."

And that he was. He had been persistent enough, but he was still here. She shook her head. That didn't mean she could marry him. She didn't care for him that way. But she did Slim. She loved Slim. It would never work.

"There...isn't going to be a wedding." She pushed out the words, fearful if she thought on it for any time, she would not be able to say them.

"No?" A sly grin filled his face. "I say, I never took you for one to elope." He leaned in, moving his mouth toward hers.

She pulled back, pressing her hands against his chest to create much needed distance. "You're not hearing me."

He frowned. "Sweetheart, I don't understand. Are you shy because we are not chaperoned?"

"No!" The word came out sharper than she'd intended. She jerked free of his grasp. Then she faced him once more. "What I mean to say is that I can't marry you."

His features became stoic. "Can't what?"

"I can't marry you."

"Ada, I know you are reluctant because I haven't your family's permission. But I believe they will be all too thrilled that you found—"

"Stanford!" She stomped her foot. The man was infuriating. How could she have ever entertained tender thoughts toward such a self-centered man?

His eyes were on hers then, a bit widened.

"It has nothing to do with permission. Even if you had their blessing, I still would not marry you. I can't. I love someone else."

He balked. Would he have been any more shocked if she had slapped him? She doubted it. "Love someone else? I don't understand, I—" He paused. "You don't mean the ranch hand."

She looked to the side. There was no way she would let him see her reaction to the mention of Slim.

"It can't be."

Looking back at him, she held her mouth in a thin line. "But it's true."

His eyes hardened. And he lashed out a hand to grab her arm. "Listen to me. I will not be put aside for some lowlife."

"How dare you!" She pulled against his hold. His grip was too firm. "Unhand me."

He jerked her against his chest. "You cannot embarrass me like this. Half the town knows of our connection. I will not be humiliated like this."

"I can't speak to that, but I own my mind and my heart. And I don't love you."

"Love?" he sputtered. "It's not about love. You are such a child, Miss Miller," he stressed her name. "It's about the right match. And I believed you were it for me."

"Let me go," she seethed through clenched teeth. "I will not be treated so."

"You won't be treated so? What about me? Can you imagine the sacrifices I've made for you?"

This was hopeless. She pulled and jerked and still couldn't free herself. "If you don't let me loose, I'll scream."

His eyes darkened. "Who will hear you?"

"I will."

Ada tried to peer around him. Mrs. Wilmont stood just outside the still open door.

Stanford released her. "Aunt Lottie!"

"Yes." Mrs. Wilmont inserted herself between Stanford and Ada, facing off with her nephew. "And I won't stand by anymore and let you bully your way through this town. You've made a name for yourself. And not a good one. You are a mark on the Wilmont name. And I am not certain you should be managing my husband's claim any longer."

What? What was Mrs. Wilmont saying? Had Stanford's wealth been dependent on Mrs. Wilmont this entire time? How had Ada not realized this?

Stanford's face reddened. He stepped to the side to look directly at Ada.

"You!" He raised a hand to point at her. "This is your fault. You've turned my own blood against me."

"To the contrary," Mrs. Wilmont said, stepping closer to him. "This is all your doing. Yours alone."

Ada watched with widened eyes as Stanford glared at his aunt.

"You'll be sorry." He directed at his aunt. "This won't be the end." Then he spun and stormed out.

Ada set a tentative hand on Mrs. Wilmont's arm. "I can't believe you did that for me."

Mrs. Wilmont turned to face her. "He had it coming. For a while now. I'm just sorry you got tangled up in this mess."

Ada nodded and looked down. How had everything around her fallen apart? And so quickly? If not for Mrs. Wilmont, she wasn't sure what would have happened with Stanford. Where could she go from here?

Time crawled by. And yet, days blended one into another. Ada filled Slim's every waking thought. And each coming evening, he became uneasy about the night ahead. How would he make it through another horrible night into the next day? For Ada visited his every dream. There was no solace for him.

And these dreams were always the same: they started with pleasant thoughts of the time they were together. Then something—a wave, a rush of horses, a wagon, a train—would take her away. Then all was bleak. It was not unusual for him to wake from these bad dreams and be unable to find sleep again. Instead, he would lie and think of how quickly it became impossible. And of how he regretted leaving her.

What was the answer? Would he forever be thusly plagued?

"Slim," a voice called. It seemed strange, as if the noise traveled through water.

Then reality rushed to him, and he opened his eyes. Had he been dozing? Images of Ada and the feeling of dread lingered. Yes, he must have been asleep. And not just for a moment.

"Slim?" the voice insisted.

He turned toward the higher pitched sound and found Amanda Miller watching him.

"Mrs. Miller!" He straightened. What was he doing? He remembered coming into the barn to saddle his horse. Then he'd sat down for just a minute. Only...that minute had turned into several. He rose and faced her. "What can I do for you?"

Her eyes on him were kind. And concerned. "Are you all right? You haven't seemed yourself these last couple of weeks."

He looked at the ground. Would there be any use in hiding the truth? "I...am distracted."

She nodded. "Ada?"

His head shot up, and his eyes caught hers. "I don't think that I..." He considered his words. And let out a breath. "Yes."

"I had hoped it wouldn't come to this." Her tone was gentle.

He wondered at her words. Hoped what wouldn't come to this? His confusion must have been easy to read as she soon continued.

"Tell me...what keeps you from going to her? From telling her you were wrong?"

He widened his eyes. How could she know his heart? But he knew —Brandon had shared much with his wife. And what wasn't told had been plain to see in Slim's behavior. "I...just can't. I have to live with my choices."

Amanda set hands on her hips. "Is that the way of it?"

"I mean...how do I know she didn't accept Stanford's proposal after I left?" Slim gave voice to his greatest fear—that Ada's regard for him had been fleeting. And he was easily replaced.

"You know that's not true." Her words were simple. And hard.

"Do I?" he challenged.

"Don't you?" Amanda appeared rather exasperated. "Come on, Slim, you know her better than that. Your heart knows better."

And, though some doubt remained in him, he couldn't hide behind that excuse. Not really. "I don't even know where I would start."

"You might start by working through whatever this trouble is that you have with yourself. And then you could write her. Tell her how you feel."

He swallowed. Could he do that? How could he express such a thing?

Cook hollered for Amanda from farther away.

Amanda looked off in that direction. "Oh, I promised to help Cook with dinner." She turned back to him. "But this isn't over. Think about it."

Then she turned and walked out of the barn. And he was alone with his thoughts once more.

What might he do to show Ada what she was to him? Tell her how much her encouragement and support had always meant. And then he realized—his stories.

He hadn't felt much like writing or creating more since returning. Not even at Samuel and Nisto's insistence. But now, his fingers itched for the paper and ink. He would write them down. Just as she had wanted him to. For her.

Ada had spent long enough hiding in her room. She was stung by the events of the day. How had it come to this? Stanford's actions had left her wondering where she'd gone wrong. How had something that looked and felt safe become a thing that was so erratic?

Still, she had to go and face the world sometime. It might as well be now. Pulling herself together—as much as possible, at least—she rose and moved to the door.

She had just stepped into the great room when she heard Mrs. Wilmont's knitting needles clanging furiously. How had Ada not heard it within her room? The sound was surprisingly loud.

Ada watched her for several minutes. Was the older woman so upset? And why shouldn't she be? This day had cost her.

Without turning, Mrs. Wilmont spoke. "Are you planning on standing in that doorway all evening?" Her voice was gentle and teasing.

Ada looked down, and her face warmed.

The knitting stopped.

As Ada lifted her eyes, they met Mrs. Wilmont's kind expression.

"Come, sit." The woman patted the arm of the chair beside her.

Ada moved farther into the room with slow steps. Her body weighing several pounds more than it should. Or was it due to the heaviness of recent happenings? It dragged at her.

At last, she reached the armchair and fell into it. And then found herself fighting tears. Why? Was she so on edge?

"Oh, dear, it'll be all right." Mrs. Wilmont soothed.

Ada nodded but couldn't form words.

"I know you had your hopes set with Stanford. But isn't it better you know now? Before you are joined in the eyes of God?"

Ada looked at her. Is that what Mrs. Wilmont thought? That she was upset because she'd lost a future with Stanford?

"I promise that there will be others. You need more than Stanford could ever give you."

Ada sniffled. Would Mrs. Wilmont understand Ada's desire after Slim? Especially when she thought Ada needed even more than Stanford was able to provide.

"What about that Slim?"

"He..." Ada cleared her throat. "He left to return to Wharton City."

"Oh? Just up and left?"

"He was only in Tombstone to help the Hayworths on their ranch."

Mrs. Wilmont's smile remained. "Perhaps, all is not lost. There may still be hope there. I know he cared for you deeply."

She searched the older woman's face. "I don't understand. He can't provide half as well as Stanford could have."

"What's that to do with anything?"

Now Ada was confused. "You said I needed more than Stanford could give me." More tears broke through.

"My dear, I am not talking about the things money can buy. I'm talking about love. You need security that comes in knowing you are cherished, wanted, and loved for who you are. Those are the things that make a marriage. Not money."

"But..." Ada had a question on her tongue but nothing came. Mrs. Wilmont was right. Slim had really seen her. And still pursued her. Until Stanford made the difference of their stations in life an issue.

Mrs. Wilmont reached over to pat her hand. "You deserve those things. Every bit and for the rest of your life. Trust me. I had them with my husband for thirty-six years before the Lord called him home. And that kind of life is worth fighting for."

Ada allowed herself to imagine, for a moment, that she could gain Slim's trust and love. It comforted and thrilled her in the same moment. Was it possible?

Slim sat against a tree on the hillside near Uncle Owen's pond, looking over his work. He had written the last story down. There was nothing left but to submit it and see if a publisher might be interested.

Part of him doubted, but another part of him...a part that he was just learning to trust, said differently. He had just as good a chance as anyone. Hadn't he received enough encouragement from Samuel and Nisto, Brandon, the class in Tombstone, and Ada? Their words, their belief gave him reason to hope.

Ada's belief in him. She had not thought less of him because of who he was or where he came from. Why hadn't he trusted in that? In her?

Instead he had walked away...rather ran away. He certainly left in a hurry.

Movement several yards away drew his attention. It was Brandon and Amanda. On an evening stroll? Had they seen him? If not, shouldn't he make his presence known?

They moved closer to the pond, their voices soft. What were the words they spoke to each other? Were they tender things? Words of love?

For his part, Slim couldn't help but remember another stroll. The one he and Ada took, walking about the Hayworth property, even by the stream where they had shared part of their pasts. All had been calm and easy. In his imaginings, when he looked into her eyes, he saw his future. His life stretched out before him, and it was blessed. Could he have that life? He wanted it...badly.

Voices interrupted him. Had Brandon and Amanda seen him? Were they talking to him? He looked in their direction to find that they had moved closer. But they seemed to still be unaware of Slim. It was past time for him to let them know he sat here, listening. Eavesdropping was not something he wished to be doing. But as he opened his mouth, he heard Ada's name. And though he had decided not to, he stilled his thoughts and continued to listen.

"I just don't know what to do for her," Brandon was saying. "She is rather out of sorts."

Was she? Had she been so unhappy after his leaving?

"Her birthday is next week. Maybe you could surprise her with something," Amanda offered. "That saddle sure fit the bill for me. I couldn't have picked better myself."

"That wasn't so difficult. I knew what you wanted. But Ada? What would she like?"

"She loves to read. Perhaps something from her favorite author?"

Brandon remained quiet. Was he considering Amanda's words? They continued past Slim. He held his breath. Now that he'd overheard part of their conversation, he had no desire for them to know of his presence.

They moved past him and continued on around the pond. As the distance grew, he exhaled, mindful to keep his breathing slow and steady. But there wasn't a hint of them turning. Had he successfully avoided them?

When all was silent once more, he considered their words. Ada's birthday was that soon? Perhaps, it would be a good opportunity to make a grand gesture. He considered her possible reaction upon opening a packet from him with his writings in it. Would she be pleased? Or more upset? Regardless, he had to take the chance. It may be his last opportunity to show her. To tell her.

He looked down at the pages. If he intended to send them off for consideration, they would need a dedication. Taking a moment to think, he let all of his memories of her, of time spent with her, have full rein in his heart. Then he looked to the blank page and moved the pen over the surface. There. That would speak truth to her. In the best way he knew how.

CHAPTER 18

Ada settled herself in her desk chair. The students had left for the day, and she was alone. She'd made an effort to straighten her desk. And now the only thing that remained was to tend to the classroom. But something caught her eye—Slim's package. Mrs. Wilmont had insisted she open it sooner rather than later. Only...she couldn't quite make herself do it.

She lifted the thin, flat, brown package and considered it. Slim's name was there in the return address. What did he wish to send her? And on her birthday, no less. Would it lighten her spirits? Ruin her day? Or serve to make their separation harder? There was no way to know.

But if she didn't open it now, she only delayed the inevitable. It had to be done at some point. She might as well face it now.

Pushing out a breath, she was resolved. She tore at the edge of the packaging. An envelope fell from among the many pages stacked together.

Leaning down, she spotted it under the desk. She reached for it and sat upright once more. As she slipped a finger in the seam of the letter, her eyes caught on the stack of papers. The top sheet held only a few words. And one of those was her name.

For Ada, whose faith in me spurred me on. Always in my thoughts, always in my heart.

She halted her movements and focused, reading the print again. It was, in fact, as she had thought. Those words that spoke volumes were scrawled there in Slim's handwriting. Could he mean that? Did he feel that way about her? A tingling warmth rushed through her. It was a powerful sensation, stealing her breath for a moment. Dare she hope? What if this was some cruel misunderstanding?

The letter became all the more important. Sliding papers from the envelope, she couldn't help but remember their early acquaintance. And how much his letters had meant to her.

She unfolded the papers and pored over the pages.

Dearest Ada,

Yes, you are so dear to me. I know it is the most unfair thing for me to say it in this way. I wish I could look into your lovely eyes. But then again, that may make this impossible.

I love you. Of course I do. The admiration I felt that day on the train platform at our first meeting has grown until it has taken over my heart.

If only I could...

A sound at the back of the classroom pulled her from the words. She lifted a hand to her misting eyes, catching a tear prepared to fall.

Who could that be? Perhaps, one of her students forgot something.

She rose and walked toward the door, glancing over the room with a careful, searching scan. There wasn't anything left behind that she could see. At least not—

The door burst open.

Three men filed in. They all wore the red sash of the Cowboy Gang.

All the life drained from her. What could they want? She stepped back. "This is a place for children. You have no business here." Even though she hoped to exude a fair level of defiance at their intrusion, her voice trembled.

The men looked at one another, amusement on their faces.

If only she could wipe those sneers off. But she was too fearful. This could not end well. Would it be her end? Or something worse?

The man in the middle moved directly toward her as the other two came around opposite sides of the room. Was she such a danger to them that they needed to cage her in this way? It was laughable.

"You will find nothing of value here." She pushed out, uncaring that her voice wavered. Her time was running short. And her options were few.

"Quite the contrary, Miss Miller..."

They knew her name?

"We think there's something rather valuable indeed."

She could not back away anymore. The other two cronies had flanked her and now came up from behind. Was there any chance she could escape? She had to take it. Shifting her weight, she sprinted to the right, dodging a desk and maneuvering toward the door. If she could make it outside. That was her only chance—to run for it.

As she lengthened her stride, an arm grabbed her, and she was jerked against something solid.

Then the leader's hot breath came down on the side of her face. "Nice try. You ain't goin' anywhere, darling."

Slim got off the train. Would he beat his letter? It had taken longer than it should have for him to decide he had to see her. Had to plead his case. Ask for forgiveness. And make her his wife.

While he certainly was nervous about the prospect of rejection, he would not turn back. She needed to hear this from him. To turn him aside in person. Not through some piece of paper.

He left the station and moved to the edge of town. Then on to the schoolhouse. She might still be there. The school day was done, but she often lingered. If not, it would be a simple thing to go on to Mrs. Wilmont's cabin. Still, he could hope that she might be at the school. It would be best to have this exchange without an audience.

As he neared the small brown building, however, something uneasy crept into his awareness. An eerie feeling overcame him, and the hair on the back of his neck stood on end. Was there any reason to think something was amiss? He narrowed his eyes to better take in the area ahead. As he moved his gaze over the building, he noticed the door was ajar.

His heart stopped. Something was not right. Panic filled his gut, though he tried to push it down. But it had taken on a life of its own. He couldn't restrain himself from running to the schoolhouse and into the large room.

Some of the desks near the back were askew. And Ada's desk sat empty.

His heart pounded, and his pulse thundered in his ears, making it impossible to hear anything.

She would not have left the classroom like this. Never.

He stepped to Ada's desk. Might he find some clue there? As he moved closer, he saw his package and letter atop the other things. Had she just opened it when something interrupted her?

A heavy, ominous feeling overshadowed everything as he scanned the room. There must be some detail...something...that would give him an idea what had happened here. As he looked, maneuvering about the room, he couldn't find anything but further evidence others had been here. Others that were not expected. Larger muddy footprints covered the floor.

What had happened to his Ada? Was she hurt? In great danger? Dead? His heart rejected that. Somehow, he would know. He had to believe that.

He came around to her desk again. Then stepped toward her chair. Something crumpled under his boot as he did so. Bending, he lifted the single paper. Handwriting he didn't recognize covered the front.

Slim made his best effort to read it though the words had obviously been written quickly. They were difficult to discern. But he did try. And began to make sense of the situation.

This was a ransom note. The perpetrators demanded that Stanford pay two thousand dollars for Ada's safe return.

Slim froze. What could be done if not to include Stanford? Slim was ready and willing to risk anything...everything to rescue her. But prudence begged another answer. If he went off on his own, going up against any number of men, it could prove disastrous for her. Ada's life would be what hung in the balance. That was unacceptable.

He had to find Stanford. Now.

Ada sat on the outskirts of the small camp, her hands tied and a rough-looking man standing guard over her. Every time he looked at her, he leered. What was in that head of his? As if she didn't know. But she had heard the leader tell him that she was off-limits...until they had their money.

Her heart dropped. Who would come for her? Perhaps, Mrs. Wilmont would get help. Maybe she could find a way. Ada had to hope.

She had nothing left but to sit with her thoughts. And think she did. Over her life, her choice to come out here to this God-forsaken land... But mostly, she thought about Slim.

Why did she let him go? Had she been so uneasy about the prospect of a life without the security money afforded? She had. So much that she'd turned Slim aside. What must he think of her? Yes, his letter said he loved her, but did he really? Did he have regrets about his feelings? He must.

It mattered not. She might very well die here. And Slim was miles away. Unreachable. He didn't even know what had happened to her. Closing her eyes, she prayed for the courage and fortitude to make it through this. If God was benevolent and saw to her rescue, she would throw herself on Slim's mercy. Beg his forgiveness for the coward she had been. And offer him her heart forever.

"Are you sure we can't have a little fun?" One of the other men in the camp came closer. He watched Ada with a sinister glare as he threw his comment to someone farther away.

"Keep your hands off the merchandise. For now." Was the response.

The man continued, moving nearer.

This caused the larger man guarding her to stand and face the ruffian down. "You heard him. Bide your time. And mind your turn."

Her stomach twisted, and she tasted bile. Would Mrs. Wilmont find her in time? Before these men lost all sense that she was more valuable unscathed? Or would they lose respect of the leader's instructions? Mutiny?

At one time, she had wished to live in the kind of action found in the stories she read. But now, she regretted that impulse. How empty-headed she had been! Now, all she wanted was her freedom and to live an uneventful life. With Slim.

If he would have her.

Slim had never been to Stanford's place of business. In fact, he had determined a while ago to never set foot in the establishment. But this changed everything. Ada needed him. And she needed him to appeal to Stanford's good graces. He needed Stanford to help him rescue Ada.

Thinking about her, with those men, unprotected and unable to get away...it was more than he could bear. But he must. For her. And he would make every effort with Stanford and promise him anything—even if it meant Slim had to lose Ada to him.

Slim stepped to the office that displayed Stanford's shingle: Stanford A. Wilmont, III. Was it Slim's imagination, or was Stanford a bit proud of his name? His full name.

Gathering himself as best he could, he then knocked on the door.

"Who is it?"

Would Stanford let Slim in if he knew who it was? Slim was uncertain.

"Who is it?" Stanford called louder, frustration seeping into his tone.

Slim started to answer, but the door jerked open.

"Oh, it's you." Stanford released the door latch, spun, and moved back into the office that was larger than Slim would have thought.

Slim tried not to let Stanford's dismissal bother him. Stirring up trouble between them was not going to help Ada.

Stanford moved to the large desk, which had papers scattered about. Piles of papers scattered. How could the man find anything? As Slim watched, Stanford pushed through stacks here and there before lifting a page to look more closely at it.

"What do you want?" Stanford's words were clipped. He didn't so much as glance at Slim.

"It's not me. It's Ada." Slim was filled with a renewed sense of urgency.

Stanford looked at him. "What?"

Slim pulled the note out of his pocket and held it up. "She's been taken. By the Cowboy Gang. And they are demanding you pay two thousand dollars for her safe release."

Stanford's gaze lingered on Slim for a moment.

Slim held the paper toward Stanford to allow him to read it himself.

But Stanford peered back at the columns of numbers on his page. "And what does that have to do with me?"

Could he be so dismissive? Did he not care?

"She needs you."

Stanford continued to move the piles about on his desk. What was he looking for? And how was it so important in this moment? Had he not heard Slim? "Listen, ranch hand, she made her choice. I fail to see how any of this is my problem."

Slim worked to keep his temper from flaring. To keep anger out of his voice. "You can't be so heartless," he said flatly.

Stanford didn't acknowledge the comment or the fact that Slim was still there.

In a few long strides, Slim rushed to Stanford's side.

Stanford, eyes wide, backed away. Did he think Slim would hit him?

"Won't you help her? She is in trouble. I know you care about her."

Stanford set down the papers in his hands. "See, that's the thing. She set me to the side. I don't see why I should do any different."

Slim clenched his jaw so tight he feared his teeth would crack. But he dared not let himself speak the words that were on the tip of his tongue. Not if he had a hope for Stanford's help. And he needed the man.

Stanford continued to comb through his papers. It became more than Slim could bear.

"Can you not put that away? For a moment?"

"I can. But, like I said, I see no reason to entertain this any longer." Stanford's eyes narrowed.

The ransom note crumpled as Slim's fists tightened at his sides. He had never wanted to hit someone as much as he did in that moment.

"Run along. I have real work to do." Stanford faced him, daring to lean toward Slim.

Slim's ability to keep his hands off Stanford was becoming rather taxed.

"I said, go. Find someone else to bother. She's worth nothing to me now."

One moment Slim was looking at Stanford's face, too near his. The next, Stanford was lifting his hands to his bloodied nose.

"You hit me. I can't believe you hit me."

Slim raised his fist to examine his hand.

Stanford jerked away. Did he think Slim would punch him again? "Get out! Go. Leave me alone."

Stunned...both at Stanford's complete disregard for Ada and at his own actions, Slim backed away. "You're the worst kind of scoundrel— one that pretends he's something but is really hollow inside and rotten to the core."

Stanford, still nursing his bleeding nose, met Slim's gaze. "If you don't leave now, I will call for the sheriff."

"Don't bother...I wouldn't waste another minute on you." With that, Slim turned and walked out. He hoped he'd never see Stanford again—there was no way to know how he might react to the coward.

But the truth remained that Ada was in a desperate situation. How was he to help her? There was no way he could secure that kind of money. He'd have to try something else.

And whatever that plan was, he'd need help.

CHAPTER 19

Confrontation

The Hayworth ranch was ahead of him. Slim had pushed the borrowed horse hard enough. He was grateful the blacksmith had looked on his situation with sympathy. As he jerked the mare to a stop, he dropped down and fairly flew into the house.

"Dan!" he called. "Dan!"

Lily stepped into view from the far side of the house. "Slim? What are you doing here? Aren't you supposed to be in—"

Slim held up a hand. "Yes. And there's no time to explain. I need to speak with Dan."

The door opened behind him. He spun. Dan's features appeared as shocked as Lily's had been. "What are you doing here? I thought you were—"

"No time. I need help. Now." Slim pressed out the words. He could not abide any more delays.

Dan's brows furrowed, his eyes full of concern. "What can I do?"

Slim let out a breath. Relief flowed through him for a moment. He wasn't alone. But the urgency of the situation swept through him in the next moment. "Ada's been taken. By Cowboy Gang members. They left a ransom note, and they are demanding payment in order to release her."

253

"How much? We'll do whatever we can to help."

"Two thousand dollars."

Dan's features fell.

But Slim had known that was not likely an option anymore. He began to pace. "What can we do? How will we get close enough to have even a chance to free her?"

Dan frowned and exchanged a look with Lily. Her eyes had filled.

"There must be something we can do." Slim was exasperated. But he was not discouraged in his quest. He would do anything, even if he must risk his own life.

"You know I would do anything for Ada. But how do we even know she's still..." Dan's words trailed.

Slim stopped and stared at Dan. "Alive? How do we know she's still alive?"

Dan nodded. "Sorry, Slim. There's a good chance she's not. These men...they aren't like your average villain. They are ruthless. And without conscience."

Slim nodded. How could he ask Dan to risk so much? Especially now. Of course, Slim would do what he could, but that didn't mean Dan had to.

Dan's features smoothed. "If there's even a chance, I'll be by your side." The words were a balm.

Slim felt crazed with worry. It was difficult to focus. "How will we gain access? Without the money?"

Wagon wheels crunched outside.

Who was coming? Dare Slim hope that Stanford had changed his mind? He prayed it would be so. Stepping around Dan, he rushed outside.

Mrs. Wilmont pulled her horse to a halt near the borrowed mare. She met Slim's gaze. "I came as soon as I heard."

She didn't seem the least bit surprised to see Slim. Only set on joining the conversation.

Slim helped her down.

"I had the hardest time getting any details from Stanford. But what I did learn, I...just knew I had to help."

Slim looked at Dan. Did he think as Slim did? How could Mrs. Wilmont help them? Still, Slim would include her.

"What I don't know," she said, her eyes darting between the men. "Is where to make the exchange."

"What? Exchange?" Slim was confused.

"For Ada." She seemed restless. "I have the money. We need to get to her. Now."

Had Slim heard her correctly? "Did you convince Stanford to—?"

"Never mind him. We have the money. Now, we need to get her home."

A sense of calm came over Slim. As if dark clouds parted and a beam of light peeked through. There was hope. "I think I have a plan..."

The afternoon dragged on. Ada had watched the sun move across the sky. It would darken soon. What might happen to her then? She feared the men might lose any ability to follow orders. What would become of her then?

She had been observing the men around her...watching for any patterns. But it was difficult to determine any sort of regularity to their movements. Was it so hopeless?

There was, too, the real fear that if she tried to escape, any hold barring them from her person would evaporate, and the men could use that as an excuse to work their misery out on her. So, what was best? Taking her chances with escape? Or complying and hoping against hope that someone would come through?

The man guarding her took a long swig of what she could only guess was moonshine. He had surely drunk half the jug. Would this provide the opening she needed? He had consumed it all in the last hour and gave no indication he would be letting up. Would this bode well for her in the way of an opportunity? Or prove to lower any resolve he had to obey orders?

Perhaps, she could work on the rope that bound her. Freeing her hands would only make any escape plan easier. She moved her wrists back and forth. Could she loosen the cords...even just a little? How she wished she had been thinking more clearly when they tied her bindings. Perhaps, she could have turned her wrists and made a little space. She shifted her focus to the knots. But had to stop periodically when the guard looked over. Which was not as frequently as she'd have thought. The drink had become all absorbing to him.

Releasing the knot seemed to be the most effective course of action. So, she tugged at it. Then she considered the rock beside her. Could she use it to work the knot loose? As she maneuvered her hands nearer the ground, the guard nearby shifted and stood. She glanced in his direction to find two of the outlaws coming closer—the one giving orders and another of the men who had taken her. She halted her efforts and sat straighter.

"It's time," the leader said to her guard. "Bring her." They turned to move back toward the small camp.

The larger man swayed a bit as he moved toward her. How much had he drunk? When he stumbled, the leader looked over his shoulder. "Have you been at it? Can't I trust you with anything?"

"Sure, boss," the man slurred. "I'm fine."

The leader frowned. "No. I need clear-headed men. Men that can follow orders." He took out his gun and shot the guard.

Ada screamed as the large man fell.

The leader jerked his head in Ada's direction, and the other man came to where she sat, grabbed her arm, and jerked her to her feet.

Ada was reeling. Had the man really shot one of his own? Her face drained, and her stomach turned. Would she faint? Lose the contents of her stomach?

"Nobody crosses me. Nobody." He eyed Ada.

She didn't know how to respond, so she didn't. Would he kill her regardless of what happened with the ransom? That seemed likely. Her desire to find some way out of this increased. Ada prayed an opportunity would present itself. And that she would have the nerve to take hold of it.

Slim stood in the open area that was the rendezvous point. What would the moments that followed bring? Would Ada be freed? Or would they all make their final stand here? He couldn't think like that. He had to have hope. He had to trust. Still, as the thunderous sound of hoofbeats neared, he found reason to pray. And pray hard.

Soon enough, a cloud of dust gave way to multiple riders. Slim searched the group for Ada. At first, he couldn't see anything that resembled a woman. Then, as the riders spread out, he spotted a flurry of long blonde hair.

His heart lurched. She was alive. But for how long?

He watched only her as the horses came ever closer. Was she well? Had she been hurt? Then he took a breath and focused on the present. On the plan. It was difficult to keep his eyes off her. But he needed to turn his attention toward the man in the lead—the man who had, at one time, pressured him to join the Gang.

As the riders came closer, several broke away and held back. The leader and the scoundrel that held Ada on his horse moved closer, stopping only a few feet in front of Slim.

A look of surprise washed over her features. Then concern. Did she know something of the Cowboy's plans? He wanted to call out to her, to assure her in some way. But that would only jeopardize their situation.

"You're not Stanford Wilmont. You're nothing but a common ranch hand."

Slim squared his shoulders. He would not be defined by these vile men. "I thought you were here for ransom. Does it matter who brings the money?"

"No, it don't." The leader sneered. "Just as long as it's all there."

"I want to see the woman first."

The lead man waved a hand to his side where Ada and the second man were positioned. "As you wish. She's right here."

"I want to talk to her."

"No. I don't think so."

Slim swallowed. "I need to make sure she is well before I hand over this money."

"You can hand it over now, or she gets another hole in her head."

The second man drew his weapon and held the barrel against Ada's neck, pushing her head to the side as he put pressure on her jaw.

Slim held up his hands. "All right. Just leave her be."

"Let's do this right. Toss your gun."

It wasn't something he relished, but he trusted that his friends were backing him. So, he unholstered the revolver and tossed it to the left.

"Where's the money?"

"It's right here," another voice said from behind Slim.

Slim turned. It was Tom...and Dan. They emerged from where they had been tucked away. Dan stepped forward, his movements awkward. What was happening? This wasn't part of the plan.

When Ada spotted Slim, a rush swept through her only to be doused as she realized that he, too, was now in grave danger. Her heart called to him, but would he hear it? Could she express her feelings before all was lost? She caught herself...this was not a time for her storybook fancies. This was time to watch. Carefully.

As he exchanged words with the leader, she had become only more concerned. When her captor drew his weapon on her, she fought to hide the dread filling her. Was this it? Then Tom and Dan came out from hiding. What was this about? What manner of plan was this? Slim kept his cool, but she had seen it—a flash of uncertainty. Had whatever ideas they had about this exchange fallen apart?

Tom, however, did not seem the least bit bothered. Though Dan was. As they came into the clearing, she spotted Tom's gun, pressed into Dan's back.

Was Tom...? Had he betrayed his boss? Was he a Cowboy?

"I knew we could count on you," the leader said. "I am glad to see my faith was not in vain."

Slim's eyes widened and his hands fell to his sides.

The terrifying truth pushed through her weakened defenses. This was not going to go well for them.

Tom, pushing Dan, neared. "Drop it."

Dan let a satchel fall to the ground. How had she not noticed it before? Was it the money for her ransom? Could it be anything else?

Tom backed away from his former boss and toward the Cowboy leader's position, holding his weapon level, aimed at Dan's chest.

"Put her with the others," the leader said, laughing.

"But—" the man behind her in the saddle protested.

"I said," the leader snarled, jerking his head toward them, "Put her with the others."

A sickening feeling overtook her. This would be it.

Tom came alongside the horse and jerked her out of the saddle. She nearly crumpled to the ground, but his firm grip kept her upright, though wrenching her shoulder in the process. He pulled her nearer Slim and Dan, thrusting her at them.

Slim caught her. His hands comforted her. But only for a moment. For he would share her fate.

She leaned into him, wanting desperately to touch him. And would, if not for her bindings. "Slim..."

"It's okay." He pulled her to his chest.

"Enough of that," the leader snapped. "Count my money."

"It's all there," Tom said, tossing the satchel to him.

The man thrust it back, knocking Tom off balance. "I said, count my money."

Tom opened the flap and pulled out the bills, displaying them for the man as he counted it. The moments were torture, knowing that their lives had a time limit.

Slim continued to hold her near. At least, there was that solace—they would meet their end together.

"Good," the leader said as Tom finished counting. "Now, where were—"

A gun blast pierced the air. The leader slumped over.

What? Who? Was this more of Slim's plan?

Another bullet whizzed by, taking out the man who had held her in the saddle.

Slim jerked her to the ground and covered her head moments before massive gunfire filled the space.

CHAPTER 20
Relief

Who exactly had fired upon the Cowboys was beyond Slim. He had almost given up when Tom was revealed for who he was. But now that the second Cowboy had been hit and the remainder of the Gang readied their weapons, Slim knew more was coming. And he needed to act. He had to get Ada down. Now.

Pulling her to the ground, he used his body to shield her. There was no way he would waste this—whatever had happened to turn the tide. Nor would he risk her in the crossfire. If they could survive at all. But he would give Ada her best chance.

They remained as they were until the shooting stopped.

Only then did he peer up and around. The Gang members had been massacred. Who had come to his, Ada, and Dan's aid? He rose tentatively, looking around to discover their rescuers. Nothing.

Then a man called out, "Stay where you are."

He had heard this voice before. Then he remembered. Could it be... Wyatt Earp?

"We are innocent," Slim yelled in the direction the voice had come from.

Slowly, a few men stepped out from behind trees and rock structures. When had they come? How had they managed to remain hidden this whole time?

Slim looked to Ada. "Are you hurt?"

Her eyes were wide and filled with moisture, but she shook her head.

He moved over to Dan, who also assured Slim that he was well.

Wyatt Earp came closer. He was examining the small group. Recognition lit his features as he laid eyes on Slim. Signaling his men to stand down, he stepped toward Slim.

Dan moved toward Earp. "How did you know? What—?"

"Let's just say we're doing a little clean up out here."

Earp's confidence astounded Slim, but there was more...something underneath. Perhaps, an unsettled anger. Maybe it was just him imagining things.

"How can we thank you—?"

"Slim!" Ada cried.

He spun to find Tom's arm wrapped around her torso, his gun against her head. The man was bleeding from his side, but that had not deterred him.

The others drew their weapons in an instant.

"Don't," Tom seethed, "Or I'll make sure she doesn't take another breath."

Fear gripped Slim once again. "Don't hurt her."

"That depends on you." Tom stared at Slim. "On all of you." He scanned the area. Not just the men facing him down, but the fallen Gang members. Did he realize just how hopeless his situation was? He couldn't honestly think he would walk away from this and have his freedom. "Drop your weapons."

Earp and his posse looked at each other. Then the lawman laid his gun on the ground. The others followed suit.

"What do you intend to do?" Slim tried to gain Tom's attention. He kept his hands visible, but he stepped forward. His gun lay on the ground just a few inches ahead and to the side.

"I—I don't know." The man's voice wavered.

"Please." Slim continued to walk toward him. "Let me help you. I think we can come to some kind of resolution." He tried to get Ada to look at him.

She met his gaze, horror in her eyes.

He had one chance. It was not good, but it was all he had.

"Let's talk about this," Dan added.

Tom tightened his grip on Ada.

She gasped.

Tom glared at Dan. It was now or never.

Slim ducked into a roll, moving toward his gun and gripping it as he came near. Then, as he rose up onto one knee, now closer to Tom, he fired.

Tom fell, a bullet in his head.

And Ada crumpled to the ground.

Ada was falling. Forever it seemed. Numb. All sound muted.

The shot had been fired. And then nothing. Had she been hit? She didn't know.

Slim was over her in the next moment. "Ada!"

She tried to turn toward his voice, but she was being lifted. And then she was in his arms. Had anything ever felt so good, so perfect?

There was no pain. Was this heaven?

Then her body was slammed with sensation. She ached, she hurt, but nothing seared her. Surely, she had not been hit.

"Ada darling," Slim's voice was laced with concern. "Are you all right?"

She looked into his eyes. Those blue eyes that she had longed to gaze at once more. "I...I think so."

He seemed to be doing his own inventory of her body, searching for anything amiss. Then he pulled her tight against him. "Thank God."

She prayed that this was it. That this moment was reality. That he loved her and would never let her go.

He pulled back and gazed at her. "I...it was..."

"I know," she said, her throat tight with the tears she held back. "But you're here. I will never wish for another thing."

The edges of his lips lifted.

There were the distant sounds of men's voices and movement, but all she knew was this moment and this man.

How had they survived? Slim was still amazed. But he was grateful. God had provided. Now he stared at the door to the clinic, waiting for the doctor to assess Ada. She had insisted she was well enough, but he would not have it any other way.

And there was much for him to think through—Tom, the Earp posse...everything. Things had gone so badly so quickly. But they made it. Because God had a better plan than theirs.

The door to the clinic opened, and the doctor stepped out.

Slim was on his feet in a moment. "How is she?"

The doctor moved back a step. "Other than some scrapes and bruises, she is fine."

"Can I see her?" He itched to touch her, to feel her in his arms, to tell her...

"Yes. She's right this way." The doctor opened the door wider and let Slim pass.

No sooner had they stepped within then he spotted Ada sitting on the edge of the exam table. He rushed to her, reaching for her hands.

She slid them into his.

"I was so worried," he confessed. "So..."

She nodded. "I know. I was, too."

"And I almost lost you. Without ever telling you how I—"

Her brows furrowed. "But your letter—"

"Is not enough. I need to tell you."

Her gaze softened. "Tell me."

He glanced toward the door. The doctor had disappeared. Had he stepped out to give them a moment? Another provision. Turning back to Ada, his eyes rested on her features. "I love you. So completely. Without holding anything back...maybe without much sense about me. But I do."

She watched him, her eyes intense.

He leaned forward and pressed his lips to hers. The kiss was everything he wanted, but still not enough. At length, he pulled back and set his forehead against hers. "Ada Clara Miller, I need to ask you a question."

"Yes."

"Would you..." His words caught in his throat. He swallowed and continued, "be my wife?"

"That's what I meant...when I said 'yes'." She smiled.

He kissed her once more. She wrapped her arms around his shoulders, drawing him closer. And, in that moment, he knew that he belonged. He was home.

Epilogue

"And you've finished all the arrangements?" Lily asked, looking at Ada.

Slim should have known such a question would have little to do with him.

"I think so," Ada said, beaming at Slim.

He, too, couldn't stop smiling. Tomorrow couldn't come fast enough.

"My mother has certainly been a little too helpful." Ada took a sip of her tea.

Lily nodded, chuckling. "I had noticed."

Slim glanced around the café. They had lingered so long that the lunch crowd had gone. Even Brandon and Amanda had begged off, wanting to get the small ones out where they could run around.

The foursome was nearly alone in the dining space.

Slim considered the last two weeks and the wedding preparations. Had it only been fourteen days since their near fatal encounter? So much had happened in the time, and yet it seemed the intense experience was only yesterday. Would he ever feel they had gotten adequate distance from it?

That was one reason they decided to marry just after the school year had ended. No sense waiting. At least, not on his account.

Ada set a hand on his arm. "I don't know how I will ever be able to sleep tonight."

Slim clasped her fingers and pressed a kiss to the side of her head.

Soon enough, the two women were chatting away about the preparations. He looked to Dan. "You having any luck finding another ranch hand?"

He shook his head. "It's not so easy."

Slim understood. With his child on the way, Dan wanted to make sure he could truly trust the person he hired. The whole business with Tom had disturbed him on a deep level. How had neither of them known? Were the signs even there? They must have been.

"What would you think of an old buddy asking you for that position?" Slim peered at Dan, watching for his reaction.

Dan's eyebrows shot up. "Truly?"

Ada had started to put down roots in Tombstone. After she broke it off with Stanford, the townsfolk had become much more welcoming and accepting. It changed Ada's perspective on settling here. And, while she was willing to go to Wharton City, he knew her heart wasn't in it.

"Yes." Slim glanced at his bride-to-be and then back at Dan. "I think we're here for keeps."

Dan seemed to consider that for a moment. "I'm afraid I can't take you on as a ranch hand."

Slim startled. He couldn't give Slim a job? What could be the cause for such? But just as he shifted and started to open his mouth, Dan spoke. "But I could offer you a partnership."

The women stopped talking.

"Partner?" Slim thought on that for a minute—a part owner in the ranch. What could be better?

Ada tugged at his sleeve. "We need to make sure it affords you plenty of time to write."

Dan cocked his head. "Does this mean...?"

"I'll be published by this time next year." Slim could hardly believe it, even though he'd read the letter more than a dozen times. "And they are already talking about another edition."

"I didn't doubt for a second," Dan said, leaning forward.

And why he had doubted himself for so long, he didn't know. The acceptance and encouragement of his friends, and the deep love of the woman next to him had given God space to work in his heart. And work He did.

Could Slim have imagined in his wildest dreams that life could be so good, so blessed? But sitting here with his friends and with the woman he would spend his life with...

There was no other word for it.

Bliss.

Keep reading for a preview of the next book in the Convenient Risk Series!

Thank you, dear reader, for for reading along with me! If you enjoyed this story, I would sincerely appreciate if you would submit a review. It would mean so much to me!

To read more about these characters, follow along with the Convenient Risk Series. Find it at:

https://saraturnquist.com/convenient-risk-series/

Author's Note

Hello, readers! What a fun book! I have enjoyed yet again pairing Romance with historical happenings. I never tire of it. And I love that this book found us in Tombstone with a nod to the happenings at the OK Corral.

For this book, I knew ahead of time I wanted to include these events as my placement in geography and time for the other books in the series put me so close. It really was "convenient" to the story.

So, what is truth here? The facts? Many are at least somewhat familiar with Wyatt Earp and the shootout at the OK Corral. Popular movies have made that bit of history all the more accessible.

Tombstone was a fast-growing town after it was established. By the time my story takes place, it would have had the Birdcage Theater (mentioned in the book), an opera house, an ice house, ice cream parlor, gambling halls and saloons, and even a bowling alley. Hard to imagine.

The shootout itself occurred on October 26, 1881 around 3pm in an empty lot on Fremont Street (near the Old Kindersley horse corral). It was between the Earp brothers (and John "Doc" Holliday) and six members of the Cowboy Gang. Billy Clanton as well as Tom and Frank McLaury (all members of the Gang) were dead when the dust settled. Ike Clanton and two other Cowboys escaped.

An attack on Virgil Earp (which he survived) and then, later, Morgan Earp (leaving him dead) led to Wyatt Earp and Doc Holliday with others riding out on a vendetta mission against the Cowboys. This vendetta is alluded to in the book, but in reality, the vendetta ride would have been a little bit later than depicted (taking place in March 1882).

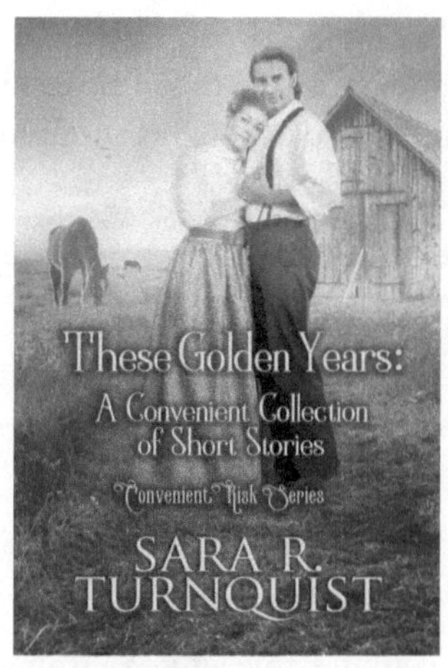

Dorothy "Cook" Miller fought the urge to snap the reins and encourage the aging horse to pick up her step. That would only increase the bumping of the cart. How would her own aging bones handle that?

As it was, they ached for home. For a comfortable seat and her sweet Owen to dote on her. Just thinking of him brought a smile to her face. It always did. The old coot.

The roof of the cabin peeked over the top of the hill. She was almost there.

Shaking and ricketing, the wagon protested the final climb. But it was sturdy. Owen made certain of that. He wouldn't risk his Dorothy, as he said so often. Yes, he was a kind-hearted man...even if he was a lot of trouble.

She smiled to herself as she pulled up to the simple log structure that was her home. And then she waited for Owen to come out, greet her, and take the horse to the barn.

But nothing happened. No one came.

So she waited.

And waited.

Was Owen all right? The old goat. He must be sleeping. Fine thing, that. She'd been working her hands calloused and he was napping the afternoon away!

But she couldn't be cross with him. He'd had his share of hardship over the years. She couldn't begrudge him some peace and rest after what he'd put that body of his through in his younger years as a ranch hand. Too many years abusing it.

It took more effort than she'd have liked to stable the horse and secure the barn, but she did it. Without thinking bad thoughts about her husband. Well...not too many at least.

She stiffled a laugh in spite of the ache in her back. They did pick at each other. But that was their way.

Opening the door slowly, she then glanced about the cabin. There were no lanterns lit within. And as the sun had begun to set, the interior had dimmed.

She made quick work of remedying that. Then she tiptoed to the kitchen and pulled together a few foodstuffs to prepare a simple meal. Dare she rouse Owen to eat? Dare she not?

If there was one thing she couldn't abide it was a stomach growling, complaining it hadn't been fed on her watch.

Nope, she'd wake him all right. There'd be no tummy grumbles in her bed tonight.

She had just put the meager stew together and started heating it on the stovetop when sounds outside disrupted her concentration. Or what was left of her concentration to disrupt.

Who would be visiting at this hour?

"Owen!" she called. She would much rather he receive than she. It was best.

No response.

"Owen!"

Nothing.

Well now, didn't that beat all. He was dead sleep. She knew the kind. And it was just like him, too.

She wiped her hands on her apron and moved toward the door. But as she neared the window, she spotted the figure, blurred by the dimness and her declining night vision, move into the barn.

The barn?

Was there a thief upon them? Come to steal their horses from right under their noses? The cad!

The man had another thing coming if he thought she was going to stand by and let a common ruffian take her old mare. Why...she never!

"Owen!" she called again. Whatever was wrong with that man? Did he have cotton in his ears?

Uneasiness prickled at the skin on her arms and she swallowed. Would it be up to her to defend their home? Could she do that?

She closed her eyes. *Dear Lord, give me the strength to do what I need to. And the sense to know what not to.*

Then she snatched for her broom. A fine weapon. She'd beat back many a beady-eyed mouse with it.

But a horsethief was not mouse, her mind warned.

Maybe they weren't quite so different, she told herself. Both bullies. Only this one was taller.

Movement beyond the window belied that the man came toward the cabin. Did he think this humble house had valuables? Why? Would he try to harm she and Owen?

Even as she peered, she couldn't make out more than his form as he came closer. She pressed her back to the wall. No sense in giving away her position. And she gripped her broom stick until her hands hurt.

The moment that scalawag stepped in this house—*her* house—she'd whack him with this broom with all the force she could muster.

Yes, that was a good plan. Sound. Doable.

A thickness rose in her throat as the steps to the door creaked. She couldn't do this.

The door latch jangled.

She had to. She would. She raised the broom and closed her eyes. Wait...if she kept her eyes closed, how would she hit him square in his detestable face?

Open eyes. Yes, that was better.

The door opened and...

She swung, smacking the door with the broom hard enough it sent a tremor through her arms and she landed solid against the wall. And all the wind went out of her.

She gasped for breath.

Someone spoke to her.

In a gruff voice.

"Dorothy?"

Hands were on her arm.

She flung an elbow back.

There was a satisfying "*Hummpff.*"

She turned.

And Owen worked to catch his breath.

Owen?

How? Why?

How?

"Oh dear!" She grabbed for his arm to help hold him up, dropping the broom as she went.

He held up a hand. "I'll be fine."

"Owen, I'm sorry...but you were a horsethief!"

He looked at her, an eyebrow quirked. "A horsethief? When? In a past life?"

"No...just now when I saw...well, you see, you...oh, nevermind." Her cheeks burned and she couldn't seem to get the words out.

He rumbled.

Was he coughing? Fighting for breath? Had she killed him?

"Owen?" She grabbed for his arm.

He took her hand as he continued to shake, head down.

After some moments, he glanced at her, his whole face lit up as he released his laughter at last.

Laughter? This was funny to him?

"Owen Miller, I might have killed you!" She shook off his arm.

He howled louder. "Most certainly, my dear. And I deserved it. And more I'm sure." His eyes gleamed.

"You most certainly did!" She crossed her arms, failing to see the humor. "You scared me something terrible."

His laughter faded and he met her gaze. "I apologize. I had no idea you would be so concerned."

"Well, I thought you were asleep." She moved back to the kitchen. "I hadn't a thought who would be traipsing around in our barn at this hour. Unless it was someone up to no good." She shot him a look.

"Sounds like me, all right." He winked.

She stirred the stew, it had begun to burn. Couldn't anything go right this evening? "I am sure glad you're amused."

His smile faded and he walked to her. "Don't be mad. I won't live long enough to work it off."

She couldn't help the grin that tugged at her lips when she peered at him. "Maybe. But you could try."

He rubbed her upper arms. "I hereby solemnly swear. I will work my hardest to make it up to you."

The grin that threatened overcame her features.

"Til death do us part." His own smile filled his face.

She leaned into him and let the tension of the past several moments slip away. All was forgiven and forgotten. Except...where had he been?

Pulling back, she opened her mouth to ask.

"Shall I...set out the bowls?" He looked at the pot.

She found herself too tired and unwilling to further muddy the waters with another discussion. Perhaps it was his business where he had been. Maybe he'd just been for a ride. Or over to visit Mr. Hayworth. It was no matter.

She sighed. "Hope you like your stew a little on the burnt side."

"I'll take it. As long as I get to sit at the table with you."

To read more, find *These Golden Years* here:

https://saraturnquist.com/these-golden-years/

A Less Convenient Path (Book 3)

She is in a hopeless situation. He doesn't have a chance.

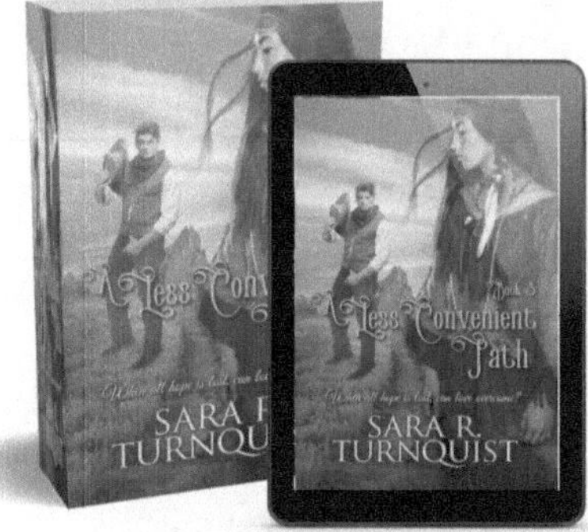

Mariena's native nation has been ordered to a Reservation but her tribe was attacked en route. She and her young brother wander in a wilderness filled with dangerous animals. Until...

Cutie happens upon them as he flees his own demons. Can Mariena awaken something he never expected? Even bring him to believe in himself once more?

A story of two people without peace. Will they find in each other the very things they are missing?

A Convenient Escape (Book 4)

She has nowhere to go. He has nothing to lose.

Lily has known hardship and rejection. Her brother takes a job at the Miller ranch. Now with no ally, she becomes desperate to get away...by any means necessary.

Dan is prepared to do whatever it takes to ensure Lily is cared for... even if that means proposing marriage.

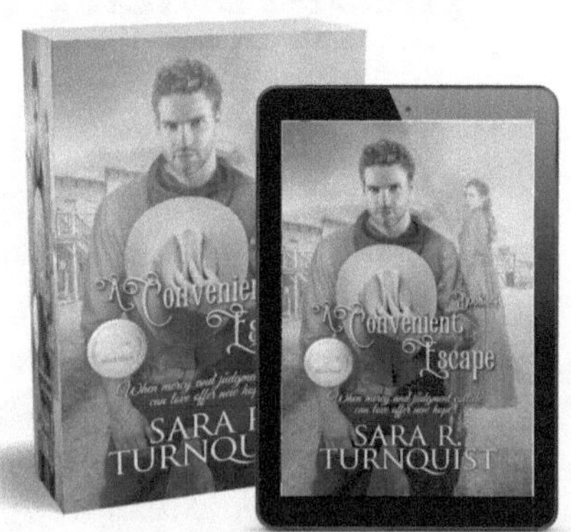

Will they make it to the church? Or find themselves victims of lies, disillusionment, or the ire of an Apache rebel?

An Inconvenient Acquaintance (Book 5)

She wants adventure. He needs a place to belong.

Ada the new schoolteacher in Tombstone. Her desire for independence stems from tales of the west. But she never expected to find herself torn between two men—one who promises safety and security, the other's future is uncertain and offers excitement.

Slim is determined that he will not become involved with a woman of privilege, Ada's fiery personality intrigues him. And soon he is vying for her heart with a man he'd rather not trifle with.

Will they find what they seek in each other? Or will they become caught up in a shootout at the O.K. Corral?

These Golden Years (Book 6)

A collection of short stories through the year.

Dorothy "Cook" Miller and "Uncle" Owen Miller are living their best life and marriage. Though it is not without bumps along the way. Join them as they walk through the year together with its measure of mishaps and laughs. This collection of short stories shows that marriage can be fraught with misunderstanding. But also has its share of lighter moments.

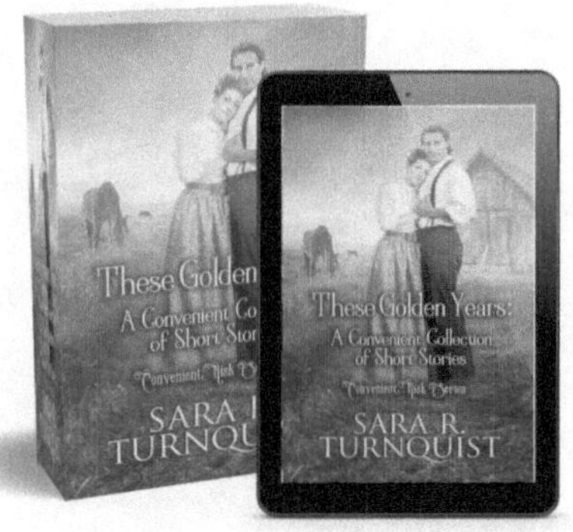

An Less Convenient Arrangement (Book 7)

She has lost all hope. He has little desire to stay by her side.

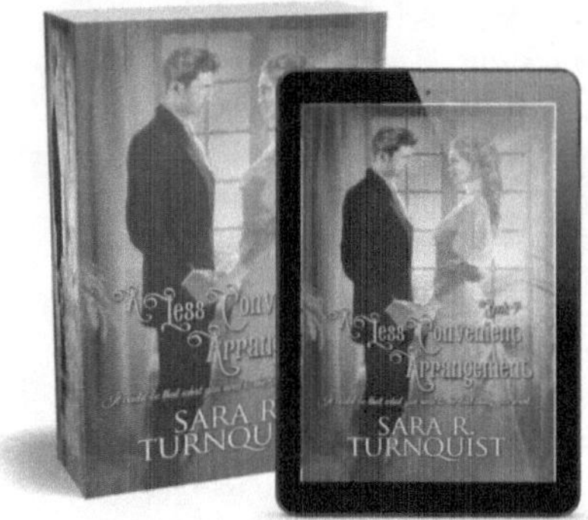

Sadie finds herself in dire straits after her father absconds with everyone's money. Her mother's failing mental stability also becomes a trial she is not certain she can overcome. Is there anywhere she can turn?

Though his one goal is to return to Richmond and a partnership in his father's law firm, David is drawn to Sadie and softens to her plight. He offers what help he can, but resists being pulled into the mess that has become her life. Until he starts to care beyond that initial attraction.

Can she stand strong against the challenges facing her?
Will David risk following his heart regardless of the cost?
Or take the first out offered to him?

Ranch Hands Collection

Four Stories from the Miller Ranch

Acknowledgments

There are so many people who have influenced and touched my life while pouring into this book. They are just too numerous to count. So, to everyone who asked about the process and let me talk about it or share my characters and story in development, I thank you. It is true you are part of the creation of this work in a unique way.

I can't forget my craft partner, Kelly Hollman, who listened and read my work each week and gave me valuable feedback that has honed me as a writer and allowed me to sharpen my skills and present better work for the world.

My Advanced Reader Team, you all are more appreciated than you know. You make my writer heart so happy!

Hannah Conway, my writing mentor, who is part of every book through advice and letting me bounce ideas off her. You are so inspiring...and I hope I can be one millionth the assistance for you one day.

Cindy Smith, your feedback has been incredibly valuable. Thanks for trouble-shooting and plotting with me. Your contribution to this book cannot be overstated.

My editor extraordinaire, Julie Sherwood, I don't know how I would be where I am as a writer without you kicking my butt and keeping me honest each and every novel. Keep it real. Every. Time.

Cora Graphics, you turn out a cover that amazes me each time. And I adore your talent and love for what you do.

VerBull Photography, thanks for getting my "good side" :-)

My husband and number one fan, Greg Turnquist, this quarantine has been nuts, but you still made time for this book to happen. You are it, babe. We're doing it.

For my sister, you make me want to be better. For my dad, you make me feel so good to have achieved this dream of writing. For my mom, I will love you forever. And for my kids, you give me every reason to smile.

Last, but certainly not least, my readers, you give me a reason to keep writing.

About the Author

Sara is a coffee lovin', word slinging, Historical Romance author whose super power is converting caffeine into novels. She loves those odd little tidbits of history that are stranger than fiction. That's what inspires her. Well, that and a good love story.

But of all the love stories she knows, hers is her favorite. She lives happily with her own Prince Charming and their gaggle of minions. Three to be exact. They sure know how to distract a writer! But, alas, the stories must be written, even if it must happen in the wee hours of the morning.

Sara is an avid reader and enjoys reading and writing clean Historical Romance when she's not traveling.

Please follow along with her journey through her newsletter at: http://saraturnquist.com/list

Happy Reading!

facebook.com/AuthorSaraRTurnquist

instagram.com/sararturnquist

x.com/sararturnquist

youtube.com/@SaraRTurnquist

pinterest.com/sararturnquist

Also by Sara R. Turnquist

CONVENIENT RISK SERIES

A Convenient Risk

An Inconvenient Christmas

A Less Convenient Path

A Convenient Escape

An Inconvenient Acquaintance

These Golden Years

A Less Convenient Arrangement

Ranch Hands Collection (ebook only)

CRIPPLE CREEK SERIES

Hope in Cripple Creek

Christmas in Cripple Creek

Faith in Cripple Creek

Love in Cripple Creek

~Prequels~

Leaving Waverly

Leaving Stoneybrook

LADY OF BOHEMIA SERIES

The Lady Bornekova

The Lady and the Hussites

The Lady and Her Champion

The Lady and Her Secret

RAILWAY ROMANCE SERIES

Laura, The Tycoon's Daughter

www.ingramcontent.com/pod-product-compliance
Lightning Source LLC
Chambersburg PA
CBHW061653190726
48289CB00006B/1861